THE GODS OF VENUS X

BY RAYMOND A. J. BEDARD

Acknowledgements

THANK YOU

To the many people who have encouraged me through the two years of creating this work.

In particular, to my wife, Nicole, who never once said I was spending too much time at the computer.

To the Green Valley Writers Group, who taught me so much!!

To my daughter, Cherylann, and her husband, Larry Pierce; without whom the book would never have been published.

I am indebted to one and all.

May 15 1994

U.S. Commander Glen Ross took a deep breathe to compose himself and strode confidently into the room. From behind an oversized mahogany desk, Air Force Colonel Colin Croft eyed the tall, muscular naval officer walking towards him trying to get the measure of the man.

"Welcome Commander Ross. Please have a seat. Can I get you a coffee or something?"

No thank you Colonel, I just had breakfast before coming in," Glen eased into the brown, leather chair.

"May I call you Glen?"

"Certainly."

"I hope your flight was comfortable and your accommodations at the Holiday Seaview are satisfactory?"

"No problems, sir."

As the suntanned Colonel opened a file folder and scanned the data, Glen Ross looked around the room to hide his surprise. He had expected to face a panel of interviewers. The one-man review board bolstered his confidence.

Croft began a series of introductory questions meant to disarm the applicant. Glen guarded his answers carefully. He had sworn to himself that this time he would be perfect and they would have to accept him.

Colin Croft, having interviewed hundreds of applicants, had an uneasy feeling in his gut that this one was too cool to be real. In fact he found Ross almost cold-blooded.

The Airman silently searched his mind looking for a clue to melting the icy veneer hiding the man, Glen Ross. Fondling his sunglasses Croft spun his chair to face the side window to his left. "Tell me who you are, Commander." Swiveling the chair achieved its purpose. Ross felt a tremor of rejection.

Quickly recovering his outward composure Glen slowly crossed his legs picking a piece of imaginary lint from his knee.

"Well most of the pertinent statistics are in the application form and the resume." As he continued with some details Ross thought, what kind of question is this? That file had all the info anyone should need. His deep resentment against academy officers, for him, symbols of rich and powerful men who oppress the have-nots, roiled in the pit of his stomach. Who am I? Why you pompous ass, I'm the best pilot you'll ever see!

It took all his self-control to shield the mounting anger. He could not afford to blurt out words that could cost him the assignment, words that once said he could never retract or explain away.

"I come from a large, first-generation, American family. My dad came over from Russia when he was twelve. He lived the American success story. He married a girl from his hometown in the old country. One of those arranged marriages. I am the fifth of a half dozen kids; the only one to go to college and to serve in the military."

Closing his eyes Croft feigned boredom but his trained ear listened to every tone and nuance in the iceman's words. He sensed a chink in the armor would come from this line of questioning. Abruptly spinning his chair to face the Navy Commander, he said firmly, "Commander! Who are you?"

Glen Ross sat up straight in his chair. Irritated by the question, his every muscle stiffened. Only a Herculean act of will allowed him to focus on analyzing the question for the answer Croft wanted to hear. What does he want me to tell him? The humiliation Dad lived with having to change his name from Rochevsky to Ross so he could find work? I'll bet Croft never had to renounce his heritage to feed himself.

"I'm not a very complex man," denying the deepest truth he knew about himself. "I like 80's music, a meat and potatoes diet, fast cars and beautiful, young women." He hoped a touch of humor would mask his growing uneasiness. Ross's mind raced through his struggling college years: working six nights a week in a pizza house, studying until three in the morning to get ready for the next day's classes. I earned my Summa Cum Laude degree in Electronics, he mentally told himself. I'll bet this Colonel never worked a day in his life. Rich old Dad probably paid for everything including the appointment to the desk job he has now.

"I did not feel challenged enough working in the electronic industry so I earned a B.S. in Aeronautical Engineering." No need to tell him how many times he had to prove to management that he was as good as or better than MIT or CAL TECH engineers. The corporate bias on the college or university where one graduated was the strongest motivation for Ross to look into a military career. His love of the sea swayed him into the Navy.

"It gave me the opportunity to accept a Navy Commission. I've logged 5000 hours flying Navy high performance jets and helicopters."

Colonel Croft shuffled the forms as if looking for something. After what was infinity to the applicant, Croft glared across the desk. Like heat laser rays, his dark, brown eyes pierced into the stiff-chin, stone face before him.

"What is at the center of your life Ross? What makes you hum? I still haven't heard who you are, just a bunch of details that I can get from your resume. What's in your gut mister? Who's the man Glen Ross?"

Glen began to rise from the chair. Only a vise-like grip on its arms kept him from racing out of the room. This desk-jockey, bus driver masquerading as a soldier has gone too far. He probably never saw combat, Ross thought. I'll bet the biggest danger he's been in is spilling a hot cup of coffee on his manicured hands.

"Colonel, flying is my life. It was probably the prime cause of my wife divorcing me. Right now the project I'm managing is all that's important to me. We are testing combat feasibility of a mother helicopter controlling multiple sonar sensing drones at distances out of line-of-sight of their base destroyer or carrier. We're in the final six months of the evaluation. This experience qualifies me extremely well for your project. I'm your man. No one will do better than I." Ross had managed not to lose his cool.

"If it's all that's important to you why did you apply to NASA? Are you ready to drop this all-important project for ours? Will you leave us for some other job?" The acid tone in Croft's questions shook Glen's calm. He had meant to sound totally dedicated and Croft put a different spin on it.

"I, uh, uh, applied to NASA before I received my present assignment. To be an astronaut has always been my ultimate dream.

The submarine detection project is near completion and my assistant project manager is fully capable of taking project responsibility. If you look at my track record you'll see that I always have run the race to the finish with all I've got."

"MMM, yes, well, we'll see." Croft looked at his watch as if pressed for time. He gathered the forms and stuffed them in the manila folder. Ross's anger at himself masked the utter disappointment he felt. He had blown the opportunity he lived for. He would never go on a space mission. Croft looked up from the folder and studied Glen's face. The iceman did not look so cool now. Maybe there was blood in his veins after all. "Fine, that will be all."

Ross uncoiled himself out of the easy chair, saluted and walked slowly to the door. As he turned the knob he heard the voice from behind the desk say,

"Commander Ross, we will cut orders for your transfer to Kennedy NASA facility immediately. Welcome to the Venus Astronaut Training Program. Good luck!"

Chapter 2

Glen Ross had to keep himself from shouting at the top of his lungs. I've made it, I've made it, I've made it, he kept repeating to himself. I'm going to be an astronaut! All his life this was the dream, to soar in space, to far off planets. Now his dream was about to become a reality.

Glen could not get out into open air fast enough. It seemed like he could hardly breathe, so excited was he at the realization that he was accepted for astronaut training.

Bursting through the outer door he crashed into a young woman about to enter. Her purse went flying as he knocked her to the ground.

"Oh my God! I'm so sorry," Ross muttered as he scrambled to help her to her feet. Without looking at her he reached down to pick up her purse. As he handed her the lavender bag he looked into the most penetrating black eyes he had ever seen.

"Are you hurt? Are you all right? It was all my fault. I'm so excited, I, rushed through the door not thinking that someone could be coming in." He could not take his eyes from hers.

"I guess I'll survive. Tomorrow I'll have all the bruises to remind me of the white uniform that ran over me."

Ross stepped back as the golden skinned woman moved toward the door. As he did, he saw her five foot four inches filling to perfection a short-sleeved lavender blouse and straight white skirt trimmed with lavender seams and hem. The matching high heel shoes accentuated well-rounded calves.

"Do you need help? Are you sure you're ok? I can't tell you how sorry I am to have hurt you. However, I have to say that it's a pleasure to meet such a beautiful woman."

"Yes, well, I prefer more gentle meetings; if you'll excuse me."

"I don't always rush through doors like that but I'm too excited and a bit out of control. You see I've just been accepted for astronaut training and it's my dream come true"

"That's nice but if you keep knocking people over they may decide you're too much of a klutz to fly in a rocket. You better slow down sailor."

Before he could ask her name the lavender blouse disappeared behind the closing door. Glen rushed through the parking area and jumped into the rented convertible. He did not hear lavender blouse say, "I have an appointment with Colonel Croft."

The trip to the hotel was just a hazy blur as Ross sped out of the Cape Kennedy Compound and through the busy sun-splashed streets. He couldn't wait to pack and fly back to San Diego. He knew that time would hang like a pall over him until the orders came to free him to relocate to the space center.

He threw the few items of clothing and toiletries into his carryon bag. A quick call to the airport confirmed his reservation and seat assignment on the 8:30 PM flight to the coast. With three hours to kill before boarding time Ross decided to take a stroll, maybe find a small restaurant and eat a leisurely supper.

The beauty of the streets lined with palm trees was lost on the self-absorbed sailor. A menu taped to the window of a small seafood restaurant attracted his interest and Glen decided to spend some time sipping cool lemonade; once seated the waitress handed him a menu.

"I'll have lemonade and the crab claws appetizer to start, and then I'll see if I'm hungry enough to eat the catfish entree."

"Yes sir. I'll hold off on the catfish until you decide."

Ross not only ate the catfish special but topped off the meal with a large piece of key-lime pie all the while lost in his daydreams about space flights. He strolled back to the motel, settled with the desk clerk and drove to the airport to turn in the rental. The forty five minutes to flight time dragged on then finally it was boarding time. Glen relaxed and soon fell asleep.

"Excuse me sir but we have just landed at St. Louis. Your connecting flight to San Diego will depart from gate 27. Have a safe trip."

The second leg of the flight proved uneventful and soon the Commander was in his quarters. He spent a few hours, before going to bed, planning the next day's work schedule for the project crew.

Chapter 3

After five hours of fitful sleep, Glen decided he might as well get up. Shaved and showered, he drove to the flight line an hour earlier than normal. He kept himself busy cleaning the files. When the orders would come he would be ready. At seven hundred hours he called the briefing to order.

"Gentlemen, I'm sky high this morning because I learned, yesterday afternoon, that NASA has accepted me for their astronaut training program." A resounding cheer filled the room.

"Thank you very much. In light of this impending assignment I am recommending that Lt. Commander Bill Jackson take over management of this project. I will brief him immediately after this session so today's first flight will be delayed until O-nine-thirty. From now on Bill will pilot Mother Hen. I'll sit co-pilot until my orders come in."

The terms Mother Hen and chicks had become the daily jargon the crew used instead of Control helicopter and Drones.

"This morning's first flight will be the last

check of the chick spacing control system. Let's be on top of every moment of every phase. You all know how imperative it is that the drones keep their relative positions plus or minus one foot. If the SCR's (Spatial Control Radars) won't hack it then we must find a more accurate system, maybe lasers."

Ross found he had to continually refer to his notes to fend off the distraction of yesterday's events. "We'll take the chicks out 45 miles and position them 1.5 miles apart to triangulate on the sub target 15 miles due west. Don't neglect the surface current drag. Mother Hen must compensate for this and keep the chicks fixed in place. Gentlemen, let's make this a red-letter day. I'm too excited to handle anything less than perfection. No questions? Fine let's hit it."

In a flurry of shuffled pads and pens and the scuffling of feet the room emptied leaving Ross and Jackson to the task of turning over controls of the project.

"Look Glen, I would prefer you stay in command until the orders are here. I'm flattered by your choice and I must say that I've dreamed of running such a project."

"Stop right there, Bill, this is not a point of discussion. You know there's nothing worse than a lame duck project manager." Both men knew that ambivalence sets in and the crew begins second-guessing, wondering if the new manager is going to change everything. Glen could not allow this with the project so close to success.

"Tonight, you review the program schedule and we'll meet at six hundred hours to go over it. At seven hundred you'll lead the briefing. The transition must be swift and clean. No doubts in anyone's mind about who's the boss."

"So be it. Thanks for the chance to lead this program."

Chapter 4

The ground crews prepped the ships with more care and efficiency than usual. The atmosphere was somber at the news that the man, as they had come to call Ross, was leaving.

Ross and Jackson suited up silently alongside the rest of the flight crew. Both had experienced leaving good friends behind when the Navy reassigned them to new locations. They knew this was a time to think about the friendship. The silence must be respected. Words must be weighed. The last days were too precious for triviality. Both knew they might never serve together or even see each other again.

The man of war can't look back. His is to go forward and serve. They knew this and now it was that time again.

Ross climbed into the left seat as Jackson took his seat in the pilot's slot. The exchange of roles went off smoothly as the two professionals executed the pre-flight cockpit check. At the same time the ECM tech verified his equipment's performance. The Sonar tech and the drone control engineers set up their gear. With all systems go Mother Hen got clearance and took off. Jackson guided the ship to a buoy marker.

The pilots on board the drones took off and flew to rendezvous with the helicopter. In ten minutes the four aircraft were in position and control of the three drones was switched to Mother Hen.

Bill Jackson steered his ship smoothly towards the exercise area as drone controller Henson deftly lined-up the drones in single file behind Mother Hen. To early sunbathers on the beach the scene was reminiscent of watching the duck hen leading her brood of ducklings across a placid pond.

The exercise went off without any hitches and target coordinates were achieved with high accuracy. Unfortunately the SCR's did not hold the drones in a tight enough relative formation. The return flight to Miramar Naval Air Station was technically flawless but the optimistic mood which had pervaded amongst the crew at take-off was subdued. They realized that the project might be in jeopardy unless a better control system was found. Lt. Commander

Jackson may very well have inherited a failing project. The roller coaster of emotions driven by failure and success was never more in evidence then on the flight back to base.

The de-briefing apprised all project crew members of the unsuccessful flight. At Glen Ross's suggestion, Jackson decided to give the SCR's one more try so he scheduled an afternoon sortie repeating in every detail the morning flight profile. The results were the same despite the efforts they made to optimize the signal capturing sensitivity of the SCR's.

"Gentlemen, Commander Ross and I will discuss this situation and then inform you of the direction we'll take in the morning at the briefing. Meeting's adjourned." Jackson was not taking over the project at an opportune time. As the crew filed out Glen pulled his replacement aside.

"If it's ok with you, we could contact the subcontractor quoted in the General Avionics proposal and request they talk with us about the Navy evaluating their Laser Control System. Sleep on it and let me know what you decide. Let's meet for breakfast at 6 hundred hours. OK?"

"Fine, I'll see you then with my project plan. By the way,
Congratulations on your selection by NASA. I'm envious as hell but proud to say that I served under your command. I wanted to say that before time skips by and you're long gone. Good luck."

For four hours Bill Jackson worked on what he hoped would be the best plan to finish the project on time and under budget. At one point he realized that his concern whether Ross would agree was affecting his decisions. It was then that the confidence and leadership perceived by Ross came to the surface and Lt. Commander William E. Jackson became of age as all choices became his and his alone.

As he sat waiting for Glen to get his breakfast through the chow line Bill felt a new sense of respect for Ross. Here was a man who had the confidence to trust others with responsibilities that could have serious impact on his own career. A lesser man would hold the reins until released while generating a lengthy advisory report to cover his arse avoiding responsibility for future failures. Glen Ross was not of this ilk but rather a man of extraordinary courage.

As the two men reviewed the new plan, Glen had only superficial recommendations. They agreed that Ross would handle liaison details through the Procurement Office to convince Laser Consolidated Inc., from Grand Prairie, Texas to supply three units as described in their original proposal. He intended to cut a no cost contract for the units. If they met or exceeded the requirements of the flight profile the Final Project Report would recommend their company be designated sole source for first buy and first buy spares. Jackson would run all other facets of the program.

Ross commended Bill on his decision to use the time until the new equipment arrived to test the "loss of control communications" from the mother ship. This would give them time to respond to any unexpected results.

At the Crew briefing, Jackson instructed the team to prepare for a thirteen hundred flight. The object of the mission was to have Mother Hen shut off its transmitters to the chicks. The drone on board computer should sense the loss and issue correct commands to fly the drones back to home base control.

Seated in the co-pilot seat, Glen enjoyed the view of the Pacific Ocean as Jackson and his crew positioned the drones. The three drones hovered each at a point of a one-mile triangle. With intense concentration on the chicks, Bill Jackson shut-off the control transmitter.

For what seemed like forever, yet it was only ten seconds, the drones retracted the sonar sensors. The two ships furthest from the Mother Hen made right turns in unison maintaining their original separation while climbing from 100 feet to a thousand feet. They came out of the turn at precisely the right moment to fly a straight-line course to home base.

Unexpectedly, the third drone turned left which put it on a direct collision course with Mother Hen. The chick's climb rate uncannily was precisely correct to intercept the control chopper at five hundred feet.

Jackson pushed down hard on the collective while jamming the control stick full left. Like a gull diving after some unsuspecting fish, the craft plummeted toward the sea. At one hundred feet above the water,

He yanked up on the collective and forced the control stick to center position. Both men watched the drone flutter over them, a scant ten feet above their ship's rotor blades. That distraction almost cost them their lives for in those few seconds their ship flared out and barely cleared the water.

With all his experience Bill Jackson fought the controls to keep the ship level while applying power to gain altitude. The waves, like the tentacle of a giant squid, lapped at the wheels. After a few hectic moments the pilot won the battle with the hungry sea. Slowly the ponderous helicopter rose out of danger.

Meanwhile the third drone pilot over rode the radar autopilot and forced the chick to climb the hundred feet, just enough to avoid the fatal collision. He was able to steer to home base safely.

The de-briefing session was deafeningly somber as everyone on the project realized they must never again overlook even the least possible scenario. It could cost the lives of all aboard Mother Hen as well as losing the ship and the drone. It could mean the end of the project. Jackson assigned the control tech the task of re-programming the drone computers, so that in all circumstances, the ships would turn away from the control chopper while keeping their initial separation. The tech also changed the profile so that the drones would fly single file until coming into control range of home base.

The next morning Jackson announced that Ensign Waters would fly co-pilot for all remaining flights. This would assure a trained pilot to replace Commander Ross when his orders came. What Bill intended was to assure that no flight incidences would jeopardize Ross's chance at Astronaut training, the solicitude of a true friend.

Two weeks later the orders came transferring Commander Glen Ross, USN on detached duty to NASA, reporting to Colonel Colin Croft no later than twenty four hundred hours 1 July 1994, transportation by personal vehicle reimbursed at a rate of thirty cents per mile. Glen immediately applied for a ten day leave which would allow him to drive to Florida at a leisurely pace, enjoying the vastness of America. He contacted the Transportation

Office to arrange shipment of his personal belongings to Cape Kennedy. After a rowdy farewell party Glen left Miramar NASA, San Diego Ca. June 15, 1994, destination SPACE!

June 18 1994

When Glen reached San Antonio he decided to call Sybal. "Hi. Look, I'm on my way to Cape Kennedy and I'd like to spend a couple of days with Andrew. I know that it's not part of the custody agreement but it would be a good time to take him to a ball game or something. He's 14 now and maybe I'll find a way to relate to him better."

"When do you want to do this? We have vacation plans." The icy words reminded Ross of the bitterness that accompanied their divorce. The healing had never taken place between them. Glen wished he had phrased his request to make it advantageous to his ex-wife. He still did not know how to manipulate her.

"Well, I'll be passing through Houston in a couple of days. Would that fit into your schedule? "

"No overnight stays. He comes home by 9:30 and you can only pick him up after his breakfast; say 9 AM. That's the best we can do. I'll also want to know where you'll be going with him." She would maintain control over the situation and make Ross accountable. She would do anything to squeeze out some bit of vengeance for his leaving her for his mistress, flying.

"That works for me. I'll be there in a couple of days. Thanks for being helpful about this. Bye."

The ride to Houston gave Glen a chance to review how the marriage had fallen apart. Maybe most of the fault was his. His obsession with flying had blinded him to what was going wrong in their relationship. Sybal no longer wanted to live as a military wife with its frequent re-locations and his long stays at sea.

He had handled the trial separation ok until he discovered she had spent a weekend with her lawyer's assistant while he and Andrew stayed in a motel watching TV. He had raged with jealousy at being cuckolded. From that moment he did everything wrong despite himself and he lost his wife and son. Now he wished he could reconcile with the boy but Sybal stymied him at every turn. Somehow, this time she had been cooperative. And he was thankful.

The last time he had seen his son was

the first week of January when his ex-wife had allowed Andrew to come out to San Diego for a week during winter school vacation. Glen wondered if the first meeting with Mitch, Sybal's new husband, would be difficult. It would be the first time he saw their new home. It had been their third wedding anniversary present to each other.

As he turned the corner onto a quiet street lined with trees and well-trimmed lawns, Glen spied the number on the mailbox. Pulling over he secured the MG and strode up the cement walk admiring the neatly mowed lawn that framed the ranch-style house. Mowing the lawn and house repairs were not Ross's strong suit yet a constant irritant to Sybal. Well, no sense in mulling over what should have or could have been.

Mitch opened the door at the first ring and invited Glen into a well-appointed living room with everything perfectly coordinated. The strong odor of furniture polish told Glen they had prepared for his coming. The two men would never be anything but civil with each other. Sybal had made sure that Mitch knew Glen was the cause of the divorce and all the emotional pain she had suffered. They exchanged introductions and small talk about the drive over and finding the house as Andrew joined them.

Glen was stunned at how tall the boy had grown in six months. The high school freshman had spurted to six feet. His stooped shoulders and downcast look expressed his shyness and awkwardness at suddenly becoming the tallest boy in his class.

"My gosh Andrew, you're already taller than your old man," Ross blurted making Andrew even more self-conscious. Glen was not sensitive to the boy's feelings and the barely audible, mumbled, "Yes sir," told the father that he was off on the wrong foot again.

"What do you say to some tennis this morning and a swim at the lake after lunch?"

"If you want to Dad." the boy murmured. Losing badly to his over competitive father at tennis was not his idea of fun. To make matters worse, being seen with only a swimsuit to hide his skinny 130 pounds would be as embarrassing as it could get.

Nevertheless Andrew gathered his gear and off they went. The ride in the MG was the highlight of the early morning. He was proud to drive by the school where some of his classmates were setting up a sandlot game of baseball. Next time he would see them they would have much more to talk about than cars and their boyhood dreams of owning such cars.

As they donned their tennis shoes and discarded the racket covers Andrew decided he would hit every volley and every ball as hard as he could. Just once he'd like to win a game. After losing the first set six love Andrew's stamina and determination waned. Suddenly the look on his son's face reminded Glen of his youth when it had been impossible to do any task well enough to please his fussy, nit picking father. This was the role model that had formed Glen into a perfectionist and the highest rated pilot in the Navy.

"Let's take a break, son. I can use a drink." They opened their thermos jugs and took long swallows of cool water. As they sat on the bench in the quiet of the deserted court, Glen Ross searched his mind for the words to break down the barrier his almost non-existing fathering had built between himself and the son he wanted to love.

"You've improved a lot, Andrew, soon you'll beat me at my own game. I'd like to suggest a few ideas that may help you. Do you mind? "

"No. What am I doing wrong now"? The boy replied in a voice that carried both a touch of sarcasm and a sense of "what do you care?"

At Officer Candidate School, Ross had learned to turn negative responses by accentuating positive traits and talents of subordinates.

"I didn't see anything wrong in your game but you are not using some of your strengths to your advantage. When you're serving, you are not using your height. You need to toss the ball higher and a bit more in front of you. Force yourself to reach to the limit of your tiptoes. Also, don't try to put all of your pace on the ball. Let your opponent do some work. Concentrate on hitting the forehands longer to the base line and when you hit a hard shot deep to the other guy's backhand rush the net to capitalize on a possible weak return to put away a volley. You'll be beating better players in no time."

"Thanks Dad I'll try to remember your

advice." Andrew was surprised at the affirming way his dad had spoken. No put-downs. No derision.

"If you want to, why don't we practice some of what I've suggested?" This pleased Andrew and for an hour they worked on his game rather than playing a match. After a quick shower they enjoyed a short swim. Then they dressed and strolled into the club dining room. They were more at ease with each other than Glen remembered they had ever been.

"Well, Andrew, what do you feel like eating?" Taking a long time to check the menu, the boy said "I don't know. I'm more into Big Macs and shakes. What do you suggest?"

"How about we get out of here and find a McDonald's. I love their fries and shakes."

"That's cool with me, Dad."

Driving down the shaded gravel road out of the Country Club, Ross felt a new closeness to his son. He did not dare express it for fear Andrew may reject it. Instead he tried small talk. "What do the kids in school call you, son? Andrew or Andy or what? "

"This year they call me Stretch 'cause I'm the tallest in the class."

"Are you playing any sports or in other activities?"

Andrew answered slowly. Uncertain of his father's views on sports he said, "I played JV basketball but not well. I rode the bench most of the year. The coach said I wasn't aggressive or mean enough under the boards. He really likes kids that are vicious with the elbows and play dirty. It's not the way Mom raised me and to be honest, baseball is the game I really love. I hope to make the JV team this year."

Then his enthusiasm for the game burst forth in his excited voice, "I'm spending a lot of time at the batting cages and fielding throws at first base from my friend Skeeter Fields, who wants to be a shortstop in the majors, some day. I don't think he'll make it because he hasn't got the arm and he's not a real good hitter. I get lots of practice fielding his wild, erratic throws but it's good for me. Mitch takes me to see the Atlanta Braves when they come to town to play the Astros. That's my dream…to play for the Braves someday."

The father beamed with pride as he listened to his son's hopes for the future. "You know Andrew, I'm proud of you that you are willing to practice so hard to make the team. You might try to have somebody pitch a whiffle ball to you when there are no cages available and no one to shag the balls you hit. This will train you to follow the pitch all the way because you know what dips and curves the whiffle ball takes. Use your regular baseball bat-that will increase your bat speed."

"That's a good idea, Dad. Anymore tips? I didn't know you played baseball."

"You might try using a little league batting tee to concentrate on the pitches you have trouble with, like knee high inside or tight on the hands. Everybody has trouble with those two." Glen stole a quick look at his son to see if the boy was interested in the advice. Andrew had turned in the seat to face his dad and was smiling as he listened intently. "You're tall. You may have trouble with low outside pitches but if you practice enough I'm sure you'll soon handle them very well. Most importantly, never forget that the best hitters of all time only batted between .333 and .360. Never get discouraged by one time at bat. Every time up is a new contest against the pitcher and you can win it. I'm looking forward to seeing your first game with the Braves." Reaching over he squeezed the boy's forearm in a gesture of pride and love.

"Did you play in college or in the service?"

"I didn't have time for it, son, I had to work after school and all summer but I saw how the good players improved their game and that's what I've shared with you. I hope it helps you achieve your dream. I'm lucky. I will get a chance to live mine when I go on a space mission. That's why I'm going to NASA now. It's all I've wanted from the first time I soloed."

Father and son sharing their dream wiped away much of the resentment Andrew felt. He now saw his father as a better human being than his image of just a flyer, a view blurred by the feeling of rejection. Andrew's mother did not paint a kindly picture of Glen for her son. She never resolved her feelings of anger and rejection nor entertained any remorse for her adultery. Rather she passed these on to Andrew. Now he had taken the first step toward seeing his father as not all bad and his mother as not all perfect. He began to understand how important a space flight was to his Dad.

The next two days saw the man and near man enjoying each other's company with little tension and much enjoyment. Too soon Glen hugged his son with the promise to see that first game and drove out of Andrew's life once again. This time the boy did not feel angry at the separation but was at peace with the newfound knowledge that his Dad really liked him.

Chapter 6

Marita Diaz loaded her luggage into the light blue Ford Escort. It was like stuffing a 6-pound chicken with ten pounds of oyster stuffing. The hot desert sun belied the TV weather report that it was 98 degrees. The thermometer on the sun-drenched porch was pegged at 120 degrees. Small rivulets of perspiration ran down her sides under her light blue blouse. The sweat from her forehead trickled into her eyes blurring her vision. Finally the last cosmetic case filled the front passenger seat.

As she hugged her mother goodbye, Marita realized how much she would miss mama holding her against her plump breasts. She had been comforted many times in the arms of the soft, chubby, dark-skinned woman. Slowly, Marita pulled out of her mother's embrace.

Turning to the stocky man with the weather beaten face, she wiped a tear from her father's cheek with her kiss. The sultry, gold complexioned Marita, the pride of the Yaqui tribe, walked slowly to her car.

Starting the engine she took a long look at the low row houses baking in the hot Sonoran Desert sun. The residents, standing in front of them, waved goodbye shouting encouragement and well wishes. Leaving the Yaqui Pueblo was extremely difficult for she knew how much her medical skills were needed. Fighting her tears, Marita Diaz drove onto the dirt road that would take her to the access road connecting with Valencia. From there she quickly entered the eastbound ramp of I-10.

Full of ideas about the next two weeks of cross country driving, she did not see the red MG streaking at her in the inside lane until the last moment. She swerved the hatchback into the breakdown lane braking in time to avoid crashing into the guardrail. The MG driver steered his vehicle to the left most part of his lane and cleared the Ford by mere centimeters.

Shaken by the near collision she edged the only car she had ever owned into the traffic lane, blending in and accelerating to stay with the flow. If the rest of the trip was going to be this nerve wracking, Marita doubted the wisdom of driving versus flying. Soon calm returned and the petite, stunning, dark-eyed surgeon began to enjoy the steady rolling drive.

Diaz had never been east of Arizona. This two-week vacation was going to be uniquely special. A couple of days to walk the parks and ride the canals of San Antonio, then a look at the gardens from the top of the state capitol in Baton Rouge. She planned a couple of days in New Orleans for dinner at The Court of Two Sisters and a midnight cruise up the Mississippi, then on to Florida and Disney World. "It doesn't get any better than this" she thought.

When she pulled into the parking lot of the motel in El Paso, Marita caught a glimpse of a red MG parked in one of the room slots. "I wonder, if that's the road hog that cut me off in Tucson? ---Probably not. At the rate he was moving he's probably half way to Dallas by now."

Rising early the next morning Marita ate breakfast and was on I-10 east headed for San Antonio by six AM. On the afternoon of her second day in San Antonio while floating down a canal she spied a red MG parked in the shade along the canal. As the boat slipped under a bridge she noted that the car had a California license plate.

"I'm getting paranoid about red MGs," Marita thought, "Who cares if I see one every now and then." She decided to enjoy the rest of the day. Tomorrow she would leave this beautiful city and head for Baton Rouge. Two days later Marita Diaz was standing on the observation deck of the Louisiana state capitol building breathlessly viewing the gorgeous gardens below. The rest of her trip stayed true to plans and on June 30, 1994 the Yaqui Indian surgeon reported to Colonel Colin Croft at NASA headquarters.

June 30, 1994

After a short time of small talk, Croft gave Marita directions to the East Dunes motel where a block of rooms were reserved for the new batch of astronauts. With instructions to attend the initial briefing meeting at 0-nine-hundred the following morning, the Colonel ushered her out of the office explaining he had to greet other reporting astronauts.

The short drive to the motel gave her a chance to assess the man, Croft. He seemed like a nice enough person. His dark brown eyes were soft and had made her feel at ease. She had been surprised at his six-foot height when he rose from behind the desk to greet her. When seated, his broad shoulders and barrel-chest gave the impression of a short stocky individual. She gauged him to be in his early fifties from the few gray hairs at his temples. The ring on his left hand told her he was married. Not much in his demeanor to reveal why he would be chosen to head up a Space project. She would come to know of his organizational skills backed by a strong will. She would learn of his courage to back his decisions and a deep loyalty to his people. These were the traits that NASA authorities had seen in Colin Croft.

Marita settled in the room unpacking and showering. Since it was early afternoon, she decided to take a swim. Slipping into a skimpy white bikini that complimented her gold colored skin; she gave herself an approving look-over in the full-length mirror. Though petite, her figure was perfectly proportioned except for slightly fuller breasts. In the eyes of admiring men this was no defect at all.

After a cooling swim she relaxed in a chaise-lounge, amusing herself by trying to guess which swimmers were part of her astronaut class.

"Hi. Could I use this lounger?" The voice was well modulated, resonant. Marita looked up into a smiling, ruddy face with flashing eyes. The small scars, hardly noticeable in the bushy red eyebrows, and the broad flattened nose suggested the man had participated in some contact sport-football or lacrosse maybe. Not waiting to hear a no he sat astraddle the chair. "Sean Murphy's the name. What's yours?"

"Marita." she answered, secretly

scanning the strong biceps, powerful legs and weight lifter's chest through her mirror sunglasses.

"Are you here on vacation?"

"No. I'm here on business." She had decided not to reveal her assignment to a stranger who was obviously hitting on her. Probably some stud trying to make every girl at the pool.

"What kind of business? I see you as some kind of executive-marketing manager or something."

"Or something."

"Look, how will I get to know you enough to take you to dinner if you play miss mysterious? I'm here to attend astronaut training. I'm a Captain in the Marines, been piloting jets for the last five years. Now I've been accepted by NASA and I can't wait to blast-off. What do you say? Have dinner with me. I'll meet you in the lounge at seven."

"If I'm not there by seven, start without me, Marine." She turned on her stomach. She lowered her straw hat to shade her face. The conversation was over. Sean Murphy knew a brush-off when the ice engulfed him. Rising, he strode to the pool and executed a perfect lifeguard surface dive, his powerful body sliced through the water, scarcely causing a ripple, and emerged at the far end.

Later in her room Marita debated with herself what to do for dinner. She did not know the area or available restaurants. Slipping into her kelly-green cocktail dress and high heeled, white and green shoes she armed herself with a matching clutch purse and descended to the lounge walking in at 7:05.

The Marine Captain caught his breath at the beautiful vision walking towards him. She had come! She really had come! After cocktails, Sean and Marita found the motel restaurant and spent the next three hours swapping anecdotes of their lives. Marita purposely left out her selection as an astronaut. Her pixie sense of humor demanded that she see the look on Sean's self-confident face when they met at the indoctrination session the next morning.

July 1, 1994

Marita had a light breakfast in her room and did a meditation exercise to relieve the tension of this first day as an employee of NASA. When she drove out of the parking lot a red MG, with the same plates as the one in San Antonio, cut in front of her car. To her utter amazement she followed the vehicle to the NASA parking lot. As she alighted from her Escort, she saw a handsome Navy Commander ease out of the red nemesis and stride into the executive building. She followed him into the very conference room where the indoctrination meeting was scheduled.

In a few minutes twenty-five eager candidates filled the seats designated for them by nametags. Under each plasticized tag was a blue folder. The trainees barely had time to peruse the first few pages of logistical information when, at exactly nine o-clock, Colin Croft and three assistants marched in. They took their places at the head table. The candidates put the folders aside as a strong, attention-demanding voice filled the room.

"Ladies and gentlemen I want to

welcome you to NASA," began the Air Force Colonel. "The folder before you will give you all the necessary information you need as to rest room facilities, dining rooms and detailed maps of the complete complex. Familiarize yourselves with it as quickly as possible during the first break at 10:15."

Croft looked at his notes for a moment. Sean Murphy took the opportunity to lean over to attract Marita's attention. She smiled, and then turned her attention to Croft as he began to speak.

"You have been chosen to compete for selection as flight crew on the most aggressive space flight ever proposed. As of this moment everything you hear in this meeting is top secret. Please sign the last form in your folder swearing complete secrecy regarding this project."

Croft waited for the signing process to be completed before resuming. Everyone complied though they had no idea what they were swearing to keep secret. It mattered not for each would sell everything to fly in space.

"Please pass those forms to the right so John Gilooly can collect them. John is my

Administration Assistant and you will get to know him very well before this training is over." John collected and checked off each form against his list of attendees.

"This form is binding until you personally receive a standard release form after the project is completed. Then you'll be able to write your memoirs and go on money making speaking tours." The trainees chuckled reservedly at Croft's wry statement.

"Now to the business of why you're here. You 13 men and 12 women were chosen out of 500 applicants. I can say that at least 50% of the other candidates are eminently qualified for any NASA project except this one. We call this project Venus X to make it seem as innocuous as possible to prying eyes and ears. The project quite simply is to send a crew into space to orbit the solar system. The mission objective is to track any large comets or meteorites coming from outer space or other galaxies. Should they be on a collision course with our planet, the plan is to destroy them by means of nuclear rockets."

Croft paused, poured a glass of water from the pitcher in front of him. He drank slowly and deliberately to allow what he had announced to sink into the minds of the listeners. To be sure that everyone heard him correctly he spoke slowly articulating each syllable.

After this session you will have the chance to sleep on your decision whether you want to continue with us or take another assignment with NASA. No one will think the less of you if you decline. "The reason for secrecy is that we do not want to alarm anyone about the possibility that large objects from space could crash into the earth and cause catastrophic damage and loss of lives. The second reason for secrecy is that the mission is to last twenty years."

The stunned silence was as powerful as a bomb explosion. The irrepressible Sean Murphy broke the dead air.

"Sir, did you say 20 years or is my hearing playing tricks on me?"

"If your hearing was suspect you would not be here. Yes you heard rightly Captain. We are offering you the opportunity to explore the universe in a way no one has dared to think possible. As we speak, the space platform

Venus X is in orbit and in its final assembly

You will undergo an intensive six month trial after which time a flight crew of 4 men and 3 women will be selected. We have scheduled shuttling the lucky seven to Venus X on March 3rd, 1995. The mission will leave earth orbit March 8th, 1995."

All sat stunned as they listened to Croft detail various aspects of the mission in general terms. He briefly described how life would be sustained for that long a time, which planets the ship would approach, what the spacecraft looked like etc. Colin finished the first session by reaffirming the importance of total secrecy regarding the meeting.

"Please wear your name tags at all times while in the NASA compound. Check out the folders. We'll break for a half hour. When we return we will bring you up to speed on what we have accomplished so far."

The trainees rose slowly, filing out of the room into a long drab hallway. No one spoke as they walked to the rest rooms and a snack area. Each pored over the folders while trying to rationalize the plausibility of the mission. This was not the simple two-week space shot they had expected! "20 years, my God, that's a quarter of my life" thought Sean.

Croft held three more sessions that first day and at lunch and breaks there was a buzz of conversation among persons who until this day did not even know each other. "What do you think? Can they pull this off? Have they found some new way of feeding people? How can you carry that much oxygen? What do you do for 20 years in space?"

At the end of the day they had some vague reassurance that the mission, 80 times longer than Columbus's journey 500 years before, could be accomplished. The group returned to their motel with instructions to check out in the morning. If they wanted to continue with the program they should report to the briefing room with their luggage ready to move into the facility NASA would provide. If they chose to not continue, they should report to Gilooly in room 235 for reassignment to other projects or severance, if so desired by the individual.

That evening room service did record business for supper meals as Marita, Sean, Glen and the others stayed in solitude to consider the irreversibility of their decision. At the check-out desk the next morning, no one could tell who was buying in and who was bailing out. None had the temerity to volunteer their choice, nor ask others about their decision. They would ride accompanied only by their thoughts not wanting to be deterred from their choice by the opinions of others.

As Glen entered the briefing room, he saw Marita gazing out of the picture window. She looked beautiful as the sunlight highlighted her complexion. Glen was awe-struck at the beauty of this woman. The women in his life mother, sisters, girlfriends and his divorced wife were attractive and pretty but this petite, dark-eyed beauty was special. He quietly walked to her side and introduced himself. She turned and looked up into his bright cheerful face. For reasons she could not understand, Marita suddenly felt safe and secure in her decision to train for the mission. Their conversation was cut short by Sean's energetic entry.

The Marine was anxious to tell Marita of his surprise when he saw her in the previous day's meeting.

"So this is your secret assignment, eh? and you let me brag about my selection all the time knowing you had been chosen too. Pretty lady you owe me a drink for that trick. How about supper tonight? "

"If we're allowed to, I'd be willing to buy that drink," she replied with an impish glint in her eye. Glen felt shut out and resented it for he had hoped to take her to supper. He listened to Murphy glibly flirt with Diaz as twenty trainees filed into the room. Croft's appearance at the door ended the conversation.

"Please take your seats. We've got a full day's work ahead. I congratulate you for your courageous and pioneering spirit. At the end of this session we ask you to take your bags and follow Sgt. Doyle, your supply person. He will guide you to your quarters. You will all be housed in a single bay with 4 foot high walls partitioning the area into individual personal living quarters."

"Is there no end to these surprises? Sean whispered to the tall blond woman seated next to him."

"We insist that the men enter the living quarters by the east entry and that the women enter by the west. This is to give the appearance that separate areas have been provided. We must draw as little attention to our project as possible. If any of you have a problem with the living arrangements, we suggest you consider that on board Venus X there will not be private sleeping arrangements."

For the rest of the session, the trainees gave short biographies telling their new colleagues their occupation, education, family background and reason for accepting this assignment. As he dismissed them for the morning Colin Croft instructed them that all meals would be served in the dining hall specified in their packet and only at the times listed. There would be no outside dining and socializing except as organized by the staff.

Croft closed the session by explaining, "This is necessary so that, in the short six-month training program, intolerable personality conflicts can emerge and must be dealt with. We cannot afford violent confrontations in space and twenty years is a long time to control deep seated dislikes and irritations."

Sgt. Doyle led the group to the west end

entrance of the two-story cement block building which would be home for the next six months. The women filed in and to their dismay found that the cubicles were assigned just as the seats in the conference room had been. This control did not sit well with many of them but they were willing to tolerate it for a chance to go on a space mission.

The women barely opened their suitcases when the men entered with the ensuing confusion as each searched for his assigned area. As fate would have it, Marita's cubicle was between those of Sean Murphy and Glen Ross. Soon strangers were befriending strangers, aware that their lives may be intimately shared over the next twenty years.

During a short interchange Diaz mentioned the coincidences of the red MG. Glen blushed and said, "Oh I do remember a tight squeeze going through Tucson. I'm sorry if I gave you a real scare. I was distracted with thoughts of this assignment and I drove with the pedal to the floor most of the way. Please forgive me. I hope we both make the team."

"Well no harm no foul. All's forgiven and forgotten. Good luck."

As the twenty assembled at the dining hall, most resented the place cards designating where and with whom they would eat. Glen sat joined by a tall, longhaired, blond with a contagious smile.

"HI, I'm Glen Ross." She barely said, "I'm Nancy Flowers," when Colin Croft set his tray on the table. Behind him came a stocky, round-faced, Air Force colonel who introduced himself as John Pennington.

"Where did you get your electronic background, Glen?" Pennington had memorized all the educational summaries given at the morning session. This gave him easy conversational openings.

"Well, I matriculated at Brooklyn Polytechnic but I couldn't get the flying bug out of my system. I got a degree in Aeronautical Engineering from University of Illinois in Chicago. While working as a design engineer, I applied for a Navy commission and was assigned to flight training, how about you, John?"

"I majored in Mathematics and minored in Physics at the Air Force Academy. From there I attended Flight Training School. I can't wait to see this Venus ship. His enthusiasm radiated and swept-up the others at the table. Nan, what's your story?"

Nancy Flowers overlooked the use of a nickname by a stranger. "I'm a biologist with a minor in math from Cal Tech. I've always had a love of flying in hot air balloons." Her voice was soft and melodious which   attracted the men to listen more attentively. "I decided to apply to NASA since a space flight would be the ultimate free floating flight. I'm excited to get a chance at this project, though I must say I'm stunned at the twenty year figure."

"We anguished over the length of flight," Croft responded. "This project will revitalize the interest of the American public in space technology. It's most important that we stay at the forefront of space travel. Our country is the only one rich enough and with the technology to pioneer in this area."

Changing the subject abruptly, Nancy asked, "Colonel Croft do you really believe that we trainees need to be controlled so closely that we can't choose our own dining companions or adjacent roommates or social friends?" The look of agreement on the other two trainees told Nancy that she had asked the question no one had dared to speak. It was a dangerous moment for Flowers, because Croft could see this as an attitude of rebellion or a lone-ranger personality.

Colin saw it as courage and the willingness to delve into the why of things. "Those chosen will have shown a trait that will guide them to always put the good of the mission ahead of any personal agenda. Each must realize that factions or cliques will jeopardize the mission. In these short six months we must see the relational skills of the individual with everyone else. We must assess this one-on-one as well as in small groups and with the whole class. We have designed the training to do this as effectively as possible."

At that moment Ross, Flowers and Murphy had been told unequivocally the traits that could cause them to be de-selected. In his own way the Program Manager would convey this message to every trainee at the appropriate time.

July 8, 1994

During the next week Ross and the others learned that each trainee must become proficient in every task to be performed including piloting the space ship. Each astronaut would take turns at every task over the complete length of the mission. Everybody does windows on this voyage, Croft kept saying.

Three trainees at a time would spend a two-week stay in Biosphere 2 in Arizona. This would be the best preview of what Venus X life would be like. The formation of the three person groups would in no way indicate possible selection or teaming for the mission.

Marita was selected in the first group with Jim Barnes, a black all-American halfback with degrees in Physics and Metallurgy from Indiana University. The third trainee was Sam Hershburg, mister intense. Sam was "Winner of outstanding graduate in Chemistry" and was a doctor of internal medicine. After twenty years in academia and ten years building a national reputation as a foremost diagnostician in the field of nutritional deficiencies, Sam was just beginning to experience other facets of life which he had missed. Hershburg's social life had blossomed in the last two years and he was considered a prime catch for some pretty young woman.

The two weeks flew by as they tried to assimilate as many details of biosphere life as possible. Marita's two partners were engaging and entertaining conversationalists. She found herself thinking that they might be good companions if chosen.

Upon her return Glen became more and more attentive to her. He took every opportunity to speak with her. Ross found her exceptionally intelligent yet unpretentious. Despite her remarkable skills as a surgeon, she maintained a modest demeanor. Glen realized that he was beginning to love her. He knew this was stupid or at best unwise. What future could they have if only one of them was chosen for the mission?

For her part Marita was most comfortable with Glen and enjoyed his friendship best of all the trainees. However, she was so attracted to Sean Murphy that she only saw Glen as a co-worker and friend. When she was with Sean, she could hardly contain her physical desire for him. Had there been no structure to prevent it she would easily have considered a sexual relationship with the Marine. Just touching his rock hard biceps turned her on like no man ever had.

Ross sensed the competition and though he liked Murphy, he envied the look in Marita's eyes when she gazed into the good-looking Irishman's face.

July 27, 1994

As part of the program Colonel Croft designated Wednesday night as command attendance social night. All trainees and staff members would go to a restaurant for dinner then go to a night club for a few drinks and dancing. The week after Marita returned from Biosphere 2 Glen made sure he sat next to her at dinner and at the nightclub.

The conversation was cheerful and exciting for the sailor. As the evening wore on and the drinks flowed Glen and Marita danced slowly and sensually. He thought she had the same feeling for him that he had for her. This illusion vanished when Sean asked Marita to dance

Glen watched jealously as the dancer's bodies became as one. Marita gave herself willingly to the undulation of Sean's body. When a second song started, Glen tapped Murphy's shoulder and said he was cutting in.

"Some other time, Ross. I've reserved Marita for the rest of the night."

"No way Garine," Ross spit out as the jealousy triggered the rivalry between sailors and Marines. The sarcasm did not escape Captain Murphy, USMC.

"The Marines have landed, swabby, and the situation is well in hand" as he pulled Marita tightly against him. Cool Glen Ross lost it completely and pulled at Murphy's arm. Sean swung a backhand at Ross. Marita screamed. The two men grabbed at each other losing their balance more from the effect of the drinks then anything either one of them did.

Others in the party quickly jumped in and pulled the two scufflers apart. At that moment Colin Croft stepped in and took charge.

"You two are an embarrassment to NASA, report to the gym at 0700. We'll resolve this the way gentlemen should. All trainees will report to the gym as well. No one better miss this call. Now go back to your quarters and there better not be any more fighting tonight. Is that clear Ross and Murphy? DO YOU HEAR ME?"

"Yes sir" they responded as one voice.

Marita was furious! Where did those two men come off deciding with whom she would dance? When they arrived at their quarters she laced into them.

"Who do you think you are, cave men fighting to see who gets to drag the woman off to his den?" "If you've cost me a chance to go on this mission I'll make you both pay through the nose. Don't either of you speak to me except for duty tasks. Grow up! Your immaturity is embarrassing."

Her words slammed through their angry minds awakening the realization that the episode could cost them being chosen for the mission. So much hard work destroyed in one heated moment; life-long dreams evaporating in minds clouded by liquor and lust. Tossing and turning sleeplessly it seemed like morning would never come, yet it dawned too soon for either of the men.

July 28, 1994

The trainees filed silently to the gym after a breakfast no one could enjoy. Sean and Glen avoided each other purposefully. They must maintain their animosity or surely lose the fight. Croft arrived precisely at 0700. He was all business.

"Gentlemen, this is how it's going to go down. You will wear 8-ounce gloves, fight 2-minute rounds until one of you quits. There will be no referee and no other rules. Understood?"

The men went to the locker room and changed into boxing shorts. When they came back to ring side Croft laced up their gloves and they silently slipped through the ropes. Each knew that win or lose their chance of going on the mission was very slim.

The two were almost equal in size and weight, however, Sean had a much more muscular body than Ross's wiry frame. Murphy had been here before as light-heavy weight NCAA boxing champion. Most of his fights had ended in knockouts or technical knockouts. Glen had his fighting experience on the streets and playgrounds of Brooklyn. No finesse, just brutal survival fights.

The first round started with much feinting and feeling each other out but after 30 seconds the Marine began to land telling stiff jabs to Ross's face. Suddenly, Glen rushed under a jab and head butted Sean under the chin forcing him to hold on until his mind cleared. So much for Marquis of Queensbury rules, Sean thought. That butt signaled the start of elbows, thumbings in the eyes, knees to the groin, kidney punches and any other painful act that would give one or the other an advantage. By the end of the first round both men were splattered with their own and the other's blood.

The spectators sat stunned at the battle they were witnessing. Could these men be civilized? They belonged in the Roman Coliseum not in a modern space ship. The watchers kept sneaking glances at Croft hoping he would stop the carnage. He sat as if made of stone. The second, third and fourth rounds just became more vicious. First one then the other would have a slight advantage only to have the other reach into some deep reservoir fueled by the instinct to survive and turn the tide and regain the advantage.

The fifth round saw both warriors spent of any strength and the struggle became one of wrestling, pushing, pulling, and tripping accidentally or purposefully. At times they rolled on the mat with stark terror in their eyes, fearing that they would not be able to get up and the other would.

At the end of the round the men stood facing each other. As if on cue they bit the lace of first one glove then the other pulling the ties loose. Pulling the gloves off, they faced each other with an admiration that only a true warrior has for a foe that would not be defeated. Smiles slowly crept over their bruised, puffed up faces. All the hatred and venom was washed away by the blood and sweat that was splattered over them, the mat and the ringside spectators.

Croft stood. "Meet in the briefing room at 0800 people." He walked out followed by his staff. The whole affair had lasted 15 minutes. The trainees walked back to the dorms conversationally reliving what they had witnessed. All feared that they probably had lost two friends to de-selection. Murphy and Ross walked to the shower room together.

"You're one hell of an animal Ross. I

don't ever want to fight you again."

"Same to you, Sean, I really thought you had me in every round. Can I buy the first drink next Wednesday?"

"I've never passed up a free one from a friend."

July 29, 1994

Everyone sat in silence waiting for Colonel Croft to speak. The tension hung like a pall over the room.

"The last 8 hours could be a cause of division in the program. You all realize that if such a fight occurred on board Venus X the mission could be destroyed. The prime concern of the staff is to be sure that those chosen will be compatible enough to resolve differences peacefully, acknowledging the other's right to differing viewpoints. I don't know how much this will affect the staff's view of Commander Ross and Captain Murphy as potential astronauts. It certainly won't be on the positive side of the ledger. As of this moment the affair is over and I don't want to hear talk about it. Now let's get back to work."

As the weeks sped by Sean and Glen became close friends based on the respect each had acquired for the other in their brutal combat. Encouraging and cheering for the other to excel in all phases of training, they focused on mission goals and did not discuss Marita. She avoided spending any time with either one. She did not want to risk being cut from the program by causing a second fight between the two men.

Murphy and Ross with Sandra Meyers were the last team to train at Biosphere 2. She was a gentle woman and vestiges of her Georgian accent added to her natural charm. A graduate of Georgia Tech with a major in Biology and a Doctorate in Internal Medicine, she had an IQ second only to Pennington's. Her adaptation to Biosphere living and her facility in assimilating all the information supplied left the two macho men in awe. They returned two weeks before final selection.

A week later Croft and his staff began daily meetings comparing their views on who should go aloft. With only two days left before final selection the team had trimmed the choices to ten candidates. All were equally qualified so a lottery could be justified. The choice now fell on Croft's shoulders. The glory and prestige of Program Manager now exacted its price.

That night erudite, cerebral, logical Colin Croft had a dream. In it the candidates and staff were at a western dance. A line dance started and all joined in. At the front of the first line and leading the dance with great exuberance was reserved, quiet John Pennington, in real life the worst dancer in the group. When Croft awoke from the dream he wrote down the names of those in the front line and went back to a restful sleep.

The next morning Croft read the names he had written during the night to his staff omitting how he had chosen these individuals. The staff accepted his choice with some reservations about two names that had been left off and one name that was on the list. They re-assessed the list one last time. In the end they stayed with Croft's dream choices. The fate of ten individuals and a multi-billion dollar mission was decided by a man's subconscious voice speaking to him in the still of the night.

February 16, 1995

At 1300 hours, Croft assembled the twenty candidates. It would be the last time they would all be together for only seven would go on to share the next twenty years in space.

"Ladies and gentlemen we have arrived at the final selection-not without much serious consideration and evaluation of each of you. We wish you could all go on this one. Those selected will have two days before lift-off. You don't need more time because you're as ready as you'll ever be. The rest of you will be assigned to monitor positions as first contact with the passengers. Should a selected candidate voluntarily turn down the assignment then one of you on monitor duty will replace him or her. As I name you please stand and remain standing so your colleagues can acknowledge your deserved accomplishment. I am most proud to present to you the crew of Venus X.

-Jim Barnes; Nuclear Energy Plant Manager and Mechanical Systems Manager

-Nancy Flowers; Electronic Systems Manager and Statistician

-Sean Murphy; Computer Systems Manager, Lead Programmer and Physical Wellness Manager

-Sandra Meyers; Agricultural Systems Manager and Dietician

-Marita Diaz; Chief Medical Officer and Atmosphere Control System Manager

-Glen Ross; Chief Pilot and Flight Control Systems Manager

-John Pennington; Mission commander and Chief Navigator

-Sam Hershburg; First alternate

Each man and woman standing had teary eyes as the realization of their selection overwhelmed them. Those not chosen sat in admiration of the crew while feeling an oppressive sense of disappointment. As Croft placed the list on the table in front of him, the ten not selected rose to their feet. Loud cheers rang out as they swarmed around the crew; congratulating them with hugs and handshakes.

"There will be a formal reception tonight at 0700 at the main ballroom of the Bay View hotel. I presume you know that attendance is mandatory. I want a few moments with the crew. The rest of you get the day off." The seven sat down while the others leisurely said their goodbyes and filed out of the room.

Croft went to each astronaut and shook his or her hand, warmly congratulating them with words uniquely suited to the individual. Then facing the whole group he said," We are sensitive to the needs of your families. Between now and tomorrow night we want you to write two letters to your nearest relative or closest friend. The first should tell the reader of your selection for a twenty-year mission. Write what it means to you and your feelings about how it will impact them. We will mail them the day that you lift off to rendezvous with Venus X."

"The second should detail what you want to take place if you do not survive the mission and what you want to tell the world. These will be kept under Top Secret security and mailed only if necessary. Are there any questions?"

Jim Barnes asked "Sir, are we restricted to only one person to whom we can write?"

"Jim, we will mail out as many copies as you wish but we suggest only one text, if possible. That way we won't have two dozen different stories circulating about the mission, any other questions? "

"Obviously, we will not get a chance to say goodbye to anybody." Glen spoke with sarcasm in his voice. "You have to control down to this level eh, Croft."

"Ross, we need to maintain security until after lift-off to prevent any do-gooder, self-serving politician from trying to delay or cancel the mission. Your constant disagreements not withstanding; all the controls were dictated by the staff's view to assure mission success. This included selection of those most qualified to fly."

Croft's irritation with the naval officer's continual questioning of procedures and controls had never surfaced until this moment. The tension in the room squeezed the breath from everyone's lungs. No one spoke or moved. The incensed Croft quickly regained his composure. In a firm, sure voice he said "If there are no more questions we'll adjourn for the day." The crew slowly rose from their chairs as if the tension weighed too heavily for them to stand. As they filed out Ross trailing in the rear, Colin signaled him to stay behind. Once alone Croft looked directly into Glen's eyes. He remained silent for a minute.

"Ross, I hope you understand that I treated you more strictly than any other candidate because I expected perfection from you in all facets of the mission. You demand it of yourself and those around you so I demanded it of you. I hope you will be more tolerant of the men and women on the mission with you. They need it and so do you. I know you have no love for me but I chose you for performance not friendship. I suspect your dislike for me is not solely personal but rather a reflection of your animosity toward all authority. You must resolve this issue or you'll have a miserable twenty years taking orders from Pennington."

"You know, Colonel, I was beginning to like the way you operate until you made Sean and I fight each other. That turned me against you but I vowed I would not let my hatred for you prevent my selection. Are you going to change your mind and pull me off the crew?"

"No, Ross, you are still the best man for the chief pilot's slot. As for the fight, it served two purposes. Both of you displayed the ferocious courage it's going to take to live out in space for such a long time. The rest of the crew now knows you two are men they can trust in times of danger, and there will be many in your flight." The complementary words softened Glen's surly mood. Croft continued as he watched Ross's reactions. "Then, I needed to find a catalyst to unite the candidates into a team which would sacrifice their individual, selfish desire to be selected for the success of the mission.

By getting everyone to hate me for putting you through the ordeal they united in one goal. They would not let me break them or force them to quit. They would see it through to the end. In the process they helped each other to perform to the best of their abilities. I did not savor the role but the end justified the means."

"Why did you pick Sean and me? There were confrontations between others before our squabble."

"Ross, you and he had to resolve the woman problem before you could qualify for the mission. More importantly you have the heart of a warrior and so does he. The others have scientist and humanist hearts; without you two they could not carry out the mission.

I'm entrusting the success to you two. Don't fail me or yourself."

"If Sean and I are the heart of this mission why didn't you choose one of us as Mission Commander?" Glen challenged.

"Pennington is Mission Commander because he is calm under fire and we judged him to be the best decision maker among you. He's the one I'm relying on for stability and wisdom in the critical moments."

"It wouldn't be because he happens to be Air Force, like you would it?" The sarcasm cut through Croft's professional calmness.

"Listen Ross, I flew with Pennington in Desert Storm. I trust him as my wing-man ahead of any other pilot I know. Make your choice! Do you want to go on this mission or not? If you do then get with the program and start acting like an officer." From their first meeting Croft had tried to avoid this confrontation. Ross stood silent staring at the symbol of all authority before him.

"Oh no, I won't quit, I'm going on this flight and when I get back you'll see who turned out to be the coolest under fire!"

"Fine. If you have no further questions

you can go. I'll see you at the reception." With this, Colin turned away and picking up his briefcase he strode out of the room leaving Ross and the anger behind him.

That afternoon there developed new strata in the relations among the candidates. The crew felt closer with each other. Yet they were humbled, aware of how fortunate they were considering the talents of their fellow candidates who now must fade into the background. The ground support people treated the crew with respect and deference. The elite were elevated to their proper place in the NASA community.

At the reception everyone danced with everyone else, the tension of six months of training drained from staff and candidates alike. Pennington made sure to speak to each candidate affirming, reassuring, encouraging, even laughing and joking. He was the consummate leader and had been well chosen for the job.

February 23, 1995

The crew would shuttle to Venus X in two space shots. Pennington, Ross, Flowers and Barnes would go first on the 23rd of February then Murphy, Diaz and Meyers would follow on the 2nd of March. The seven selectees spent the remaining days reviewing those systems which would be their area of prime responsibility.

The imminent blast-off carried with it deep significance for them. Each knew the chances of returning to earth were less than even money.

As Glen Ross suited up for the flight he knew this was the day he had lived for. There was no fear in him, only the supreme confidence that this was his destiny. He would prove to the world once and for all that he was the best pilot of all time. He knew he would be the man who would see the mission to completion. It was as if he could stand straighter and taller, head more erect, shoulders back. Glen Ross was pleased to be Glen Ross today. The loss of his marriage and the impending long separation from his son and parents were a small price to pay to achieve his dream. "This is what life is all about," he shouted and the other three suiting up gave him thumbs-up.

Pennington was confident and excited. He was commander of a mission of hallmark importance for all future space exploration. John did not allow himself to dwell on the life he was leaving behind. No, the choice had been made and now he focused on the moment at hand, while reviewing in his mind the blast off procedure and the ensuing link-up with Venus X.

Nancy Flowers was uncharacteristically quiet and pensive. It was as if her whole being was in a hush mode. She wondered if her father would finally see her as important and significant or would he still be so self-absorbed as to be oblivious to her. She too had a need to prove herself, if to no one else, at least to her father. Her outward confidence hid the little girl who wanted Daddy to love her and pay attention to her.

As the aides helped him secure the cumbersome space suit, Jim Barnes' mind flitted to a time when he was four years old. His mom was helping him fasten the hooks on his bib overalls as he stood on the red Georgia clay. He could feel the cool, wet dirt ooze between his toes. A morning downpour had soaked the front yard. He felt his mother's lips on his cheek as she said, "You play nice out here now and I'll fix you a biscuit by-and-by." He wished she were here now so she could say, "You go play in space now and I'll fix you a biscuit when you get back." It was not too strange that this memory should intrude into the high tech conversations that were taking place. When he had first arrived at NASA, his Mama had sent him a plastic sandwich bag with some red clay from her front yard. The simple words she had penned on the yellow note-paper, "We're so proud of you. Never forget where you come from" had touched Jim deeply. He slipped the plastic bag inside the left breast pocket and secured the Velcro flap in place. "I won't forget Mama."

Lift off went perfectly and with every mile the astronauts were carried further and further away from any connection to the realities of living on earth. The ship sped them to a life of isolation and deprivation they could not envision in the farthest stretch of their imaginations.

The night before her flight Marita visited the local priest for absolution and a special blessing. Now she felt ready to leave mother earth. As she pulled on the movement-restraining space suit a peace and certainty of the correctness of her choice enveloped her. She had the feeling that she had been wrapped safely as her mother wrapped her and carried her in the sling on her chest when she was a baby. Soon the world would know that the Yaqui Indians still existed and were capable of anything an Anglo could do. She was gambling her life that the young men and women of her tribe would have the courage to become all that they could be.

Sean Murphy had to tell at least a dozen Irish jokes to release the exuberance he felt that blast off morning. Sean had faced death in combat and had come to grips with his mortality with a sense of "Que Sera Sera". His motto was "don't sweat the small stuff and there ain't no big stuff." "Think of it," he told himself. "In space for twenty years with three beautiful women and all that time to make love." He broke into a grin as he thought how upset Croft would be if he could read his mind. Life was beautiful today!

For Sandra Meyers, this was the moment she could safely release the "Tomboy" held captive in her soul for all these years. The genteel southern beauty had never been allowed to fully be herself. "No dear, you can't play lacrosse it's not lady like. No Sandra baseball is a boys game, come in the house and practice your harp lessons...Sandra dear, concentrate on your swimming if you have to compete in sports at college." Now she would be an equal in all ways. She knew more than any of the others about the ship they would cohabit for the prime years of their lives.

She was ready for whatever would confront her. Mama was not pleased with her choice of career but then again she had never liked any of her men friends either; unless she was the one who had introduced them.
The flight to meet with their space home was uneventful, if a space flight can be described this way. Like all previous astronauts, they experienced the awe and joy of seeing the earth grow smaller until finally they sighted the

immense, gray structure where they would soon rendezvous with their companions.

Venus X was exactly as the simulators had depicted. The days were long and so busy that the new comers to space had no trouble sleeping when their work shift ended. On the ground Colin Croft and his crew were as busy and more tense because they were no longer in full control. Now Mission Control depended on the crew for most decisions in these final hours. Always hovering in the back of Croft's mind was the thought that soon he would have to announce to all of America the full scope of the mission. He knew that the media would swarm down on the Cape and his privacy would be nonexistent until some lurid murder case became the new focus of interest.

March 8, 1995

Morning arrived quietly over sunbaked Florida and vacationers went about their routine while Colin Croft gave the final command for Venus X to escape orbit and begin its 20-year journey touring our solar system. Only two days before, Croft had given the crew a third purpose for the mission. The crew would be testing the efficacy of newly designed nuclear rocket boosters which would propel Venus X at speeds of 60 million miles per hour. This was a quantum leap over the 43 thousand miles per hour of Voyager 2.

The news was disconcerting to the flight crew since no theories had been discussed as to what they might expect to face at these speeds. It was of paramount importance to test this capability over an extended period of time, if some day, man was to successfully explore the limits of the universe.

They soon resigned themselves to the fact that twenty years in space was twenty years no matter how fast you were going or where you went. The newness of weightlessness and the many non-habitual tasks took all their energies. The sleep hammocks beckoned them and rest was all they thought of when their duty shifts ended.

By the end of March 2000 all on board were settled into work and free time routines. Pennington made a few necessary corrections to schedules while Sean was assiduous at seeing that each astronaut performed the designated exercise routine tailored to each individual. Marita had to spend more time than most as copilot and pilot under Glen Ross's supervision because she was the weakest of the crew in that area. This pleased Glen and Marita found herself more and more comfortable in his company.

In a fateful twist of scheduling, Sean Murphy and Marita had the same off duty hours. They spent time working out, sharing books they were reading on the computer screen and conversations about their pasts as well as their present life. It was after working out one day that Murphy took Marita in his arms and kissed her gently on the lips.

Feeling his rock hard body against her, she responded willingly. They found their way to one of the sleep hammocks and hooked the lanyards to their belts so as not to float around. The lusty desire she had been harboring was sated as the Marine proved himself a willing and capable sexual partner.

For a few months they met daily and satisfied each other's physical needs.

July 1, 1995

The passengers of Venus X met daily for status reports and discussions regarding anything that was of concern to one or more of them. After a few months the reporting become routine and data had to be markedly different than expected for the crew to respond enthusiastically. Boredom brought on by the sameness of each day began to set in. To combat this Pennington set up teaching seminars every day with a grading system so as to stimulate the competitive spirit of his people. Each astronaut took turns at presenting material in his or her field of expertise.

John also encouraged them to become creative in their preparation of meals. The one-acre farm area was multi-layered to reap the most production out of the minimal space. It had been seeded six months before the crew came aboard and was already producing carrots, beets and turnips. The tomato plants and wax bean bushes offered tasty, albeit smaller than normal vegetables.

As the years went by, this phenomenon resulted in smaller and smaller sized crops of fruits and vegetables. For the time being they afforded an adequate variety to satisfy the daily nutritional needs of all. In addition the miniature goats gave plenty of milk and the flyers soon were experts at making cheese and churning butter. The chickens supplied a half dozen eggs a day and the rooster and mini-Billy goat performed their siring duties with gusto.

The mission plan was to survive as long as possible on the produce of the farm. When the yield became too meager for the crew to survive they would begin to eat the frozen food that was stored underneath the outside skin of the ship. This food had been attached outside to benefit from the extreme cold in outer space. A great deal of effort and planning had arrived at what was estimated to be eight years of survival diet for the crew.

Sandra Meyers became a key factor in the lives of all as they realized the criticality of the farm if they were to survive the mission. Her seminars were of deep interest to all. Marita and she became close friends as the Yaqui Indian shared folklore agriculture she had inherited from her ancestors. Also the environmental control system was germane to successful farming in space.

Sean Murphy was drawn into Sandra's work as they collaborated to compliment diet and exercise. The genteel Georgian was charming company. Her seeming southern naivety was betrayed by a quick wit and rapier repartees when others teased her. She carried her 125 pounds in an erect; lithe 5 feet 6 inch well-proportioned body. She fit the mental image everyone has of southern aristocracy.

Graced with a flawless complexion, light brown hair, which fell to her shoulders in soft waves, and piercing black eyes encased in almond shaped lids, Sandra Meyers was stunningly attractive. This beauty did not escape Sean's roving eye. One day, after sex, Marita looked at Sean and realized that as sexually satisfying as their affair had been she no longer lusted after him as at first.

"Sean, do you love me?"

"Marita, you are the greatest. The best I've ever had."

"I didn't hear that four letter word, Murphy."

"Look this mission doesn't lend itself to love. No long-term commitments can survive because we're too confined. We need to be there for each person when they need us. None of us can monopolize one partner to the exclusion of another's needs."

"Are you saying that I've monopolized your time? Or do you want to spread your talents to the other women you think are panting for your tool?"

"What I'm saying is that I want a little variety. I'm not saying I won't be here for you when you need me but I can't be fenced in when it comes to sex."

"Well, fella, it's clear that we need to walk away from a good thing, before we hurt each other and we jeopardize the mission. So long, Garine, it's been good to know you. I'll see you around. Good luck with Sandra."

"How do you know I'm really turned on by her? Is it that obvious? "

"Only to the one being dumped, its o.k. Sean I'll always like you and your company but I've cooled off to our sex and as you said we all need our space. She unhooked herself from the lanyard and the addiction that had been Sean Murphy. The affair, like all relationships based solely on sexual infatuation was doomed from the start. Marita Diaz floated to the farm for some silent time to sort out her emotions. She always got help from digging barehanded in dirt, a gift from her Yaqui parents. She pondered what new twist life on the space ship would bring.

October 1, 1995

Sitting in the Mission Control Center, Colonel Colin Croft stared at the report, the CEO of Nuclear Power Industries, had just presented to him. He was totally distraught at the damaging news.

"Are your people absolutely sure of these findings, Mr. Volk? This is not another computer error or erroneous data input some engineer made?"

"Colonel, if there was any way that I could disprove these findings I would spend the resources of NPI down to the last penny. However, the results are irrefutable. The seals on the Nuclear Waste Dissipaters may leak prematurely. If this happens, nuclear radiation could seep into the main structure of the ship. All on board would be contaminated and surely die, if not from the radiation but from eating the contaminated food." He continued, fingering the zipper slide on his briefcase. "The life expectancy of the seals is dependent on the frequency of turning the boosters on and off. It's a case of thermal shock. Going from minus 454 degrees Fahrenheit to plus 150 degrees breaks down the molecular structure. Can the mission profile be modified to reduce the use of the booster rockets until re-entry time?"

"I don't know. In the meantime no one, and that means no one, is to talk about this unless I'm present. Is that clear, Mr. Volk? I will consult with my people and you'll hear from me before the day is over. Don't plan to leave the cape for a while. Fly in your top technical personnel on this subject for consultation with my experts. Make sure those coming in are cleared for top secret and tell them to keep their mouths shut. If this leaks out, the media will be down here like flies on horse shit, and it will become extremely embarrassing for your company and NASA."

Croft's anger saturated his every word. "Make no mistake; if we have to scrub this mission because of this potential failure, you and your company will pay dearly. I've got seven special people up there and I don't want to lose even one of them. If this mission fails we'll never send another crew up on an extended flight in your lifetime or mine. Volk, if you believe in God then you'd best spend your time negotiating a miracle with him. You will hear from me ASAP."

The businessman knew enough about the man's temperament to resist any further explanations. He picked up his brief case and told Croft, who was on the phone summoning his staff, that he would leave the hotel address and phone number with the Airman's secretary. Volk left the room walking as softly as possible relieved he had come out alive.

Croft's rage had been all too evident. CEO's of major corporations are not used to being ordered around like enlisted service men. Recovering his composure, he began to frame a game plan to handle the imminent cancellation of the Venus X mission. The NPI stock was sure to plummet and result in a financial blood bath for the company and himself. Once at the hotel he called his broker and told him to sell his shares at the going rates over the next three days. Hopefully, he'd come out ok if not too many investors caught wind of his sellout before the mission was scrapped. The ever-resourceful Mr. Volk would survive. Meanwhile, aboard Venus X, the crew was planning a big celebration in honor of Columbus Day for they related to his ocean crossing as the precursor of their flight. The pioneers had no inkling of the possible seepage of radioactive waste into their living quarters.

At Kennedy Space Center, Colin and his staff studied possible alternatives. After three hours of brainstorming, deep, silent thinking, and mathematical analyses, they broke for the night. Croft scheduled a meeting with NPI staff first thing the next morning.

While Colin Croft sat in his den sipping a double scotch and grappling with the despair of having to cancel the mission, Glen and Marita were coming off duty. She had finally mastered piloting a space ship the size of two football stadiums. Her joy bubbled out of her as she found herself unable to stop talking about the last session at the controls.

Her exuberance infected Glen with unusual cheerfulness. He had been feeling this way every time they were together. His love for her had become undeniable.

"Do you want to see if any of the crew is in the kitchen area finishing the party plans," Glen asked hoping to prolong their time together?

"Sure, I'm too pumped up to sleep now, anyway."

To their surprise, the area was vacant so they sat down and shared a tomato juice. As they swapped stories about Marita's woes as a pilot, Ross studied every feature of her face. So entranced by her beauty, he almost missed her answer to why she had taken so long to qualify.

"If I did not enjoy your company so much I could have finished sooner. It was the only way I could get you to pay attention to me since we left mother earth." Her eyes met his and the softness of true caring and friendship pierced the fence he had kept between them. When she had been with Murphy, Glen had decided she only had respect and professional friendship for him. Rather than be hurt by her rejection of his love he had chosen to treat her with professional courtesy.

He moved to her and kissed her tenderly. She did not pull away. Rather, she kissed him back hard. He would remember how cool her lips had felt and the softness of her skin against his nose for the rest of his life.

"I've loved you for so long, Marita. These six months have been torture for me. I've wanted to hold you in my arms and tell you how much I loved you."

"I know, love. My time with Sean hurt you deeply. I had to work that out in the way I did. I would never have been sure that my sexual yen for him would not have burst out the first time you and I had a lover's quarrel. Please forgive me the hurt I caused you and try to understand."

"I hoped all along that you had to get him out of your system for me to have a chance with you. I don't know if I'll ever totally put it out of my mind for good but I want to forget it ever happened. I don't want it or anything else to ever come between us."

"Oh Glen, I've come to care so much for you these last few months and I've been waiting for you to take me in your arms. I believe I love you in a way that surpasses any other love I've felt before."

Ross pulled her closely to him. As they kissed they forgot about weightlessness and floated about the dining area locked in each other's embrace. She kissed his eyes and his ears while his lips caressed her neck. A tender moment typical of longtime friends who will one day discover that they are lovers. Their passions faded as Sam Hershburg's voice filled the ship over the intercom system.

"Venus X, this is Mission Control. We're seeing an anomaly in some data. We suggest you institute a yellow alert until we can resolve this situation."

So much for any romantic interludes as the new found lovers hastened to the locker area to check out their gear in anticipation of a possible red alert. Nancy Flowers and Sean Murphy were at the controls of the ship when the message came. Within two minutes Mission Commander Pennington was on the flight control deck.

"Tell Croft I want to talk to him on Red channel pronto. We have no indications of any marginal conditions on board. What can they have that's so critical?" The Red channel was a frequency reserved for communications between the Mission Commander and the NASA Mission Manager exclusively. Pennington sat at the scramble computer and typed, "Colin, John here. What's the story? All systems are "go" here. What do you guys see that we don't and why don't we?" John's paternal caring for his crew did not allow for base station earth to be privy to information that he did not have.

The truthful response was alarming. "John, we've been apprised of a weakness in the Nuclear Waste Dissipater seals. We're trying to get a handle on it with the NPI people. They assure us it's a progressive thing and the seals will hold for now depending on the frequency of Nuclear Booster firings. I suggest you avoid any firings except for emergency situations until we get a clearer picture. Your sensors will detect the seepage but we don't want it to get to that point. Hang tough for now and we will tell you everything we know as soon as we can."

"Nancy, put an electronic hold on all booster firings until I clear up this situation with Kennedy. I want to know any and all comm with NASA until I say differently." Pennington's calm and quick reactions confirmed the correctness of Croft's choice of Mission Commander.

"What's going on, John? What do they have we don't? Flowers asked-"Do you want me to scrub the last Red channel communications?" "No. It's not necessary. Assemble the crew on the control deck and I'll fill you all in."

When they heard his explanation the questions came in a staccato fashion. What's the fix? What's the margin of safety? Would they abort the mission? How come such a finding at this late date into the mission?

The commander had no answers.

October 2, 1995

At NASA the tension was suffocating as if the oxygen was slowly siphoning from the conference room. The longer the discussion the more it was obvious to everyone that the mission was doomed. It was certain death for the seven if the boosters were fired once too often. The consensus was that the seals were 90% safe up to 75 firings, 99% safe up to 60 firings. Since return to orbit could take up to 10 firings there remained only 50 safe firings to steer the ship out and back.

To make matters worse, the turnaround maneuver would consume 10 short bursts. No one in their right mind would attempt a 20-year flight under these conditions.

At 14:00 EST, Mission Manager Colin Croft decided to abort the flight. First, he would notify the two companies financing the project with NASA. Then they would hold a news conference and announce it to the world. NPI would defray half of NASA's cost and acknowledge full responsibility for the faulty seals.

Croft called Venus X on Red channel.

"John I'm very sorry but we've got to abort."

"You can't be considering this without trying some sort of fix. Why can't we replace the seals or cover them with some epoxy which would stop any possible cracks or seams to develop?"

"You know that the seals have to be resilient. We've explored every possible solution. There is none. It's time to cut the possibility of a total loss and come home."

Pennington new that Croft would go to any length to complete the mission. "I'm sure this is the only decision possible. I'll brief the crew."

"We're getting the software modified to make the return flight as foolproof as we can. As soon as it's ready we'll transmit the changes to you and get all of you back home safe. We'll be ready in 48 hours."

"Take your time, Colin; we're in no hurry to come back with egg on our faces."

The press conference was the nightmare that all NASA Mission Managers fear. Explaining failure to millions of Americans is not the way to make voters want to support funding of future programs. Typically, the funding companies not only refused to be identified to the public but they cut off monetary support immediately. Their management took the usual tact, always save your arse, and never admit guilt in press reviews.

Only one or two Wall St Experts associated the resignation of two major corporation CEO's with the NASA announcement of the aborted mission. They had the acumen to dump their stocks in both companies before the bottom fell out.

Chapter 19

Colonel Pennington outlined complete details of the problem and the impending cancellation of the mission. He assigned tasks for turn around and re-entry. As he finished, Glen Ross asked to address the crew. Failure was not acceptable to the Navy flyer.

"John, I want you to understand that I'm in no way preaching mutiny. However, I believe we can complete this mission if we change our trajectory right now. We don't need to orbit Neptune. We can make one long firing to accelerate up to 60 million miles per hour and stay at that velocity for the whole mission. Meanwhile, you can calculate a new course to cover most of the mission profile but with much fewer corrections. This will minimize our use of the boosters and still let us complete most of the mission as planned. We can get all the scientific data except the Neptune Mapping which can always be done by non-manned satellites. The extra velocity will give us a longer turn around with fewer booster firings."

"John, are you willing to put my suggestion to an open discussion with the final decision in your hands?"

"This is new territory we are exploring so I'm open to hearing all of your ideas and suggestions. Please keep in mind that any of our ideas would have to be acceptable to Mission Control. The floor is open. Say everything you have to say now, because in less than 48 hours it will be too late to override the new re-entry program."

The discussion bounced between "Why should we continue?"
To, "Can Ross's plan work?" At times passions ran so hot that Pennington had to order a few moments for cooling down.

From the start the consensus was to continue with the mission, however; how to do it was the point of contention. After two hours, they agreed to offer Ross's plan to Mission Control. Each crewmember knew that the odds of base earth accepting the new plan were next to nil.

This fact prompted Glen to approach Pennington privately and ask, "John, if you don't receive an answer from Mission Control would you give the ok to go with the new flight plan?"

John knew immediately where Glen was going with this question; he had already wrestled with this possibility. He would not allow himself to be boxed into any activity which could make him part of mutinous acts.

"Ross, if I had no answer from ground control and no new flight control program, I would be forced to assume that the Yellow alert was over and the mission would continue as planned."

The clown had jumped out of the box. The gods of Venus X were about to take control of their fate. Glen searched out Nancy and Sean to discuss implementation of his plan.

Chapter 20

Glen Ross, driven by his inability to accept failure, convinced Nancy and Sean to assist him in disabling both ship to earth communications systems in such a way that none of the others could detect the failure mode. This called for some hardware modification and for a change to the fault diagnostic program such that the error would not be reported.

They edited the data collection program so that any out-bound transmission would be recorded as if sent correctly; while all in-bound reception would be intercepted and stored in a protected file area only available to any two out of the three conspirators. In that way no one person could read incoming messages nor could a single person bypass the new code and contact mission control on their own. This meant Kennedy Space center would not receive Pennington's request to change flight plans nor could they reject it. Thus ship Mission Commander Pennington could never be accused of having disobeyed orders.

The next step was to modify the flight

program to fly a course which would steer the ship tangent to the outer edge of the Van Allen belt. They returned to their rest areas agreeing to meet in twelve hours. At that time they would decide to go ahead with their fateful plan or return the ship to original configuration and let Mission Control decide their destiny.

Two hours before they were to meet, Pennington called a meeting of the crew and told them he would talk to NASA Control and request permission to implement Ross's plan.

"If mission control agrees or does not respond in 48 hours I want your vote as to whether we implement the new flight course or turn around and go home. Take a half hour to discuss it amongst yourselves and come back here prepared to voice your feelings and your vote."

John waited to hear any responses then continued. "The vote shall be secret ballot so that no one need feel pressure on their decision. First we'll vote whether the decision must be unanimous or a consensus. That vote may be academic if I make the decision on my own. As ship Commander it is my responsibility. However, I promise you if I take that step your vote results will influence my decision greatly."

The three conspirators lobbied the rest of the crew to follow Ross's plan. When they voted that the decision to return or abort had to be unanimous the hope to continue became doubtful.

Pennington read the second ballot results slowly as if his motor reflexes were anesthetized by the ramifications that a yes vote would bring.

"Yes.... Yes.... Yes.... Yes.... Yes.... Yes! " The decision now rested on the Mission Commander's vote.

"Common sense dictates that the risks are too great to go on." A low moan barely escaped the lips of the crew. "I realize that we all knew the probability of mission success was 25%. That implies that each of us had made a choice to risk death for the chance to accomplish what no one thought possible. As Mission Commander it's my responsibility to bring you and the ship home safely."

John paused, undecided, considering all possible eventualities. Did he have the right to choose a path most likely to lead them all to a terrible death from cancer? Was the mission worth the chance to end up floating in space for eternity, lost to the rest of mankind?

"I've decided to vote yes. It may be a suicide mission but pulling this off would be the accomplishment of our generation. I want to be in on it."

Each one felt a surge of exhilaration as the adrenalin flowed. The gods of Venus X were convinced that even the risk of death was worth the chance to be the ones to live in space for twenty years without support from earth. Each astronaut believed that though the rest may not survive, he or she would make it. Each preferred to focus on his or her own possible immortality rather than consider the final alternative.

"Let's get back to our duties and I'll update you all as events dictate."
As they filed out to their tasks John took Glen aside. "Ross, see to it that NASA can't turn us around. Set the new course. When ready, I'll fire the boosters to accelerate to 60 million miles an hour. I'm taking full responsibility for this change. None of you will be accused of mutiny. Just obey my commands and you'll be

blameless. Make sure no one can get back to Croft and tell him of our plan. Make it foolproof."

Ross's underhanded effort to control the decision had been meaningless. John had robbed him of the glory. "Consider it done, John."

Pennington went to the rain forest part of the gardens. He stripped and sat there letting the warm mist soak into his skin. He hoped that it would wash away the doubts and anxieties of the dangerous choice he had made. An hour later he dressed and climbed to the Flight Control Deck ready to fire the nuclear rockets which could propel his ship and crew into extinction.

Since Ross and his co-conspirators had prepared the system before-hand it took only forty-five minutes to run the Fault diagnostic. John Pennington anguished through the longest three quarters of an hour of his life. All except John and Glen were taken by surprise when the boosters ignited. All expected Mission Control to order them home. Now they realized that Pennington never intended to turn back. Their feelings were akin to death row convicts. No control over their destiny, the "Damocles" sword of radiation poisoning hung over them. Their mouths salivated as the taste of their mortality roiled in the pits of their stomachs.

Gone was the bravado that had swept them up to vote for the mutiny. Now they looked at each other and saw the imperfect men and women they must trust with their lives. The umbilical to mother earth was cut. Their universe shrunk to a pentagon shaped three-story structure the size of two football stadiums.

With all systems functioning as expected, John Pennington left the Flight Control Deck and worked his way to Nancy Flowers' cubicle. The way he tapped lightly at the door revealed his uncertainty at the step he was taking. "Nancy, it's John, may I come in?"

"Just a minute, John."

Nancy was not ready for company. She had gone to her area as soon as the ship had begun accelerating. She chose to be alone with her thoughts in the dark silence of her quarters. Nancy clambered out of the hammock and unlocked the door.

"Yes, what is it, John?"

"May I come in?"

"Uh, yes, I suppose so."

John slipped inside the door blinking repeatedly to get accustomed to the darkness. "Is anything wrong with the boosters or the ship? Are we accelerating ok? You look worried."

"Everything is A OK so far. We haven't reached max velocity yet but the accelerometers are reporting as expected. We'll know in an hour or so if this floating egg crate can stay together at 60 million miles an hour."

Nancy sensed his nervousness and did not know how to disarm the awkwardness. John and she had never spent any social time apart from the rest of the crew. "Do you want to sit and talk for a while?"

"Yes, I'd like that. Actually, I need to hold a woman in my arms, to smell her freshness and to feel her hair against my cheek. Can you see me through this?"

Nancy understood how deep John's need for him to speak so candidly was. He had never spoken other than casually, with her or with any of the other women as far as she knew. She did not speak but took his hand. In the darkness, she led him to the hammock. There she slowly unhooked the Velcro fastener of his shirt and slipped it off his shoulders. While she undressed, he took off the rest of his clothes. The scene was painted in silence. Words would only interfere with the intimacy of the moment.

Embracing, caressing and fondling, the two souls responded to each other's need. They tried to lose themselves in the moment hoping to feel alive again, able to hope, to believe that all would work out, and that they would survive.

For Nancy, it was the first time she allowed mothering instincts, so long repressed, to seep out of the depths of her being. She could not separate the mothering from the sexual arousal. It was, in some unexplainable way, a total sensuality that she had never experienced before.

For the first time, since his wife had died three years ago, John gave in to his need for a woman. For a long time He had convinced himself that no woman could replace his Clarissa. Now, doubting the wisdom of his decision and acutely aware that each moment was sublimely important, he nestled his head between Nancy's breast and slipped into the melancholy of the little boy within.

After a time, Nancy raised his face from her bosom and softly kissed his forehead, his eyes, and his cheeks until she found his lips. With increasing ardor the kisses fueled the sexual intimacy they both needed. Locked in his arms, she felt his tears dropping on her cheeks. The giving of his body released three years of repressed emotions. For that brief moment Nancy Flowers saw into the dark sadness of John Pennington's soul.

Later, they lay intertwined allowing sleep to heal their fears; a mutual catharsis was taking place. Before John came to her, Nancy had been lying in a fetal position fighting the demon of depression. Gone was the self-confident Nancy Flowers as her thoughts had raced from one scene of destruction after another. Hope was gone. Extinction lying in wait at every turn.

For John it was a restoration of his manhood. His courage returned as the sexual release had drained off all the doubts and fears. Two hours later they awoke and dressed silently. Neither dared to speak, fearful that words might destroy what had happened between them. As he opened the cubicle door to leave, John turned and said, "Thanks, Nancy, I believe I owe you my sanity."

She looked at him and murmured, "Thank YOU, John. You gave me life and hope, knowing I'm not alone with my fears."

Quietly, John returned to the Flight Control Deck and Nancy logged on the computer to check the status of the flight profile. She needed the reassurance that the work she had done with Sean and Glen was completely correct. Self-assured Nancy Flowers was back in control.

Chapter 21

Sam Hershburg sat at the console perplexed. Twice he had tried to transmit the new flight control program to Venus X with no return acknowledgement. He called Croft at his office and explained the dilemma. Colin raced to mission control.

"Get me Red Channel right now, he commanded. John, this is Croft, what's going on up there? We can't load the new program onto your guidance computer. Do you have a malfunction showing up on your diagnostic? "

No answer. He repeated the call a second time, then a third, now a fourth. For ten minutes Croft tried to reach the ship to no avail. Angry and frustrated as he imagined the worst reasons for the silence, the usually unflappable Air Force Colonel shouted to no one in particular, "How could two different receiving computer systems fail at the same time unless it was a total power failure?"

"Sam, what does our system show as failures up there?"

"None Colonel, all systems show a green light."

"How can that be when we can't light either comm channel? What's their track? "

"That's what else is bugging me, sir. It seems their track has shifted 40 degrees left and if I believe the data; the ship velocity computer is registering an unprecedented acceleration. It's beyond anything we had programmed. At this rate they will reach top velocity in five minutes. What do you make of it?"

"It scares me to think what could be happening. Something has gone haywire on that ship and our seven people could be in great danger or maybe dead. Keep recording the track and every five minutes call them on Red channel until you make contact. I'm calling the computer manufacturer's reps and the power people down here to see what they make of it. Don't leave that console."

"Don't worry. I'm glued to this console until we hear from them."

As he waited for the experts, Croft prayed that his fears were unfounded and a quick explanation and fix be affected. The answer to that prayer was a "No." The gods of Venus X had shut him out of their lives.

For three days NASA personnel tried to raise a response from Venus X but to no avail. The press was unrelenting in seeking the status of the mission. On the fourth day the head of NASA instructed Colin Croft to announce that mission control had lost communications with the space ship but would continue tracking its flight while trying to rectify the communication problem.

That night, Colin Croft's soft curly brown hair began to show traces of gray. Soon he would sport a full head of gray hair. Relief from the press came the next week when a major hurricane swept up the South Carolina coast. The mission relinquished its front-page status as the media concentrated on the latest catastrophe.

On November 1st, 2000, NASA quietly pulled the plug on the project with a Top Secret report declaring the space ship lost in space and all aboard presumed dead. Colonel Croft and Sam Hershburg were assigned to a new space project and the Venus ground communication center was declared salvage equipment.

Risking a conflict of interest, Croft

contacted the CEO of NPI and entered negotiations to have NPI purchase the Venus X communications equipment and set it up in a garage he rented. He enlisted Sam Hershburg to moonlight with him in continuing to monitor the channels allocated to Venus X and recording the flight track as well. The two mortgaged all they had to support this activity.

As the weeks ran into months and months to years the vigil took its toll on both men. Their walk, their posture, the lifeless look in their eyes imaged their grief and despair. The ship was lost yet neither dared give up hope.

The gods of Venus X did not know the price those left behind were paying. As pioneers, the astronauts did not dwell on the sacrifices of their families and friends on earth. The unknown must be explored at any cost.

Chapter 22

The weeks following the decision to continue the mission saw the crew perform their duties more carefully as if each moment, each activity was crucial to life. Conversations were short and mostly duty related. All on board were dealing with reconciling the reality that mission failure, accompanied by the death of all, was more likely to happen than any had been willing to admit up to this time.

While working in the farm area, Jim Barnes and Sandra Meyers began to talk more freely about their emotions and how they were handling the stress. On one occasion while talking about the plants and the care they needed, Jim asked, "Do you think the animals are showing any signs of stress since we accelerated to max velocity?"

"I haven't noticed any change in their behavior. The hens are still lying as much as before and the goat's milk is as plentiful. Why? Have you noticed any differences?"

"Not really. At times I wish I could be like the animals."

"Why?"

"They don't seem to worry much. They go on about the business of being chickens or goats and it's enough for them. Me, I've been trying to be more than just a black athlete all my life. That's why I'm on this project. I want to make a difference for my kids and other black kids. If we don't make it, I may just be a forgotten black man like so many others before me who dreamed big dreams they never realized."

Sandra stopped gathering the eggs and looked at his ebony face now etched with concern for the safety of the mission and its crew. She and Barnes had not developed anything more than a professional friendship. She, the white, southern aristocrat, had never learned to be anything but distantly courteous to black men. For his part, Jim Barnes had always known that trying to get too close to her kind was trouble. He could still hear his father, Baptist Minister Luther Barnes, warning him, "Son, you make sure you're always polite to white folks and stay with your own color. Black is what you are and black's all you'll ever be. There's plenty of good wimmin in your own race." That's the way it was in Waycross,

Georgia for young Jim Barnes.

Sandra searched for words that would show him she too was concerned about the possible failure of the mission. She did not want to sound too friendly nor condescending. After all, this was no black butler standing before her.

"I didn't know you had children, Jim. How old are they?"

"I don't. I gave up that dream when I accepted this assignment. It seemed to me that this project would have an effect on more kids than raising a couple of my own and working in the community. I was engaged to a Miss America contestant until NASA called. When Croft told us about the length of the project, I wrote to her and told her I wasn't ready for marriage. It would interfere with my career. Man was she upset. She wanted to return the ring but I told her, "A gift is a gift and that no one else would ever use it but her." I hope she understands better when she reads the last letter I sent her when I was selected. It wasn't fair for me to ask her to wait twenty years. By then it will be too late to start a family.

The love and sensitivity in his words

touched Meyers. "You're right," she said. "If I were her, I would have reacted the same way." For a moment neither spoke then Sandra continued. "I did not have to make such a tough choice. I never fell in love with any of the men I dated. Most were spoiled, sons of rich families and they were either absorbed in their careers or infatuated with their self-importance. To me, they never matured past the college sophomore level. Maybe I was just as wrapped up in my career. It makes no sense to me but girls with high IQ's never fare too well in the dating game."

Barnes heard her words but was not impressed with the "poor little rich" white girl tale. However, he detected a certain disquietude in her body language and dullness in her voice. He asked, "Sandra, are you afraid that we won't make it? Outside of Ross, the rest of us are not without some fears. We've got to encourage each other to take it one day at a time. You can't mark the time on the calendar or worry about how long we have to go. Every day we survive is a breakthrough in space travel."

She interrupted him with the words no one wanted to speak. "How will any of this help

anyone if we die out here, lost in space?" Jim
had the same thoughts. "I'm going to talk to
Pennington about that. I believe we should be
transmitting our progress and findings even if
we don't acknowledge any responses. That way
they can plan future flights with better chances
of success. Do you think he'll listen?" "I think
it's a good idea. I'll go with you if you want a
supportive voice." She was surprised at her
quick willingness to join the black man, yet she
knew it was the right thing to do.

   "No, I don't think it would be wise
because it will look like we are ganging up on
him to get our way. I'll try it alone. If the idea
has merit, he'll implement it. Otherwise he'll
scrub it. In fact, I'm going to look him up right
now so I that I don't talk myself out of it. Wish
me luck."

   Brushing his arm with the lightest of
touch, she nodded agreement and wished him
success. As he left, she thought to herself, "My,
my, wouldn't Mama and Daddy be surprised at
such openness with a black man?"

Chapter 23

Jim Barnes saw a light under the curtain of Commander Pennington's cubicle. "Commander, may I have a word with you?" "Certainly Jim, come right in. What's on your mind?" "Well John, I have a suggestion." Without waiting for a response, Jim outlined his plan. The Air Force Colonel listened attentively. He promised to consider it and make a decision within twenty-four hours.

An hour later, John called the crew together. "Jim suggests we transmit status on an on-going basis without acknowledging responses from earth stations. What do you think?"

Sandra was quick to agree with the idea. Nancy Flowers objected. "I don't like it," she spoke sharply. "If we continue to transmit, the earth stations will know that we're operational. Mission Control will find a way to contact us and order us back to earth. I didn't take this mission to turn around for anything."

"Scared to go back home, Nancy?" Sandra's uncharacteristic sarcasm exposed her dislike for the statuesque blond. Beneath her southern charm hid a tigress ready to pounce and devour the enemy when she was provoked too far.

With Nancy it was the rivalry for Sean Murphy's attention. The casual friendship the two women had, during the training at Kennedy Space Center, was snuffed out as they preened and postured like mares in heat vying for the Irish stud.

Flowers never liked coy, cutesy women and viewed Meyers as one of those women who use female wiles to get her way. This Georgia peach with the syrupy drawl made Nancy nauseous.

"Are you looking for a way scuttle the mission so you can go back to the plantation and your black servants?" The gloves were off and the situation had all the makings of a catfight erupting at any moment.

Pennington spoke sharply. "Alright you two save the bickering until we're back home. I want ideas on how we report our findings and still fulfill the complete mission. "The alley cats knew that John was not going to tolerate their pettiness anymore. Glen Ross spoke. "John, this is all bullshit. Sean, Nancy and I can program the system so it will look like we lost our receivers. When we get it set up we'll train all of you," Glen continued. "Marita and Jim, we need to find a satellite system that will accept our data without it being accessible to NASA. John you and Sandra could draft a priority list of data to send."

Mission Commander Pennington had no reason to dispute what seemed like a workable plan. "If there are no objections to this plan, let's try to put this together." The crew dispersed with a revived enthusiasm for the new job at hand. The meeting was over and John Pennington had suffered the first denigration of his authority by acceding to the Chief Pilot's orders. Glen Ross, the warrior god of Venus X, had made his initial thrust and Pennington had not parried. The dual for leadership authority had begun and John was oblivious to being a combatant.

Chapter 24

During the next ten days the morale of the crew was very high. Marita and Jim Barnes relished the challenge of researching data in a science unrelated to their career fields. Nancy feasted on the opportunity to work closely with Sean Murphy for she saw a way to win his attention away from Sandra Meyers. Sean was too wrapped up in the work with Glen to appreciate the situation for he, as well as Glen, had put the confrontation between the women out of their minds.

The crew met in response to Colonel Pennington's request. He had to speak loudly to break up the animated conversations as the astronauts exchanged glimpses of the individual results they had achieved.

"What have we got done, people? Let's start with Software. Sean, give us a status, will you." Sean went through a detailed description of available computer memory. "In summary we could store the equivalent of sixteen thousand 8 /2 by 11 pages, single spaced. However, all our vital signs statistics are stored outside our control and this will always have priority on memory. My best guestimate is that we can use sixteen megabytes safely, that's about five thousand pages."

Glen Ross interjected. "That's about ten books the size of Moby Dick. Do you think we'll record that much data in twenty years?" His question was not sarcasm or humor but an effort to get the opinions of the others as to how much data they thought would be saved.

Marita was the first to respond. "If we store one page per day times 365 days for 20 years that adds up to 7300 pages. Would we need one page per day?"

Her question triggered an energetic discussion that resulted in a system that would abbreviate all words in a form similar to speed writing and pack the data for one month. The data would be culled for value and priority every month.

Jim Barnes and Marita Diaz had located only the Intastar Satellite able to receive data from Venus X. Unfortunately, the window of proximity for the two space vehicles that would permit communication between them would occur only once per year for a two day period. Jim added, "This satellite is monitored twenty-four hours a day by the BBC in London. The odds are they would not interpret the data as important for NASA."

"Is that the best connection we can make, once a year?" Pennington was not pleased. "Maybe a few more months of work will find something better but that's what we have right now," Jim offered. "Keep working on that and in the meantime we go with what we've got. Glen, you and your software team will define our abbreviation rules. I'd like the system to send a Mayday or SOS directly to NASA if we don't save data for forty-eight hours. Can we code that into the schema?"

Nancy jumped in. "I can do that. The emergency will be flagged if the Flight Control Officer on duty does not log on at the beginning of the shift and log off after saving at least one piece of data when that shift ends."

Chapter 25

Sam Hershburg dialed the phone excitedly. He impatiently drummed with his fingers on the desktop as he listened to three, four, five rings. A drowsy voice mumbled, "Hello, Croft here."

"Colin! Colin! Wake up! We just received a transmission from Venus X. I don't know why but I woke up at midnight and could not get back to sleep. I felt I had to check the comm gear and there it was a message from the ship. They're alive and continuing on a new course they've programmed. Get down here I'm trying to reach them but no response yet."

"Are you drunk, Hershburg? Do you know it's 2 o'clock in the morning? "

"Wake up, man! I'm dead serious. Get down here in case we can talk to them. You'll want to hear what they say. I'm hanging up. I'll keep on trying to contact them until you get here."

Croft got up. Swiftly pulling on a pair of faded, tan, corduroy jeans, he slipped on a dark, grey sweat shirt, tugged-on a pair of black Air Force issue socks and finally double knotted the laces of his brown deck shoes. Jane lifted her head slightly from the pillow and raising the black eye shade from her left eye she asked, "What's going on, dear?'

"Sam says we just received a message from Venus X. I have to get down there in case we make contact. They've got to know that we're still monitoring their frequencies." Colin bent down and softly kissed his wife. "Don't breathe a word of this to anyone because if it's some weirdo faking this message and we go public then the list of court suits by the survivors will look like the New York phone book. Not a word now to anyone." With that, he ran to his car for the twenty-minute drive to the rented garage where he and Hershburg had set up the communication equipment after purchasing the salvage gear from NASA.

"How do we know this contact is really from Venus X and not from some crackpot jerking us around?" the Air Force Colonel asked as he slipped through the side door and sat down next to Hershburg.

"I don't know maybe I can detect something in the message that will identify the sender."

As he reached the last paragraph Colin Croft smiled and very slowly singular tears of joy and relief seeped from his eyes and trickled down his tanned cheeks. "It's them. See this last sentence. Only Ross and I know about this conversation. They deliberately added "Those with warrior hearts will go all the way and return victorious. See you in twenty years, hard ass." That son-of-a-bitch, Ross, is defying orders and if I judge him rightly he won't let us order him back no matter what. In fact that might be why they don't acknowledge our transmissions. Let's send this scrambled message and see what happens."

"Croft acknowledges message from warrior chief pilot; NASA no longer on your frequencies. Repeat, NASA no longer on your frequencies. Hershburg and Croft only remaining contacts with your ship. Do you read? Over." The two waited for the transmission to be relayed to the ship via the communication satellite. A long four minutes later Ross's voice came crackling over the speaker.

"Glad you didn't give up on us, Croft and Sam. What's the story on NASA Mission

Control?"

"Venus X, you have been officially declared lost in space with all aboard presumed dead. Project has been dead filed for three months. No NASA authorization or funding for mission activity."

This time the return transmission was delayed as the crew realized they had been abandoned in space. Ross and Pennington discussed the situation and decided to continue as they had planned.

"Croft we never expected to be forgotten so soon. We will not abandon the mission until forced to do so by a failure mode we cannot live with. How do we stay in contact with you two?"

"Venus X, we suggest all transmissions be sent on red Frequency and scrambled per this code. If you go public you will be ordered to return to earth immediately."

"Roger, no public until we're ready to do so."

Croft and Hershburg recommended a schedule because they only monitored communications during two one-hour spans per day, 6 to 7 EST morning and night.

"Roger, earth station, we'll try to accommodate ourselves to your schedule."

The vigilant earthmen waited throughout the day and evening but to no avail. Their initial enthusiasm and joy waned as the hours dragged on and at 10:30 pm they left for their individual homes not knowing if they would ever hear from Venus X again. They agreed to disavow any knowledge of this contact. They would not divulge the day's happenings to anyone for the time being.

When Colin arrived home his wife, Jane, was sitting in front of the TV in the family room clutching a glass of scotch in her well-manicured hand. "Well, what'sh your story thish time?" she slurred. "Ish she better in bed than I am or are you turning queer and uh --- and uh making it with Sam?"

Since Jane was usually a one glass of wine at dinner drinker, Colin knew she had run out of patience with his dedication to monitoring Venus X. He tried to soothe her anger and sarcasm until nausea forced her to let him help her to the bathroom. Sick almost all night and hung over the next morning she was in no mood to listen to excuses. Venus X was still taking its toll on earthbound creatures.

Two months passed before Colin finally shared the secret of the transmission. Only then did Jane begin accepting the importance of her husband's role in the ill-fated mission. He felt forced to share it when she confronted him, "I want a divorce unless you give up this obsession with your radio ham set. I can almost understand an affair with another woman but your listening for radio transmissions that never come is too much."

On board the spacecraft Glen Ross was smugly pleased with the answer they had received from Croft. He consulted with the ship commander and they agreed to transmit the ships log on a bi-monthly basis without responding to messages from earth.

Chapter 26

Since that moment in the dining area when Glen and Marita had acknowledged their love for each other, they spent as many hours together as duty schedules permitted. They shared intimate details of their lives before NASA. Their love for each other had an element of tenderness which neither had experienced with previous lovers. However, from the night of the first contact with Croft and Hershburg, Glen spent more and more time with mission details. He would work extra shifts or extended shifts to stay abreast of the daily progress.

Marita felt that Glen was more wrapped up in the mission and his desire to be commander than with her. She hated the feeling of rejection. When they were together he rambled on at length about the work. Marita felt cut off from him and alone. This triggered memories of being made to feel second class because she was Yaqui Indian, or she was too small or not white enough. The old feelings of not measuring up or being unlovable began to take hold of her. One night she decided to talk to Ross about it. She reached over and tenderly placed her forefingers on Ross's lips.

"Love, tell me you love me. You do love me don't you? Hold me. You're so far from me when you talk about the mission."

"I'm sorry, Marita, I can't help it. I get so absorbed in flying missions that I forget everything else."

"You told me this obsession cost you your first marriage. Am I always going to be second best to this ship?"

"Marita, I don't want to lose you, sweetheart, you're the best thing that has ever happened to me. Help me to break this compulsion. Remind me when I'm going off the deep end. I truly love you." The look of love in his eyes and the sincerity in his voice assuaged Marita's fears.

"You know that if we were on earth your placing flying first would prevent us from getting married. I would leave you rather than not be first in your life. Then again maybe you would not want to marry me anyway."

"Of course I'd marry you. I want to spend the rest of my life with you. You are the main reason I will do anything to bring this ship home safely. In fact I'd marry you right now if it were possible."

Marita, imbued with the wiles of generations of Indian women, had slipped the bridle of marriage on Glen Ross and he never felt a thing. "Are you serious? You'd marry me if you could?"

"Yes, of course. Do you think we could?" as he took the bit.

"I don't know. We would have to ask John, I suppose."

"Leave it to me. I'll talk to him next shift change."

The idea seemed preposterous to the mission commander. No one on the project had ever conceived that two of the astronauts would want to marry. There was no need. All had conceded from the start that romances would flourish but the freedom from earth bound rules and customs would allow liaisons without the trappings of marriage. Pennington's negative attitude triggered Glen Ross's compulsion to be right and win at all cost. He insisted that the crew be given the chance to discuss the proposal.

John agreed, convinced that the crew would oppose the idea. "What kind of stupid idea is this? Nancy Flowers barked out. What's the matter with you two? I don't see any signs saying you can't screw unless you get married." Nancy had not like Marita from the first time she worked with her in training. She thought the Indian got special treatment because of her race. It would be great press for NASA, she thought, if a Native American were to go up in space. Now, her dislike had a reason to be expressed. "You didn't have to get married when you were laying for Sean. A married couple on board will cause nothing but disunity because neither partner will be free to make correct decisions that adversely affect the other."

The demeaning reference to Marita revealed the unconscious bias Flowers harbored. Her tirade triggered a heated argument as some took exception to the slur while others argued the pros and cons of marriage on board ship. After a while, the din of voices quieted and Pennington asked Marita to explain her desire to be married.

"Glen and I love each other very much. We have made a commitment to be faithful to each other for good. It's important to me that the rest of you recognize this." Marita tried to look at all the others to see their reactions but the ingrain Yaqui female shyness won and she lowered her eyes. "By marrying, the integrity of our vows is placed for public scrutiny. I would look for your aid and support in being true to my commitment. If I don't make the promises public I can renege without the embarrassment of your judgment."

John Pennington stopped her. "We have no right to judge each other's behavior on this trip. We have to trust each other. Your promises to each other or to yourselves are only binding on you. We are not part of that."

"Yes, that's true but women of my race place great value on the esteem of our people. Also, I'm sure we all live with the constant awareness of how slim our chances are of ever returning to earth. I want to live out my life married to Glen." There it was again; the public voicing of everyone's unspoken fear. The flight was most likely doomed. What difference did it make if they were married or not?

Glen pounced on the argument that it probably was of no consequence if they married and said, "If it doesn't matter then why oppose our desire? If we die in space it means nothing to anyone but Marita and I If we make it back it should not affect any of you once we land."

None favored their request but the couple's reasons for marrying swayed Pennington. Realizing that marriage vows, though made publicly, are the province of the couple, he decided he would perform the ceremony.

Commander John Pennington, USAF, officiated as Glen and Marita married. Sandra Myers and Sean Murphy were the witnesses. Jim Barnes was on duty in the command post. Nancy Flowers did not attend the ceremony labeling it a farce and predicting that it would have long lasting consequences detrimental to the success of the mission. All of her lobbying attempts to prevent it had failed.

On that same Christmas day on earth, Sam Hershburg and Shirley Stern, another of the trainees not selected for the mission, announced their engagement. They had been lovers since the day the mission had been scrubbed.

Except for Sam and Colin Croft, life on

earth was going on as if Venus X and its crew did not exist. A week after the wedding, Flowers and Marita were scheduled to clean out filter screens and dispose of debris out into space. The conversation was laconic and at best civil. After one of the awkward silences that interspersed the few exchanges, Nancy, in a condescending voice asked, "Well, is the screwing any better since you had your little show? Are your archaic mores soothed so you don't feel guilty when you spread your legs for him?"

Marita could not believe her ears. In the flat, monotone Yaqui women use when stating a fact she said, "Why are you so bitter and resentful? Are you jealous of me because I had Sean first and you're getting seconds? Maybe you want Glen for yourself and now you know you'll never have him?" There was no anger in her voice; rather, there was a note of sadness as if she felt sorry for the self-confident, always in control, woman standing before her.

Nancy's only rebuttal was to mutter, "Stupid bitch," glare at Marita then turn away. The rest of that work shift was completed in silence punctuated only by unavoidable work

related one-liners.

Chapter 27

The next few months saw the crew settle down to the exacting life style of space travel. The most difficult thing to deal with was boredom. The sameness of the ship's interior coupled with daily mundane tasks caused each in his or her own way to experience mild depressions. Conversations seemed less stimulating as "I've heard all this before." Even the spectacle of the universe as seen through the viewing portholes was losing some of its magic.

To stimulate the lives of his people, Pennington decided to have a Spring Festival celebration. Perhaps a united viewing of the majestic universe followed by a breakfast party at which they would vote on who was wearing the most creative hat. He hoped to restore a sociability which was missing since the wedding debacle.

All joined in the effort for it offered newness to their lives even though it seemed childish behavior for men and women of their ages and technical background. It allowed the little child within to come out and play. Even

Nancy and Marita began to talk to each other about things other than work.

Sean, in the style of a true Irishman, concocted an alcohol potion of significant strength. After a couple of drinks, everyone relaxed and the party achieved the results Pennington had hoped for. After a morning of storytelling, which seemed funnier with every sip of Sean's punch, the crew began to drift away to their respective quarters.

Sean was the last to move on after capturing whatever debris the crew had overlooked. He went to be with Sandra but found her sleeping. Rather than wake her and take a chance of rejection he went to Nancy. Feeling the effect of the alcohol she welcomed him and they both enjoyed the sexual encounter.

Marita and Glen found their way to the rain forest section of the farm. The feel of the warm, mist on their skin and the alcohol in their veins stirred deep passion within them. As they embraced and kissed, each began to slowly disrobe the other.

As they removed their steel soled shoes releasing them from the magnetic gravity walkways, they began to float about. She wrapped her legs about her husband and his strong arms held her torso from floating away. Copulating in gravity free space added a dimension of frustration due to every movement causing the other to drift in the direction of motion. Finally Glen reached out and grabbed a limb of a tree and Marita managed to hook her feet onto adjacent forked branches. Suspended hammock fashion, the water dripping from the trees diluting their perspiration, they satisfied each other's passion. The moment of climax was in perfect unison something all couples strive for each time they join in sex but seldom achieve.

At this moment the God of gods, wearing His Hermes the trickster hat, chose to use the lovers to create the first earthling in outer space.

They drifted toward the manmade waterfall. This lightly pressured flow of water, constrained by a ten-foot diameter polyurethane tube, hung from the ceiling to the floor of the rain forest area. As they slipped on the water-washed rocks that formed the base of the fall, they would float away and have to work their way back to the cataract. It took almost an hour to wash, dry themselves and collect their clothes that had floated all over the rain forest. "Do you think this is the way it was with Adam and Eve after they ate the forbidden fruit?" Marita joked. "I don't know but I still haven't found my fig leaf and you look better without one" as he looked at his wife admiringly.

Chapter 28

Marita suffered through two months of nausea and a queasy digestive system before she admitted to Glen that she might be pregnant. With minds addled by alcohol and driven by lusty passion, neither had taken any steps to prevent conception. They discussed alternatives and resolved to have the child despite the many reasons not to.

In her fourth month they approached mission Commander Pennington to reveal their secret. They asked for his agreement to keep the child. It was obvious that the other astronauts must be told immediately. Their reactions were not unexpected.

Sandra Meyers was the only one supportive of her fellow doctor's desire to give birth in space. On the other hand, Nancy lashed out furiously at the stupidity of the co-creators. "Once you solve the problem of birthing, what will you do for diapers, space gear, and potty training? Are you crazy enough to think you can raise a child in space? Don't you know that we still have 19 years to go before we get back to earth?" Her dislike of Marita, fueled by a jealousy she could not explain, incited Flowers to lash out with venom in her tone and words. "What makes you think we have food enough to feed some insatiable teenager? You've got to abort this thing before you screw up this mission completely. Commander, order them to end this pregnancy right now!"

Glen spoke coldly and with sternness in his voice which silenced everyone. "You have no voice in this. It's Marita and my decision and we will have this child. Anyone who tries to stop us won't have to worry about getting back to earth. We're supposed to be pioneers, resilient problem solvers. If you were on a desert island in the middle of the ocean instead of space would you oppose this new life?" The resolve in his voice was unmistakable.

Commander Pennington spoke softly; the words had a loudness of their own. "We have the alternative of going along with Glen and Marita or forcibly causing her to abort the child. The latter could necessitate restraining Glen for some time, perhaps for the duration of the mission, if he insisted on carrying out his threat. Could we complete the mission under this choice?" John paused to give all a chance to absorb the thoughts he had spoken. "I don't know. However, we can all concede that Ross is the best choice to pilot our ship during re-entry, if we get back to the earth's gravitational field. Unless you and Marita change your mind, Ross, you are not giving us much of a choice. Will you reconsider for a few hours and get back to me tomorrow? In the meantime, I ask the rest of you to consider the two alternatives and where you stand on them."

For Glen and Marita the decision to have the child was reinforced by the sense that it was their destiny, part of the big experiment that was Venus X. Why else would this have happened? The world needed to see that space life could be earth-like in almost all things, even childbirth.

The rest of the crew realized the impracticality of a forced abortion. People would be injured in any struggle that would surely ensue. Equipment would be damaged and the safety of the ship would be jeopardized. All agreed to wait and see if the child survived to full term. They lived with a new awareness of Glen Ross's iron will and the threat he posed to their safety if they pushed him too far.

Marita watched her health carefully, eating and exercising under Murphy's guidance. Sandra Meyers became gynecologist by default. The expectant parents busied themselves making diapers and layette sets out of some of their own clothing. The mother recorded in the ships log that other than the baby seeming to float around in her belly the pregnancy was normal.

Chapter 29

As the due date approached the astronauts became more supportive and soon each had contributed material to put together a makeshift tent in the animal pen area. The intent was to have Marita deliver the baby inside the tent thus confining the blood and afterbirth, preventing it from floating all over the ship. They stored water in sealed containers and towels inside the tent.

On the sixth day of January, Marita began to experience mild labor pains. Expecting sharper and more frequent pains she continued to work in the garden. Without warning the water broke. To no one in particular she shouted, "The babies coming," as she hurried into the tent. She remembered the stories told by the ancient Yaquis of the women having their children alone in the wild. She grasped the center pole of the tent and squatting began the arduous delivery of her child. Millions of miles from earth, this small Yaqui woman reenacted the scene played on the wilderness stage of earth hundreds of years before.

The birth was uncommonly easy and the child came into the universe before anyone came to Marita's aide. As she struggled to stay anchored to the pole and keep the child from floating to the end of the umbilical, Sandra Meyers came into the area. Sandra quickly made sure the baby was breathing then cut the cord. While the mother continued the process of delivering the afterbirth, Myers, with the baby in her arms, worked her way to Nancy Flowers' quarters.

"Marita just had the baby. I'm going back to help her. Come over after you clean him up." She left the infant with Nancy and returned to Marita's side. "Where's my baby? What did you do with my baby?" "It's ok, Marita, Nancy's taking care of it until we get this mess cleaned up and get you into your quarters." "How could you give the child to Nancy when you know how she feels about it? What if she harms my baby?" Nancy heard Marita's concern as she entered the tent. She placed the child in the mother's arms and with tears streaming down her face she helped Sandra clean the area and fold the tent material. They guided Marita to her sleep area and Sandra left to find Glen and announce the news that he had fathered a healthy baby boy.

"Isn't he beautiful, Nancy?" "Yes he's gorgeous. He has your dark eyes and Glen's nose. All that black hair. I wonder if it will fall out like the baby hair does on earth. He has your complexion too, you've done a good job," as she looked away.

Marita saw the woman's sadness and questioned her, "What's wrong, Nancy? Aren't you happy for me?" "It has nothing to do with you. It's a long story I don't talk about." "Why don't you tell me?" as the child suckled at her breast. "Maybe it's time I told somebody. When I was fourteen I stupidly had sex with the local high school hero. Some luck. My first time and I got pregnant. I didn't dare tell my mom who was a strict Presbyterian. I let the boy talk me into getting an abortion and he found some sleazebag to do it." Nancy wiped the tears from her cheeks. "Unfortunately, in the process, he caused so much damage that I can't have kids. I nearly died and my mom never forgave me for my mistake."

The tears were gone now and only the sadness in the woman's eyes revealed the hurt she carried. "When Sandra brought him to me, it was the first time I held a baby since before the abortion. You can't believe the pain and sorrow I felt. God, how I wish I had my baby to hold. I'm so sorry. I'm so sorry." With that acknowledgment a torrent of tears, buried in years of repression and guilt, poured out amid groans and sobs. It lasted 15 minutes one for every year since the cruel event.

Marita softly consoled the broken woman before her. "Nancy, you could help me raise my boy. I'm going to need all the support I can get. If something should happen to me, I want to believe that someone would take care of the boy with love. If I don't make it back could you do that?"

"I'll try the best I can."

The special moment ended when Glen came in to see his wife and son. Nancy quickly went to her quarters. Lying in her hammock she allowed the bitterness and anger to return. "How could I have told her about that? Now she'll lord it over me because she knows I can't have kids." Jealousy for Marita nestled in her soul. The hatred returned.

"I'll never let that little shit, squaw throw

it up to me. If she tells everybody, her kid won't reach the next day." Tough as steel Nancy was in residence again.

That same day the Senate Investigation committee published its final report. They declared that NASA officials were derelict in duty by entering such a foolhardy endeavor. The lives of American women and men had been sacrificed to the sorrow of the astronaut's families and all citizens. It cost taxpayers of the United States enormous sums of money for a program that had no chance of success.

The committee recommended immediate dismissal of all senior officials who had taken part in the decision making process of the Venus X project. No blame was assigned to the finance committee and the members of congress who had jumped on the bandwagon when the project looked so glamorous.

The head of NASA was relieved of duty and within a few days was hired by a large Aircraft manufacturer as a Lobbyist in Washington, D.C. Colin Croft resigned his Air Force commission. He joined Aerospace Avionics Inc. located in Daytona Beach, Florida, as a Systems Project Manager. Though offered more lucrative positions in other parts of the country, Croft chose to stay near Cape Kennedy to continue the monitoring effort he and Hershburg had set up. The man of integrity stayed true to the men and women he had sent to what universally was believed to be sure death.

Chapter 30

Glen and Marita named the baby Adam. The presence of this new fragile life, on board Venus X, drew astronauts together as the tiny one stole their hearts the way babies do. Now it was Aunt Sandra instead of Meyers. Uncles Sean and Jim and John always had excuses to seek out the infant. Each wanted to show the child new things about life aboard Ship though they knew that Adam understood nothing they said.

Glen Ross found himself absorbed in his son. He had not been that way with Andrew. As he experienced each phase of Adam's growth he savored the moments with some melancholia for having missed these times with his first son.

Nancy remained aloof. She dared not let herself become fond of the boy. The unpleasant task of cleaning dirty diapers was left to the mother and father. Jim Barnes installed a trap door in the clear water allowing it to flow into the effluent system providing a turbulent flushing system. Prior to his ingenious modification the handling of soiled diapers had been an exercise in will power and constant vigilance. At times, it was more an exercise in futility trying to prevent free floating baby doo-doo that always seemed hell-bent on escaping to the control deck.

It was at this time that Marita decided to resume wearing her elasticized suit designed to apply pressure on her body, exercising the muscles while performing routine tasks. Until now her distended stomach had made it impossible to wear the suit. To her consternation she found it too short. She took her body measurements and found her legs and waist thinner while her bust and chest dimensions had increased. She knew that her height would increase but was not prepared to find she was more than two inches taller than at blast off.

As the prime on board physician, she arranged to measure the rest of the crew. The results were essentially the same. All agreed that, when the suits became much too short or tight, a hand-me-down exchange would take place. Unfortunately, it meant the tallest would eventually end up without suits. Sean had the task of increasing the individual exercise programs to compensate for the effects the suits would have on muscle tone.

It would be two years before Nancy and Glen, the two tallest, would relinquish the gear. As the shortest astronaut, Marita would always have access to a hand-me-down. Adam never wore a suit. The whole effort became moot when most of the crew gave up wearing the suits because, with long term wear, they chafed the skin and in some cases even caused blisters. The scant supply of skin lotion did not offer any relief. This was one more important fact to note for future missions. Elastic suits don't work as presently designed.

Chapter 31

As soon as Glen allowed it, Sean began working an exercise program with Adam, geared to developing the child's strength, for no one knew how his body would develop in a gravity free environment. The time spent together every day, saw the man and child develop a close relationship. Murphy came to see Adam as his own son for he knew that he probably would never father a child of his own.

For his fifth birthday, Glen let Adam control the ship. He stopped short at arming the directional boosters with a stern warning never to fire them for the ship may become radioactive and all would die. At the celebration Sean Murphy experienced a sharp pain behind his right eye. It was as if an ice pick were driven into his eyeball. He grabbed at his eye but the pain was so momentary that he told the others he had a piece of debris in his eye.

On that day a short insert in the Houston sport pages noted that "Handy Andy" of the Houston Astros was traded to the Atlanta Braves. He would report in February for spring training with the new parent organization.

Glen's son had matured into a fine major league prospect and his dream to play for the Braves was becoming a reality. His father knew nothing of Andrew's success.

At five years old, Adam was the typical inquisitive boy with the added dimension that he was living in a weightless environment that he had mastered with more agility than any of the crew. Gifted with a photographic memory he learned about life on earth through the Encyclopedia Britannica stored in the computer, while the 50 issues of National Geographic offered him pictures of wild life and creatures of the world.

Sean and Sandra Myers taught him basic mathematics and how to play chess on the computer. Adam was a child growing up in a solely adult world, leading an uncommonly free life with few inhibitions. The boy seldom wore any clothing since all adult outfits were too large and none of the astronauts voiced any need for him to be clothed.

In this respect he was not too out of uniform since most of the crew's outfits were becoming so torn and tattered that the men only wore shorts. The women improvised bandeaus and shorts from worn out clothing, exchanging them, with each other, to break the monotony of wearing the same thing all the time. NASA had not foreseen this most rudimentary fact, ---clothes wear out. The scientific community planned redundancy in much of the hardware yet under estimated the life expectancy of clothing.

The yearly physical exams revealed a continued lengthening of the spine for every crewmember. With it came some discomfort similar to that felt on earth by teens and pre-teens that experience too rapid a growth.

Chapter 32

Over the next few months, Sean Murphy began having headaches; the sharp pain behind the eye became a daily visitor to the Marine Captain. He reluctantly approached the internist, Sandra Meyers with the symptoms. She examined him and took a blood sample that she studied under the microscope, in a most primitive fashion, compared to the sophisticated techniques available on earth.

Meyers consulted with Marita and they agreed that they could not diagnose the illness. The two convinced Mission Commander Pennington to let them transmit a microscope photo of the blood sample to Colin Croft hoping he could have it analyzed and report the findings.

During the month it took for Croft to arrange for friends at Walter Reed to run the tests and transmit the results to the ship, Sean soothed the pain with an herb tea Marita had learned to make on the reservation. The blood test did not reveal any clue to Murphy's problem. The Walter Reed staff suspected a tumor or an aneurysm and suggested to Croft that the patient should come in for a complete physical to locate the cause of the headaches and the pain. They warned the retired Colonel that the patient should not be on flight status until the problem was resolved. Colin could not reveal the blood sample source and saw some bitter humor in the irony of the situation. He imagined the laugh the Venus crew would have when he told them he was supposed to relieve Sean of flight duty and order him back to earth for a physical.

The astronaut doctors, Sandra and Marita, agreed with earth findings and examined Sean critically for any signs of lumps particularly along the spinal column, the back of the head and the neck area. They found nothing, for the problem was an aneurysm behind the ear bone caused by one of the many blows Sean had absorbed in his boxing career.

In the weightless state the blood tended to collect in that portion of the weak blood vessel causing it to expand thus applying pressure on the adjacent nerves. The blood in the expanded portion was coagulating and would sooner or later block the artery completely or break loose and cause a blockage wherever a constriction occurred. The aneurysm could also burst, flood the brain with blood and Sean would die.

As weeks droned into months the tea sedative lost its effectiveness. There were not enough drugs on board to kill the pain. Murphy's behavior became erratic and unpredictable. From moments of tranquility he could suddenly lash out verbally at whoever was present, or would lose track of the conversation and speak of things totally irrelevant at the time. He might just as quickly revert to his normal jovial self.

Pennington was forced to relieve him of flight control status which exacerbated the condition for the Marine saw himself relegated to mundane tasks. The one activity to which Sean pointed was the once a week spacewalk that the Mission Commander had instituted as a way of breaking the monotony of dull endless time.

The flyers were struggling with maintaining the simple routines of everyday life such as men shaving and women combing their hair. With Murphy sick the exercise programs were frequently ignored. The spacewalk allowed each astronaut one hour of solitude floating in space at the end of a thirty-foot tether cable. The suiting up and checkout of life support cabling consumed the better part of an hour. Adding a half hour for unsuiting and storing made for two and a half to three hours of activity which each astronaut savored.

Chapter 33

On July 9th of Venus X's eighth year in flight Sam Hershburg's wife had their third child, Jane and Colin Croft celebrated their eighteenth wedding anniversary and Andrew Ross played first base for the National league all-star team, getting two singles and scoring one run. The TV and Radio announcers mentioned his father milking the sadness of the missing astronauts for all it was worth.

While life in the good old U.S.A went on routinely, Seam Murphy donned the flight suit and slowly worked his way out of the narrow tunnel to the pressure chamber that acted as a barrier between the ship's pressurized interior and the vacuum of outer space. Jim Barnes and Sandra Meyers were his support team.

As the Marine Captain floated away from the ship and performed graceful bird-like patterns of flight the two monitor astronauts engaged in small talk nonchalantly surveying the life support gauges. Sean broke into their chatter.

"Well boys and girls, it's been nice while it lasted. Tell Adam I loved him most of all."

With those last words Captain Sean Murphy, USMC turned off his supply of oxygen.

"Hey, Sean, the oxygen flow gauge just bottomed out. Are you getting a good flow?" Barnes waited. No response.

"Sean, did you receive that last message about oxygen flow rate?"
Barnes looked at Meyers. No response. Sandra grabbed the ship intercom mike shouting.

"All hands report to the command deck immediately. Sean's on a walk and he's not responding to our calls. It looks like he's lost his oxygen supply."

The Mission Commander and Glen Ross got there first. "What's going on? Is he responding yet?"

"No, Commander, and now the heat flow gauge is down and the suit temperature has dropped to minus 10 degrees Centigrade and it's still going down. It's already at minus 40."

The shrillness of Barnes's voice cut through the uncertainty of the moment. Pennington barked out orders. "Ross, suit up and get out there quick. He can't survive that cold and no oxygen. Flowers, you and Diaz get Glen hooked up and into that tunnel pronto.

Make sure his life support systems check out before he's in the pressure chamber, I don't want two dead people out there. Barnes, keep calling Murphy. Try to get him to check his air supply and heat valves, the temp's down another 10 degrees."

"John, Murphy's suit is probably not leaking heat out into space because it's holding at minus 50 Degrees C. That's what the suit is designed to do if the heater tube gets blocked." Barnes stated in a dull matter of fact way as he began to grasp the possible reason for the emergency failures.

In record time of twenty minutes Glen Ross was moving from the craft, maneuvering as quickly as floating in space allows, toward his stricken friend.

Shutting off the heater valve was the last motion, and two minutes later the Marine's last cognitive act. Typical of loss of oxygen, Sean's goodbye wave was the last motion locked in his brain cells and nerve system. Ross had to try and catch the flailing arm as Murphy kept swinging it back and forth.

Everything was in slow motion with Ross reaching out and Murphy pulling away. Like pilots in a dogfight the two friends sparred in the dark silence of star lit sky. Then Murphy's arm extended for the last time. The macabre space dance of death was over. All Sean's vital signs went straight line on the monitors.

Pennington took the mike from Barnes's grip and said, "He's gone, Ross. Bring him to the pressure chamber entrance as best you can."

Chapter 34

Like a lifeguard rescuing a drowning bather, Ross held the dead comrade's neck in the crook of one arm and with the other hand pulled on the tether to float back to the ship. He groped along the ships surface. Sometimes he pushed too hard and they drifted out to the end of the umbilical line. He would then have to pull himself and the corpse back to the ship and continue working his way to the entry port.

It took 40 minutes to push Sean's stiff body, with the left arm rigidly extended, into the pressure chamber. Once in the ship it was obvious that Sean had deliberately shut off the air and heat valves. Though unspoken, everyone knew that the pain must have been so severe that Murphy could not live with it any longer. The Marine had chosen to no longer threaten the safety of the crew and the mission. "At least die with honor Sean me boy," he had told himself as he left the ship.

"What are we going to do, John?" Marita asked.

"What do you all suggest? We can't keep him in the ship he'll stink badly in three days."

"Maybe we can cut him adrift in space like we bury sailors at sea." Barnes suggested.

Pennington closed his eyes as he tried to weigh all the options.
NASA's instructions were to cast adrift any dead crewmember. Now he knew that he could not do this.

"We are not going back without him or anyone else who might not make it to the end of the voyage. I want you to take his suit off, strip him naked then tie his ankles together. Now tie his arms alongside his torso."

"We can't get the stiff arm to budge," Sandra said looking towards Pennington for help.

"If you have to break that left shoulder do it. Tie his wrists inside his marine belt that he liked so much. Nancy, fetch the outside shell of his sleeping bag from his quarters and a couple of six-foot lanyards. Barnes and Diaz suit up. I want you to take him out and lash him to the stanchion just aft of the starboard viewing area."

The astronauts did not move. The thought of their companion strapped to the side of the ship was too much to process in a moment.

"What are you saying, John? You want to leave him out there flopping around while we finish the mission." Nancy Flowers rebelled as her mind filled with the image of her lover's cadaver floating alongside Venus X. It reminded her of the scenes depicted in Moby Dick where they lashed the whale to the side of the ship as they sliced off the blubber and meat.

"Look, the Marines are proud of their reputation that they do not leave their wounded behind. If we were on earth we would have brought Sean to a medical facility as soon as possible. The country has a right to know if his illness is a result of prolonged weightlessness or some space travel phenomenon." The crew listened to Pennington's argument. "As soon as Murphy's body hits the minus 454 degrees F. every organ will be quick frozen. It will take considerable time for him to defrost once he's back on earth. After the medics have analyzed the autopsy report he'll be laid to rest where he belongs in the ground on earth. I would want nothing less for myself or any of you."

"Can't we leave him in the space suit, John? Marita asked.

"No. We'll need the suit for Adam or spare parts. Sean doesn't need it anymore. Now let's get on with it. We're not even sure that what killed him is not contagious."

Ross supported the mission Commander saying, "John's right. Sean deserves to finish out the flight. We've got to tie his ankles and wrists so he won't freeze in a posture which would make it impossible to get him into the ship that will take us off Venus X and ferry us back to earth."

The discussion was over. Each astronaut went about obeying Pennington's directions. As they prepared to move into the exit tunnel the Mission Commander recited a commitment prayer from the Military handbook. It took Barnes and Diaz thirty minutes in space to lash the Marine Captain securely to the stanchion tie-down and return to the safe confines of the ship.

Pennington's entry in the ships log read that a faulty hose connection was the primary cause of loss of oxygen resulting in Captain Murphy's death. This sealed his death was accidental rather than suicide. It assured that his survivors would reap all death benefits without legal entanglements.

The boy Adam was very troubled by Sean's death. For a few weeks he had nightmares and would frequently wake up crying. When awake he would mope around the gym apparatus as if waiting for Sean to come and work out with him. Sean had been like a second father to him. Explaining death to a seven year old was difficult, at best, to make sense of terminal sicknesses and suicide was near impossible.

The next time that the boy logged-on the computer he found a message from Sean. "Adam, I'm leaving you in charge of the exercise program. Don't let any of them get lazy. Someday you'll understand why it was important for me to leave this way. If I stay on board I may do something to hurt someone or break something that could destroy the ship. As you get older and face things in life you will come to crises that call for difficult decisions. At those times remember that I said "Be the man and do what's right. It's very important that you tell your Dad that the magic word is GUNG-HO. Buy good buddy."

Adam did not understand the

significance of this last instruction. When he showed it to his father, Glen realized that to the end Murphy had the success of the mission as his highest priority. Sean had taken into account that he, Nancy and Ross had modified the flight profile program and without his password they would not be able to access the code. The password, GUNG-HO, allowed Ross to access the portion of the code that Sean had written should he need to restore the ship's communications with earth to its original status.

Ross approached the mission commander with the reality that if he or Nancy Flowers were disabled or died the last of the trio which had modified the flight program could not restore the flight control computer to original status. They agreed to publish, for the rest of the crew, the details and code words necessary to re-install the original software. Murphy's death had driven home the mortality of the crewmembers.

Chapter 35

For the next year the astronauts responded to Adam's reminders to exercise but one by one their commitment dissolved. Only Glen and Nancy Flowers worked out regularly. The sameness of the available food diminished their desire to eat. All lost weight and strength save the boy, his father and Flowers.

Life for the adults was tedious. Glen and Marita had the luxury of their son's youthful exuberance and inquisitiveness to sustain their interest in the world around them. Jim Barnes and Sandra Meyers grew fonder of each other every day. Both struggled with the learned prejudice against the other's race.

Sandra fought her feelings for Jim every time she remembered the warning her mother repeated over and over. "Proper white girls don't get involved with black boys. They only want to take advantage of you and then brag to their friends that they had themselves a honkey white girl." Jim's parents had continually reminded him to stay with his own kind. "The white gals that have sex with a black man is white trash and you deserves better." Yet both knew that the learned prejudice is not to be trusted.

As they worked and spent off duty time together the attraction they had for each other grew to a point that it could not be denied. Like a pair of ten year olds, their first kiss was tentative and barely a brushing of the lips. Would she be stained by his color, she wondered. He worried whether she was using him as an experiment to see if the old saw "black men are better at sex" was true. Each knew that his or her fears were foolish and too juvenile for sophisticated adults of the twenty first century. Yet, the old wives tales had seeped into their minds.

"I'm sorry; I should not have kissed you. I took advantage of you." Jim spoke softly. He wasn't sorry he kissed her. He wanted to give Sandra a chance to end the situation before it got too far.

"I'm not. I wanted you to kiss me but we were both so shy, weren't we?" She stood close to him and he knew there was no turning back or their lives on board Venus X would be unbearable. He pulled her to him and kissed her long and hard. They would be lovers. The bias gates came crashing down and love enveloped them.

"What would our folks say if they could see us now?" she asked.

"My Mom would say, 'Boy, you better stop all this foolishness rat now, ya hear me boy?"

Chapter 36

The astronauts busied themselves with personal projects beyond the scope NASA had devised. Sandra and Jim, with common academic backgrounds in Physics, studied the effects of the gravity fields of meteor showers on the Magnetic Gravity Simulator (MGS) which inhibited weightlessness in the farm and rain forest sections of the ship. They supplied voluminous data to Flowers and Pennington who spent their spare time running math analyses using algorithms of their own design. Much of this work proved technically worthless yet it was of paramount importance in keeping the gods of Venus X emotionally stable.

The one phenomenon which proved substantive was that the soil, in the two areas studied tended to shift to the edges of the ship when in the gravity field of other celestial bodies. They allocated this to the high iron content of the soil that the design engineers had deliberately created. The metallic composition was what kept the dirt attracted to the magnetic field of the Gravity Simulator.

Barnes and Meyers offered diversion to

the other crewmembers by scheduling three dimensional chess matches against the Flowers and Pennington duo and the Glen, Marita and Adam team. These games satisfied some of the competitive spirit of the crew.

The flight trajectory of Venus X was for Glen and John a stressful concern. They spent much time checking and rechecking their course. Ross came to respect and admire John's abilities. Day by day, Glen accommodated himself to Pennington's leadership. Ross outgrew the compulsion to take over command of the mission, settling into a secure relationship with his supervisor. Parenting Adam and loving Marita along with the endless hours of space flight were tempering his obsession with flying. The Navy Commander was becoming the man his first wife, Sybel, had wanted as a husband.

Two months before the projected day to turn the ship around onto a course for home, Glen discovered that the flight trajectory was aiming the ship directly at a star not registered in the Universe Directory of Space Bodies. The star had been imploding towards becoming a black hole and had eluded observation by astronomers.

Pennington verified the data then notified the crew of the collision threat. Flowers and Ross rushed to re-program the course computer. John agreed to fire the booster rockets in order to turn away from the collision course.

--- Too late---

The gravitational pull of the star on the ship prohibited the full effects of the rocket burst. Ross and Pennington had hoped to orbit the star and then escape orbit whereby Venus X would be catapulted slingshot fashion on course to reach the turnaround space coordinates. By mere seconds the ship missed the window of opportunity for orbit and skipped off the dense atmosphere of the collapsing star like a flat stone thrown onto a pond skips off the water. The ships trajectory was now 45 degrees off course.

Pennington ran a computer calculation to determine which boosters needed to be fired and for how long to return the ship to its proper course. The results were demoralizing. The turn trajectory would lengthen the flight time by two years. To make matters worse the long booster rocket firing would consume most of the fuel allocated for home course corrections.

Except for Marita and Adam who were napping in their sleeping bags lashed to the tie downs in their quarters, all astronauts were on the control deck mezzanine.

Pennington, eyes glued to the monitor screen before him said to no one in particular, "Crew, you'd better start praying because we are running out of options. Every second we fly in this direction adds days and months to the voyage. If we don't fire we'll never get turned around in time to get back to earth before our supplies run out. If we do fire we may not have the fuel to guide the ship into earth orbit when we get there."

Ross updated the Control computer with the current data and activated the firing sequence. As Venus X turned to its port side; the collapsing star zoomed by the space ship.

The gases filled with debris being sucked into the black hole and surrounding the star were thickening in density exponentially. These struck the tail end of the craft and sent it spinning on its own axis at an ever increasing rate of rotation. The centrifugal force of rotation was so great that everything not tied down was propelled against the walls.

Barnes, who had just finished suiting up for a spacewalk prior to the discovery of the rogue star, was pinned against the exit porthole. Ross and Flowers, who were sitting at the consoles, managed to fasten their seat belts. Marita and Adam were pressed against the wall of the cubicle. Cushioned by the sleeping bags they struggled to breathe as the G forces increased.

Myers and Pennington, having no protection from their skimpy clothing, were thrown violently across the deck area. The woman landed against the commander softening the impact and sparing her from severe injuries. Colonel John Pennington, USAF was not so fortunate. As he smashed against the wall his head hit the metal stanchion and crushed his skull.

---He died instantaneously---

Meyers, trapped against him, her face crushed against his, was unable to turn her head. She held her breath as long as she could as the internal gasses of his destroyed organs hissed from his mouth and nauseated her. She felt his warm urine seep down her legs as his body lost continence. Her nostrils filled with the stench of death coming from his bleeding mouth. She forced her eyes to close. Her mind could take no more; she blacked out.

With all the strength he could muster, Glen Ross the consummate pilot, managed to reach the manual firing controls and trigger the boosters attempting to cause a clockwise force countermanding the spin motion. The firing caused violent tremors through the ship as opposing forces fought against each other.

As the rate of rotation decreased Ross gingerly controlled the booster firings so that the ship would not over react and begin spinning in the other direction.

After an eternity of 10 minutes Venus X stabilized and Barnes unsuited to help in damage assessment while Nancy Flowers led Meyers to her quarters and bundled her in her sleeping bag. On the way back she stopped and helped Marita and Adam as she explained what had happened. Together, the trio returned to the Command deck.

"Ross, Pennington's dead." Barnes spoke in monotone.

"Barnes, wrap him in his sleeping bag so no more blood will float around," Glen ordered as he, by default, took over command of the mission. "The rest of you fan out and take an assessment of the damage while I check out the electronics and control systems." To Ross's surprise and a testimony to American craftsmanship and reliable manufacturing, all systems were functional except for some of the gauges that were either stuck or the related sensors were malfunctioning.

It would take days to resolve these problems. Meanwhile Barnes found the oxygen generators working normally. The water supply and flow control systems were damaged. As he tried to trace the cause of the trouble Barnes found Marita at the entrance to the farm and rainforest area. She stood immobilized by the scene of destruction before her.

"My God," Barnes blurted out. "It's like a hurricane came through here. No wonder there's no water pressure."

"This may be the end of the mission," Marita spoke softly trying to reconcile the catastrophe she beheld. It would take a Herculean effort to salvage and reconstruct the main source of food on board Venus X. Everything that had been held in place by the Magnetic Gravitation Simulator was jammed against the outside walls.

All but two of the goats were buried under the debris. Four chickens trashed their way out of the shrubs and dirt, the rest were not to be seen. The African pigmy pig and its sow were lying under one of the trees, both laboring through the last gasps of life.

The water tanks that processed effluent water into purified re-usable liquid were empty. Some of the seams had let go from the pressure of the whirlpool effect the spinning had caused. The contents of the tanks had splashed onto the now muddy soil. The sprayed water mixed with debris along the walls and created a mush which would float around if disturbed.

As if out of some bizarre sense of humor, the collision had driven the root vegetables such as carrots, beets, turnips and potatoes into the debris transplanting them in neat rows on the walls.

On her inspection of the sleeping quarters, Flowers found chaos. As if ransacked by a thief, articles held in place by Velcro were ripped out and smashed against the walls. Some, like combs and hair brushes, were impaled into the Lexan cubicle dividers lending to the scene a weird three dimensional abstract art work.

Chapter 37

Glen Ross remained at the controls until confident that the flight control system was operating properly and keeping the ship on course. To his amazement the space craft had stabilized on the exact course to return to earth. The God of gods was watching over the gods of Venus X. Glen chose to stay this course and forego the original mission goal of turning around.

By then all but Sandra Meyers were assembled on the control deck. Each related their assessment of the damages. It was at this time that young Adam looked out of the observation window and saw the frayed lanyard to which Sean Murphy had been tied. The Marine was not to be seen. The bag was frayed into ribbons and the body, pulled loose by the centrifugal force, had been flung into space. The naked son of Eire was hurtling into the unknown of the universe at half the speed of light. The first earthling lost for eternity in the vast, empty universe.

"If we are to survive we must act quickly to salvage what we can and get the water system working," Ross commanded "Marita, help Jim suit up for a walk to inspect if any damage has been done to the exterior of the ship. Nancy, strip Pennington down and wrap him in his sleeping bag shell like we did Sean. Barnes, I want you to take John out and secure him to a tie down. This time, wrap the lanyard around the body as tightly as possible; I want to take him home if we can. Meanwhile I'm going to take a float around the ship to see the damage for myself and to check on Sandra."

What Ross saw was worse than anything he had envisioned from the crew's description. When he reached Meyers she was huddled in a fetal position inside her sleeping bag. The trauma of being crushed against her bare-chested Commander was still real. She was catatonic.

"Sandra, Sandra, listen to me. We need you to help save the ship and our lives. We need your medical skills and your expertise in Biology to salvage as much plant life as we can. We all will surely perish if you don't help us. Sandra, Sandra do you hear what I say. We've come too far and through too much to give up now. Come let me help you."

That strong, pioneer courage inherited from her ancestors, among the first to settle Georgia, stirred within the hunched body and she opened her eyes. "Was it a bad dream or is John really dead?"

"It wasn't and is not a dream, but the damage we have suffered surely is a nightmare. I'll send Marita to be with you as you pull yourself together. As soon as you are able we need you in the farm area. I'll see you there."

With that, Glen hurried to the Command deck. Barnes was ready for the space walk. After Glen read a short commitment prayer over the dead Air Force Commander, Jim went out of the ship pulling his lifeless comrade with him. Barnes secured Pennington's body to a stanchion-wrapping the lanyards around the body as Glen instructed.

Jim toured the periphery of the ship and reported, "No visible damage, Glen, but some of the thinner walls have ballooned out and we had better hope that no minuscule leaks develop that could suck out the oxygen and cause complete loss of pressure. I want to stay out here a little while longer and make sure I didn't miss anything. Alert me to come back fifteen minutes from now if I haven't called in."

"Flowers stay here and get Jim in the ship and de-suited. Don't let him stay out there for more than ten minutes before he starts getting back to the entry port. You two come with me, we have lots of work to do." Glen led Marita and Adam to the farm. They found Sandra, in her soiled shorts and bra, sitting despondently, holding a carrot in one hand and a dead chicken in the other, unable to cope with the destruction surrounding her.

"Sandra, help Marita to scrape the soil slowly along the floor, away from the wall towards the garden section and into the magnetic field of the Gravity Simulator. Get up Meyers and do it now."

The woman responded slowly and began a task that would take two weeks to complete with everyone working every waking hour.

"When you find a live animal," Ross continued, "Give it to Adam." "Son, I want you to secure every live animal in the pens that are not damaged. Pass the dead ones to me so I can butcher them immediately and salvage the meat. We've got to get to the dead ones quickly or they'll not be fit to eat so always work towards any sign of life or a trapped dead one. I'm going to start with the pig and sow that are easiest to get to."

Glen soon realized that the blood would not drain out of the animals by just hanging them since the gravity force was not strong enough. He found a way to suck the blood out of the butchered meat with the small vacuum cleaner, normally used to collect floating debris. Then he evacuated the blood into the soil hoping to feed the remaining earthworms. They would be useful in reconstituting the garden area.

"How will we preserve all this meat, Glen?"

"Well Marita, somehow, we've got to freeze it. Adam, go get the outside shell of a sleeping bag. Take all the insulating liner out of it. We'll stuff the meat inside and stow it outside like we did with Sean's and John's bodies. It will be hard work to retrieve pieces for they may freeze together. We'll worry about that when time comes. First we save it and figure out how to use it later."

Soon they were joined by Jim Barnes who reported that he had observed no other signs of damage to the exterior of the ship.

"Well, that's good news," Ross commented. "Jim will you tackle the water system malfunction and try to get the drinking water back on line first, then we'll address the effluent control system. If you need a pair of hands to help you just tell me and one of us will come."

"Fine, Glen, I think I know how to jury rig some piping on a temporary basis. I'll come back and explain what I've done after I try my ideas." Barnes's voice trailed off into silence as he floated to the water generation plant.

Ross took a moment away from butchering to call Nancy Flowers on the intercom asking her to stay at the controls for another hour assuring her he would send someone to replace her. She acquiesced and the cleanup continued.

They managed to save the meats from four pigmy goats, twelve chickens, one turkey, ten rabbits, along with all the carrots, potatoes, turnips and onions they found in the first twenty-four hours. They micro waved many tomatoes, zucchinis and peppers. Using surgical rubber gloves as pouches they poured the vegetables into them and tied them securely. Then they stored them in the sleeping bag shell.

Glen took the food cache outside and secured it to a stanchion closest to the exit port. He took the opportunity to view the damage Jim had described and was relieved that conditions were not deteriorating.
The next day they found more, healthy root vegetables and cooked and packaged them for freezing. When Ross went out to stow them in the cache he was unable to unzip the bag and had to slit the zipper out. It did not matter for all the food was completely frozen and the new supply he brought out froze hard before he finished the slit. The crew would soon learn the almost impossible task of cutting portions from this frozen mass. As time would pass it would become the most arduous and time consuming part of their survival.

It took Barnes four hours to cap off the broken reconditioned water line that was causing a vacuum lock in the water generation system. It would take him two months to restore the effluent processing system into operation. In the meantime the garden area was slowly rejuvenating as the water soaked soil generated the growth of new plant life.

Now that the bulk of the salvage work was done, Ross transmitted the monthly message to earth. "Croft, we've had a major accident. We nearly collided with a collapsing star and the ship was thrown into a cyclonic spin. Pennington was tossed like a pebble against one of the metal girders and it crushed his skull. Do you read, over?"

"We copy, Ross. What can we do to help?"

"Unless you know of some way to send up a new supply of food, I don't see what you can do. We repaired the water supply system and have preserved all of the food we could salvage." Ross ended the transmission with a terse, "We are on course for return to earth."

"Roger, understand you are on course for return to earth. Let us know what we can do to help."

Chapter 38

Colin Croft turned to Sam Hershburg. "Sam, we need to think seriously about whether it's time to tell the world about Venus X or not. It's going to take a long time to get the wheels turning to fund the program and staff a recovery crew. Can you and your wife come to the house Sunday afternoon? We'll barbecue some steaks and plan the best way to handle this. We'll expect you around noon. See you then." The five days until the meeting would give both of them a chance to consider the furor the announcement would precipitate.

The crew of Venus X knew that in disobeying the order to abort the mission and return to earth they had triggered a Senate investigation resulting in Congress cutting off all funding for the project. What they did not know was that the following year the joint Congressional appropriation committee cut NASA funds by 80%. The rationale given to the news media was irresponsible fiscal decisions such as projects like Venus X. The committee advised that NASA should not be rewarded with poor tax payers' dollars.

Colin fired up the grill while Jane set the patio table with real silverware and crystal plates. This was definitely not a plastic and paper plate day. At exactly twelve noon Sam and Shirley were at the front door. This did not surprise Colin for he knew Hershburg as fastidious in all details and particularly obsessive about punctuality. Colin escorted them to the back yard patio.

"I thought we could be comfortable out here. It will let me barbecue and be with you at the same time. If it suits you, we'll have an aperitif while I do my best not to burn the steaks."

Croft tried to ease some of the tension he, and more than likely Sam and Shirley, felt by keeping his voice as cheerful as possible. The two couples sat in the shade of the patio canopy exchanging small talk over Amaretto aperitifs and stuffed mushroom appetizers. Soon they drifted into silence. The reason for meeting was too important to stay hidden behind the veil of pleasantries.

Croft broke the ice by asking Sam if he had re-read the last transmission and what he assessed as damage to the ship.

"Do you think they've got any chance at all of making it back alive?" he asked.

"I don't know Colin, they've survived so far. I guess as long as they are transmitting to earth we have to remain hopeful. However, announcing their live presence to the world is going to open a can of media worms that may not give us a moment's peace."

"You're right Sam. I think we need to reach the head of NASA first and try to keep this Top Secret. Can you shake loose this week if I can get an appointment with Davis? I would want you aboard right from the get-go on this."

"You name the time and place, I'll be there."

"I'm concerned that we may be premature in revealing our communications with Venus X. They're still ten years from home and a lot can go wrong to destroy the mission."

In an atypical fashion Jane responded to her husband's uncertainty, "Colin, you've kept this from the world long enough. It's time you let others share your anxiety and stress. You and Sam have done more than anyone could expect. Bring in some experts and resources to help the ship get back safely."

"She makes sense to me, Colin. Besides we have no idea how long it will take to get systems on line to affect a recovery. We know that they've mothballed all the Endeavor type ships that could shuttle the crew back to earth." Sam continued as the three listened attentively. "This is assuming that Ross manages to steer the platform into orbit as planned. If he misses we need a fall back plan to intercept their trajectory so we can get them off that death trap. We need all the time we can get. I suggest immediate disclosure."

"I'll contact Davis's office first thing tomorrow morning." Owen Davis had been the Chief of Operations at the Kennedy Space Center for the past three years. "Let's have another aperitif while I put the steaks on the grill. After we eat, we'll lay out our approach to NASA and detail all that has to be done."

The meal was perfect, topped off with fresh peaches smothered in French Vanilla ice cream then followed by two rounds of Grand Marnier and digestives. After clearing the table and loading the dishwasher, Jane and Shirley joined Colin and Sam sitting at the patio table. The women beamed with pride as they listened to their men develop their approach to revealing their long time secret. Only now did they realize the enormity of their husbands' task.

Chapter 39

Croft managed to get an appointment with Davis for the following Friday at 4 PM. It was obvious from the curt conversation and the time slot of the meeting that the NASA chief had no interest in being linked with the man who had headed the disaster called Venus X.

Undaunted, Sam and Colin arrived at the Space Center office building 15 minutes early not wishing to give Davis any excuse to postpone or cancel the meeting. After cooling their heels in the entrance lobby until 4:30, the visitors heard the Security guard on the phone saying, "Yes sir, they're still here. ---Yes sir, I understand sir. I'll give them the message, sir." As he slowly placed the phone on the cradle the guard said, "Mr. Davis sends his apologies for the delay. He will be in conference for at least another hour. He suggested you may want to reschedule. I can connect you to his secretary's line if you wish."

Sam and Colin recognized the stonewall ploy for what it was. If they were put off often enough the unwanted visitors would give up and go away. Croft opted to speak with the secretary, on the guard's phone. "Miss, we are willing to wait this out so we can get a few minutes of Mr. Davis's time. When he hears why we're here, he'll set up a second meeting when he's not so busy."

"I'll see what he says." Fifteen minutes later, the clack, clack sound of high heels against the tile floor drew the men's attention to a corridor leading off the right side of the lobby. The source of the noise was a tall hazel-eyed blond walking towards them. Her tight black skirt restricted her normally long stride and the pale blue blouse was barely winning the struggle to cover her large breasts.

Croft recognized the secretary's voice as she invited them to follow her. "Mr. Davis can see you for a few minutes. The office complex is normally closed to visitors after 5 pm but he has arranged with security to extend the time until 5:15 so that you will not have wasted a trip." Her soft, lilting voice carried certain sensuality to the listeners' ears.

Croft and Hershburg sensed she was parroting time restraints ordered by her boss. "Davis hasn't lost his taste in good looking women," Croft mused. He had met the NASA chief when the young Welsh had been hired at the Cape. In a short two years Davis had acquired a Center wide reputation as an exceptionally capable Engineer with the potential of reaching the top of any career field he might choose.

Croft remembered the comments by different bureau chiefs. "The kid will go places if he keeps his pants on long enough to get the job done." Or, "If he doesn't get caught screwing his boss's wife he can have it all," and "How did he marry such a nice girl when his taste in women seems to lean toward one night stands?"

Colin thought, "Somehow he managed to juggle everything to his advantage. Here he is in charge of the whole, darn operation." What Croft did not know was that in Davis's third year at the Cape, June Landon had been assigned as his secretary. This was no majestic stroke of fate or synchronicity. The ambitious twenty-seven year old blond had sized up the potential rising stars at the center and decided the black haired, dark eyed Welshman was the best bet. She used all her wiles and charms on the Office Personnel Manager to finagle the assignment.

To Davis's surprise he soon gave up his other female playmates for June Landon's exclusive company. She was that good. For her part, the pretty Texan knew to be discreet and not to ask for more than she could get. He would always stay married for social and political reasons. Three years his senior she knew what it took to keep a power seeker, flawed by a macho drive to seduce all women in his path, on the road to success.

Landon was perfect at having her paramour attend all the right meetings, wheedling invitations to anything that would make Davis more well known in a wider and wider circle of NASA activity. The work paid off. He kept her at his side all the way to the head office. The power seekers had achieved their goals.

Colin was pulled out of his reveries when he heard Sam's response to her asking, "Did you have to travel far?"

"Not far, only fifty miles." Hershburg responded to the obvious polite concern about their time and travel. The quick elevator ride to the fourth floor was completed in silence. A few steps to the right took them into the secretary's well-appointed office. The blond woman walked to her desk in the center of the room. Lounge chairs and couches lined the walls forming a semi-circle around her desk. All that would go on in this room would pivot around the woman.

"Your guests are here, sir." she announced over the phone.

"Show them in, Miss Landon," the deep gruff voice dictated out of the speaker phone. She led them into a large office with wall to wall windows facing the door. The glare from the bright sunlight blinded anyone coming in so that the man sitting behind the lightly colored ash desk was not immediately discernible. This afforded Davis the chance to size up his visitors before they could see him. The voice behind the desk welcomed them and invited them to sit down.

"What can I do for you gentlemen? I understand you both worked here a few years back on the unfortunate Venus X Project."

"Yes, sir, it's precisely the Venus X project that brings us here." Croft continued quickly not wishing to give Davis a chance to interrupt and say he wasn't interested in anything to do with the project he blamed for all his funding problems. "As you well know everyone believes the ship and crew to be lost forever. However, Mr. Hershburg and I have been in monthly radio contact with the crew for the last ten years."

"Do you expect me to believe you've kept this a secret for ten years? What's your scam?"

"This is no hoax. We have recordings of all the transmissions and we're prepared to turn them over to you. The last message we received said they are on the return course back to earth. It is imperative that NASA begin operations to effect the rescue when they re-enter earth orbit."

"I won't act on this until I've heard the tapes and had them analyzed by my people. I don't intend to be made to look like an idiot if they turn out to be fabrications on your part."

"We understand your reluctance to believe us and we're ready to do whatever is necessary to convince you and any other NASA people you designate."

Sam cut in, "We realize the awesome task of preparing for a recovery mission what with obtaining funding from the federal government, build the recovery vehicles, man and train the crew, and fly some prove-out missions."

Croft picked up the conversation not waiting for Davis to speak. "We've come to you first believing that you would want to be in the forefront of this effort."

When Croft stopped the only sound was the whirring fan noise of the air-conditioning system. Owen Davis sat stunned by what he had just heard. Were these two men crackpots or legitimate? What course of action was most expedient and beneficial for the Welshman's interests? His animal instinct for self-preservation shouted at him to throw these two clowns out of his office, and his life, forever.

However, his consummate ego begged him to grab a ride on what could be the greatest achievement in the history of space travel. He, Owen Davis, could be the star of this show. What a way to close out a career! --- If this was true and if the crew survived the next nine years, and if they can unload them off the platform and if they can get them back to earth safely ---

"Get me proof what you are saying is

true. I want everything that substantiates your claims. NASA receives a plethora of wild schemes that turn out to be figments of some vivid imagination. Scam artists are always trying to get their hooks into the government's pockets."

"We said we'll turn over tapes of all the conversations we've had with the ship and detailed reports on the methodology and equipment used." Croft sensed the reluctance in the chief's voice. Somehow he hoped that the tapes would bait Davis to act.

Sam Hershburg, irritated by Davis's posturing, turned to Croft and blurted out, "Colin, why don't we let the chief mull this over at least until our interview with the New York Times. When the story breaks, Congressmen will jump on it just for the free publicity." Sam had set the hook in the fleshy part of Davis's ego. The dark eyes behind the desk, afire with rage, flashed Owen Davis's unspoken thoughts. Who does this guy think he is that he can squeeze me into a decision? I'll teach him not to try to put the screws to me even if it takes forever. The lure of fame may temper Davis's decision but he would do everything he could so Sam Hershburg would pay the price of anonymity for the duration of the project

"That's fine. Tapes are too easily fabricated these days to convince me of anything. Get me the tapes and call me in a couple of weeks then we'll see where we go from here, if we go anywhere at all." Davis would not give them any feeling of success. They needed him and he knew it.

"June will escort you to the lobby. Good afternoon gentlemen." Summarily dismissed the two visitors exited to the friendlier atmosphere of Ms. Landon's company. The ride down the elevator and retracing the long walk down the corridor to the visitors lobby was essentially in silence save for a few questions posed by the leggy blond. She hoped they had a pleasant meeting? Were they pleased with the results? Would they be seeing Mr. Davis again? The terse responses by Croft and his tone of voice told the inquisitor all she needed to report back to her boss. Davis had won the first round.

Chapter 40

Once out of the building the two men broke into smug smiles as they felt sure that their little charade of good guy/bad guy and the Times interview would reel Owen Davis into the Venus X boat quickly. Colin Croft's acumen at judging personalities had not failed him.

Once he realized who the NASA Center Chief was, he and Sam had planned their dialogue, for the first visit, to the very last word. The opening gambit had been successful and now they would wait for Davis's move.

When June Landon returned to her boss's office he was still steaming at the way he had been approached. Her assessment that the men had not shown any sign of satisfaction by their surly responses restored Davis's confidence that they needed him more than he needed them. If the tapes were valid; and in his possession, he would be in control. Owen called home to say he had to work late; then while enjoying a martini with his secretary he told her the amazing tale of the possible return of the lost ship. The power seeking gold dust twins had sex and planned their moves towards

achieving front page fame in effecting the
rescue. June's share of the spoils would be to
be named as Assistant Project Engineer. This
position would allow her instant access to
everything going on which in turn meant that
Davis would be privy to it all.

Three days later at the very same time
that reporters from the New York Times and the
Washington Post were flying to Tampa for
exclusive joint interviews with Croft and
Hershburg, Owen Davis, NASA Chief of
Operations at the Cape Kennedy Center, was
holding a press conference. He announced that
he had been approached by individuals with
unsubstantiated claims to have had contact, for
the last ten years, with the crew of Venus X, the
long lost space excursion platform.

"Ladies and gentlemen of the press let
me assure you that if their claims turn out to be
valid, I will do the utmost to bring about the
rescue of the crew as Venus X approaches
earth. I also will see to it that a thorough
investigation is conducted and charges
brought against the two or more individuals
involved in this pact of secrecy. In my
estimation, an assessment universally shared

by my NASA colleagues, these individuals, by depriving the mission from complete NASA support, have jeopardized the lives of every astronaut on board. I will see to it that they are held accountable for this unconscionable indifference to the safety of our American men and women who have put everything on the line for the future of our country's pre-eminence in interplanetary space travel." Davis knew how to play hardball. Owen turned the mike over to June Landon introducing her as Venus Assistant Project Engineer. She would handle all releases and conferences relating to this situation. June announced there would be an information release in a week to report on the progress of the investigation. With that she closed the conference.

Chapter 41

Later that afternoon, the reporters were sitting in Colin Croft's living room conducting the interview when Jane Croft walked in excitedly saying, "Colin you must come quickly and see what's on TV, hurry!" Croft and Hershburg rushed into the den with the reporters on their heels. They heard Davis's voice coming from the TV mounted in the dark oak entertainment center. "I will see to it that they are held accountable for this unconscionable indifference to the safety of our American men and women; who have put everything on the line for the future of our country's pre-eminence in interplanetary space travel."

Colin quickly scanned the other channels trying to pick up the whole segment. Too late, he had to be satisfied with Jane's account of what she'd heard before calling them into the TV room.

The newsmen were upset. They doubted the credibility of Hershburg and Croft, yet, they wanted to stay with the story. "What about this announcement, Mr. Croft? It sounds like the chief at Kennedy Space Center doesn't buy your story."

"Gentlemen, I assure you that we have all the proof necessary to validate our claim that we are in contact with the space ship." Croft hid his disappointment at Davis painting him and Sam as possible traitors. He was upset with himself at misjudging Davis's viciousness.

"What kind of proof, Mr. Croft?"

"Why, the tapes of every contact we've had with the ship. That's what brought you all down here in the first place."

"How can you prove they are not dubbings you've made or maybe some alien nation is using this to land one of their ships right into the heart of our space center?"

"Gentlemen, when NASA personnel contact Venus X, that will be our proof that we are telling the truth. If you don't trust us then wait with all the other journalists to report the story."

The reporters wanted to be first to break the story with this personal interview. It would give them an inside track throughout the future evolvement, rescue or fraud. Colin reassured them the best he could with details of the mission to which only he and Sam were privy. The reporters decided the story was worth writing. Unfortunately, the Davis conference upstaged their story to third page. Realizing that Davis would initiate legal steps to confiscate the tapes, Sam and Colin duplicated all the taped communications from and to Venus X, encoding a subliminal track which would identify any duplicates as copies. The originals they stored in a locker at the railroad station. Should Davis be devious enough to edit his copies they would be able to produce the real transmissions. They completed the effort in three days.

A scant 30 minutes after their return from storing the last originals, FBI agents were at their doors with search warrants that covered all buildings owned or rented by either or both Croft and Hershburg and gave authority to confiscate all materials pertinent to the Venus X mission.

Chapter 42

Two weeks after the near fatal encounter with the rogue star, Adam joined his father on the command deck. Glen had noticed how pensive the boy had been since that traumatic day. The two sat silent. The father did not want to press the son while Adam didn't know how to put words to his jumbled thinking. Glen broke the spell.

"How's it going Adam? We haven't had much time together lately."

"OK, I guess." The soft words spoke of confusion and uncertainty. "Dad, what's going to happen to Sean?" blurted out of the boys mouth as a torrent breaking through a dam.

"What do you mean, son?"

"Well, you know. Will we ever see him again? I miss him a lot. He used to make me laugh and tell me stories of elves and leprechauns, and was teaching me karate."

Glen Ross was surprised at the question and the depth of emotion in the boy's voice. He did not answer immediately for Adam stirred up a loneliness and sadness that Ross had suppressed.

"I miss him too, son. He became my best friend." Glen related the story of the fight he had with the Marine and how it had bonded them as men who could trust the other to be courageous to the end. "I don't know what will happen to him. He may be on an endless course out of our galaxy, years from now, or he may be on a course to the sun or some other planet. God only knows what will happen to him." Glen did not want to scare the boy by describing Murphy smashed into millions of tiny pieces by some asteroid or burning on re-entry to some planet or star.

"Does he?" the boy asked.

"Does he what?

"Does he know?"

"Does who know?

"You said God only knows what will happen to him. Does he?"

"Uh, that's just an expression we use when we don't know something."

"But what do you think, Dad. Do you think God knows about Sean and what will happen to him?"

"I guess I've never really thought about it. Right now all I can think about is getting us home in one piece. When I'm back on earth I'll have time to philosophize about those kinds of things. Why don't you ask your mother about them?"

Ross was not into "what ifs and maybes". His world was based on mechanics and provable hypotheses. A pilot doesn't have the luxury of reveries if he is to survive combat as well as hundreds of landings on a carrier that looks like a postage stamp in the middle of the ocean.

"I asked Aunt Nancy; and she said Sean is just another frozen asteroid, one of millions in the universe. She said when you die that's the end of useful life and you just don't exist anymore. Is that the way it is, Dad?" The boy sought answers to questions beyond the ken of mere mortals.

"That sounds like a pretty depressing view. Did you ask your mother?" Where was Marita when he needed her? Isn't the mother supposed to answer these kinds of questions?

"She didn't know about Sean but she said that if God is powerful enough to create the big bang that gave us the universe full of stars and galaxies then He would be the one that would have to solve Sean's situation."

"That sounds a bit more optimistic to me, son. I guess, if I had to choose, I'd go with what your mom said because at least there's hope that we may see our lost friend again. If she's wrong and Nancy's right then it doesn't matter that we lived with the hope anyway."

That response seemed to satisfy the boy's quandary and he slid out of the stool and floated around the command deck for a while amusing himself by reading some of the gauges aloud to his dad.

"Mom says that Jesus is God and that he's coming back to earth someday and then no one will ever die again." The matter of fact way the boy said it implied "Does mom know what she's talking about?" Glen did not wish to continue a discussion that had no solutions. He chose to acknowledge Adam's last statement with a laconic, "Oh."

The boy repeated more gauge readings "What happens to us if she's right and Jesus comes back before we get back to earth?"

"Go find something else to keep busy. I've got to do some navigational checks and computations. Why don't you see who's next to go out for the meat and when they expect to do it."

With the ability that children have to leave things as they are and move on to something more interesting, the nine year-old floated off to the living quarters to check the rosters. Ross shook his head as if to unscramble the discussion that had transpired. He quickly put it out of his mind to concentrate on his Mission Captain's duties.

Chapter 43

Croft and Hershburg watched the government men ransack their homes, garages and finally, the rented garage housing the communication equipment. The searchers confiscated all files, tapes and material they felt was connected in any way with the space project.

Sam and Colin now knew, first hand, what people in oppressed countries go through, powerless to stop the police or military, of the current regime, from destroying their property. The search lasted two days despite the continued effort by Croft to assure the searchers that all Venus X materials were in the rented garage.

As investigators left, Chandler, the FBI agent in charge instructed Sam and Colin to come to FBI headquarters the next morning at nine o'clock for questioning and to give their statements for the record. The wheels of the government investigation were beginning to grind slowly towards prosecution of the two men and their wives who were considered accomplices in the matter.

At nine the next day Sam and Colin entered the FBI offices accompanied by James David Erlich, a trial lawyer whom Croft's banker had recommended. They were escorted to Chandler's office, an antiseptic room with two 4 drawer file cabinets, a gray metal desk, one Government Issue desk chair and four padded folding chairs. The faded contractor beige walls made the room even more depressive.

At first the two friends were interviewed together and the FBI agents were polite and solicitous. Then they separated them for individual questioning. Later they brought them together again for more questioning. As the morning droned on towards noon the attitude of the agents became more and more acerbic and even belligerent.

Erlich cautioned his new clients not to answer any more questions until he had a chance to consult with them. Sam felt connected to his fellow countryman. A bond forged throughout a history of persecution for living their beliefs. His frustration showed in the sarcastic tone with which he answered the agents.

Croft knew the system, having spent

twenty years in the Air Force. Still, he became very irritated at the attitude of agent Chandler and his men. Innocent until proven guilty did not prevail in this office. They made him feel guilty for helping the astronauts. Chandler chain-smoked large Corona cigars and the air in the room became acrid and stale. Later Sam and Colin would have their suits dry cleaned to remove the stench of stale tobacco smoke.

As the interview progressed it became evident that the investigators were seeking connections, however flimsy, to any illegal activity in which the two men might have been involved. The queries invariably returned to why Croft or Hershburg had not gone to NASA at the first communication with the lost space ship. They could not reveal that, had they reported the contact, NASA officials would have ordered the crew to return to earth immediately. The astronauts would have disobeyed and could be charged not only of disobeying government orders but of pirating a space vehicle. They might all be found guilty of mutiny if the crew refused to obey the Mission Commander's direct orders.

At 11:30 am Erlich had heard enough of

the government's questions. Addressing Chandler, he spoke decisively.

"Chief, my clients have nothing more to say to you. If you want to bring charges do so. In the meantime you are not to speak to either Mr. Croft or Mr. Hershburg unless I am present. Good morning gentlemen." He rose and he and his clients left the stale stench of cigar and boorish behavior behind as they walked out. Once on the sidewalk, Erlich set a time the next day for what would be the first of many meetings to discuss defense strategy.

After months of legal research, the FBI charged Croft with subversive activity against the best interest of the United States and endangering the lives of civilian and military personnel; while in their performance of federal duty. The third charge, the only one covered by strict federal statutes, was the illegal transmission of radio waves without an FCC license.

Sam was charged with aiding and abetting Croft in illegal activities. The two wives Jane Croft and Sarah Hershburg were charged with misdemeanor offenses of acting "in consort" by not coming forth to reveal the

illegal activities.

Chapter 44

The government charged NPI, its CEO and Croft for intent to defraud the United States Government by arranging the purchase of the salvaged NASA communication equipment for the illegal purpose of setting up a fraudulent series of messages from the lost space craft.

For two months the news media had daily inside stories and reports about the beleaguered couples labeling them greedy, power hungry, publicity seeking exploiters of the endangered crew. Then a movie star-allegedly selling the services of young boys to friends and acquaintances took over the headlines and the space ship coverage became old news quickly.

Politicians, not wanting to miss the chance for free publicity, launched a Congressional investigation. Owen Davis had, in the interim, taken control of the communication equipment Croft and Hershburg used to contact Venus X. The first month that NASA responded to transmissions from the space ship, Glen Ross saw that Colin's encoded signature did not start and end the message from earth. As previously arranged Croft was to sign on and off all transmissions to Venus X with the notes of the first four bars of "Oh Danny Boy."

Ross discussed this with Jim Barnes and they decided not to transmit the next scheduled message. The astronauts and Croft had made arrangements in case Venus X missed a scheduled transmission. Croft and Hershburg would send a series of messages containing frequencies necessary for the astronauts to transmit to video satellites that in turn would be accessible to monitors in the communications garage. When the messages did not come, Ross knew that something was drastically wrong.

A complete check of the on-board communication system showed all systems working perfectly. Glen decided to resume the monthly transmission in case the ground system had malfunctioned and been repaired. When the next month's response from earth did not contain the music and, no instructions for satellite frequencies followed, Jim Barnes, who was on duty at the time, notified Ross immediately.

Glen called Nancy to the command deck and instructed her to research available TV satellite positions and frequencies. Two days of scanning the data banks on the video monitor revealed only one dish in position with frequencies compatible with the space ship's gear.

At the next scheduled transmission time, Glen had Nancy transmit thirty seconds of the first bar of the "Oh Danny boy" tune followed by the words "Where are you?" TV sets throughout the country blared out the message. Angry watchers, begrudging the interruption of their favorite programs, flooded their local stations and networks with calls.

When Colin Croft heard of the strange message, he guessed that the astronauts were not in contact with NASA for some reason. With no capability to reach Venus X, he tried to contact Owen Davis but the chief refused to take his calls.

After three failed transmissions, Davis and his staff decided that Croft and Hershburg had found a way to trigger transmissions from some spy satellite with the intent to dupe the world by claiming contact with Venus X.

Davis enlisted CIA's help in tracking down this false message and asked them to use their cryptography staff to decode the tapes. CIA personnel did not choose to reveal to anyone including the Chief of the Cape Kennedy NASA facility that they had been listening in on these transmissions for five years with the belief that it was some foreign power which was conducting a super-secret space communications project.

Meanwhile Russia had duplicated U.S. activity, suspecting America of some devious plot. Both countries had pin-pointed the location of the garage transmitter and were in a watch and wait mode. CIA had accumulated lengthy dossiers on both Croft's and Hershburg's activities but found no evidence of illegal activity.

Chapter 45

With Davis refusing to see him, Croft contacted the two reporters with whom they had interviewed initially. He read them a letter he was mailing to Davis with info copies to Chandler at FBI explaining the meaning of the TV transmission and its relevance to the Venus X mission. Both reporters asked Colin to Fax a copy before mailing the letter. The two newspapers carried excerpts on the front page quoting the proverbial "reliable source."

It was at this time that the CIA deciphered Croft's signatures. When the story hit the newsstands, CIA agents went to Davis with the proof that the transmissions from Venus X were legitimate. With their help, Davis sent a correctly encoded message to the space crew explaining that Croft and Hershburg had abandoned the project. NASA had picked up the ship's transmission and finally broke the code. The message told the astronauts that NASA would handle all communications until the crew came home safely.

Davis, a master at landing on his feet when troubles were on the verge of bringing his downfall, called a news conference. June Landon, wearing a figure revealing, scalloped necked black dress accented by a small silver heart hanging from a red choker and matching, red, stiletto heel shoes, charmed the audience as she prefaced her introduction of Owen Davis with glowing praise for the joint effort of NASA, FBI and CIA personnel which the NASA chief had coordinated.

The men reporters relished the vision at the microphone while the media women envied her. A perfect distraction while Davis weaved a mantle of glory around NASA and a tale of deceit around Croft and Hershburg. The ruse worked and NASA was praised in all the newspapers and TV stations except the New York Times and the Washington Post. The editors of these two papers, convinced of Croft's and Hershburg's integrity, decided to champion the two underdogs.

On board Venus X, the news that Sam and Colin had abandoned the project was received with disbelief and dismay.

"What do you make of it, Glen?" Marita voiced the question on all the crewmembers' minds.

"I don't know. I can't believe Croft, or Hershburg for that matter, would bail out on us. Something doesn't smell right. Let's go with NASA for the time being and see what develops." His words were not very effective in reassuring the crew that all was well with ground contact. Ross needed time to devise some way of finding out what was really going on. He trusted Sam and Colin completely. They were the most qualified to help him bring the ship and crew back to earth safely. Now they were not in the picture.

Chapter 46

On the Fourth of July 2010, Sam, Sarah and the children joined the Croft's for their traditional Independence Day barbecue. Relaxing after the meal, Colin said, "Sam and Sarah how are things with you two financially? You've told me that your practice is dwindling. Why do the patients leave you?"

"They fear I'll not be there for them when they need me because of the upcoming trial and a possible jail term. They want to protect themselves and I don't blame them very much, except it does rub me the wrong way sometimes. The worst is that my income is now at twenty five percent of what it used to be and dropping every day." "How about hooking onto an HMO facility or a hospital until this case is settled?"

"I've been trying but I'm getting form letters using standard rejections like 'Sorry, you are over qualified for the position we are filling at this time or, 'We have no openings at this time' and you've all heard the, 'we have tended offers to qualified applicants and will be hiring those who accept our package.' Sam paused a moment then continued. "Actually, most hospitals or med facilities are not even responding. I've signed with a head hunter but nothing so far. After this trial we may have to relocate where we can start fresh. How about you folks?"

"Well we're getting very low. You know that my contract as project manager will end next month and I don't expect them to give me a new project with what's in store for us. Jane and I are trying to come up with ways to earn some money. We've already used up the house equity loan option and the savings won't last more than another month or two. The lawyer has been fair in his charges but overall the negative cash flow has us on the ropes."

"Sarah and I are in the same boat. She just took a job at Burger King. Five and a quarter an hour barely pays the baby sitter and buys a few groceries. We're even considering selling the house to pay off the debts and get a little cash on hand. Things don't look good."

Croft waited a few minutes before responding. "Do you think selling the house is a good option? Won't you end up paying as much rent as your mortgage payments?"

"Probably not; because we have high monthly payments plus the taxes are $200 a month. We should be able to rent for five to six hundred a month. We are not sure we'll do this." The uncertainty in Sam's voice eloquently exposed the despondency that was slowly enveloping the two couples.

"Well, Jane and I are debating the same decision. If we sell, pay off the mortgage, liquidate the equity loan and clear the credit cards we'll barely net $10,000. That would carry us for six months at best. We are going to apply for work at every store and fast food place in town. If we both bring in minimum wages we might make a go of it."

"We're really cheering each other up with our troubles." "I wonder how Ross and the crew are making out. I wish we could talk to them." Hershburg's melancholy question brought them all to a thoughtful silence.

Colin broke the spell by pulling out the last bottle of Grand Marnier from behind the patio bar. He dropped two ice cubes each in four tumblers and covered them with a double shot of the digestive.

"Enjoy this good liqueur because it's

probably the last we can afford until this mess is cleared up," as he handed the three their drinks. Colin picked his drink off the bar and turned to the others.

"Here's to the crew of Venus X and to their safe return home."

"Hear, hear." they all chorused.

Chapter 47

Owen Davis lost no time in contacting all companies that had taken part in the Venus X mission in any way. He sent out letters to every NASA person who had worked on the project inviting them to become part of the recovery team.

The companies that were still in operation responded with promises to support the project. All asked for a bid request with the scope of their task described in detail. There was no rush to glory on their part for the risk of a failed mission was preponderant. The cost would be directly proportional to the probability of failure. Most of the original staff turned down the offers to return to work for NASA on this project. They were building new careers and did not choose to give up their equity in them.

Davis did not lose any sleep over the refusals but rather used the opportunity to hire new, young engineers at lower salaries; young persons allured by the glamour of working on this highly publicized rescue mission.

Meanwhile on board the space ship Jim Barnes succeeded in sealing the leaks in the water processing tanks. He mixed a thick paste made from crushed tree and plant leaves and the liquid from the leaves of the two small rubber plants that had survived. The sticky mixture hardened like a strong epoxy and sealed the tanks water tight. It took two weeks for the tanks to return to normal level of operation.

Restoring the garden was a more tedious process and took a year before the area was back to full size. As the crew filled portions of the bed they planted seeds to start the growth process as quickly as possible.

Now that NASA was the earth contact, the space crew communicated daily with mission control. This allowed the new ground personnel to get hands on training while learning every facet of the ships construction. Davis also released contracts to design and build a recovery space ship capable of docking with Venus X and transferring the crew for return to earth.

The reconstruction work and the exchange of data with NASA were very demanding of Glen Ross and his crew. It meant long hours of responding to detailed questions about all aspects of their space home. In addition, the task of recovering the meat from outside the ship was much more difficult than anyone could have imagined when the decision was made to salvage it in this way.

They had cut the meat in small sections that would satisfy the meal requirements for one or two days. However, they did not have individual containers in which to store the portions. Consequently the smaller cuts froze into a large mass. Breaking the daily rations loose took Herculean efforts and patience.

What the astronauts did not realize was that despite their exercise regimen they were all suffering from muscle deterioration. This was imperceptive to the astronauts over the course of the ten years in the gravity free environment. Man on earth does not realize the physical advantages in performing routine, daily tasks. We perform these effortlessly, using many muscles, keeping them toned. Moving a chair, opening doors, washing the car, walking under fourteen pounds per square inch of pressure on our bodies, all use muscles acting against a force.

In the spacecraft there were none of

these unconscious exercises. All things floated from the mere touch of a hand. The exercise program did not make up for this phenomenon since it was too easy to put off the workout after twelve and fourteen hour duties.

The astronauts were all losing muscle tone at the same time so they had no one against whom they could measure themselves. Their mass, the ratio of muscle to body fat, was decreasing continually. As the months and years droned on this condition would become the biggest threat to their survival. Would their hearts or other organs cease functioning properly? Would they lose the natural healing properties of the body such that any sickness or disease would be fatal? The return home was now a race against time. Could they live another nine years or would the space ship be a coffin with no one to guide it into earth orbit?

Chapter 48

Despite all this pressure, Ross continued to question NASA regarding the availability of Croft and Hershburg returning as members of the mission control staff. At first the answers were vague. They were not available due to other commitments. Their present employers would not grant them an indeterminate leave of absence. One or the other had health problems.

The excuses both puzzled and angered Ross. How could both men abandon the project knowing that the crew was alive and on the way home? That did not square with the nine years of communication and support they had given the astronauts.

Once in a while the possibility that Croft and Hershburg had given up on them would infuriate Glen Ross. He tried not to speak of these doubts to anyone but Marita. She in turn kept insisting that something was wrong and that Glen should press Davis to arrange communications with the two friends directly. Davis never allowed this. Eight months later the Attorney General of the United States brought charges against Croft and Hershburg. Also indicted were Senator Birdwell of Florida, ex white house Chief of Staff Conrad Smith, retired Air Force General Casey Morgan, and ex NASA Chief Ray Rincon for conspiracy to defraud the U. S. Government.

The investigation had uncovered a plot, by the men involved, to raise sponsorship for an extended mission in space which would push NASA to the forefront for federal appropriations. The mission had no real scientific value. The purported reason was the study of magnetic fields and their effects due to stellar body motions and, the investigation of Einstein's theory that exploding stars cause ripples in space called "gravity waves."

The real purpose was to install long range projects for NASA personnel in cooperation with key companies with which the last four names were financially involved. Croft and Hershburg were not part of the collusion. Unfortunately, they were sucked into this quagmire because of their long term involvement with the space mission.

The four conspirators, in consultation with their lawyers, decided to try the case in the media. They appeared on TV and spoke on talk radio programs at every opportunity, professing total innocence and explaining their interest in the space mission as personal avocation.

Croft and Hershburg under the advice of their lawyer no longer gave interviews after they first revealed the contacts with the space craft. Now they were not even approached since the media hounds had more famous persons to pursue.

With the return of the indictments and a trial date set, Davis sent word to the Venus X astronauts. The message was cold, and terse, "Croft and Hershburg indicted for criminal activity. Neither can be associated with the Venus X mission." It was calculated to cut off further requests, by Ross or any other crew member, regarding the two alleged criminals.

This news devastated the morale of the astronauts. When Ross queried mission control about the charges and details of the trial, Davis would simply respond that they were under court order not to discuss the case because NASA personnel were potential witnesses.

Three months later four of the insurance companies that had paid death benefits to the survivors of Venus X crew members brought joint civil suits against Croft, Hershburg and NASA for intent to defraud the insurers by alleging the deaths of the astronauts and not disclosing the crew was alive.

Obviously none of the beneficiaries could return the money. The companies wanted to squeeze a large judgment against NASA knowing that neither Croft nor Hershburg would have any money left after the criminal cases were settled. Hershburg's and Croft's lives were crumbling and they were helpless to stop it. With their homes mortgaged to the limit and unable to meet legal fees, they sought work fruitlessly. No one was interested in hiring men who could be found guilty and sent to jail. Sam and Colin met with their lawyer. He reviewed their finances and advised them the only action he could suggest was to file bankruptcy. This was a shameful concept to the two men. Both were successful professional men and now they had to concede to failure.

Depressed, they went home to their wives reluctant to share the bad news. The two had no alternatives and filed bankruptcy. It was during the many discussions about finances that Jane Croft developed a chronic cough. The doctor diagnosed it as a scratchy throat and suggested over the counter cough lozenges and cough syrup at bed time. Nothing worked. The cough persisted.

Sarah Hershburg began to slip into spells of depression. The strain of mounting financial difficulties and three children under seven years of age, demanding her attention when she got home; after working the counter at Burger King, wore her down physically and mentally. She needed more of Sam's aid and support. Instead, he became absorbed in surviving the onslaught of the suits against him and was less and less helpful as the days wore on.

Chapter 49

With the garden planted and the water supply repaired Marita; busied herself in doing a trend analysis on the health of the survivors. Except for Sandra Meyers the others seemed well enough considering the circumstances. Sandra did not fully recover from the Pennington collision. She suffered some physical brain damage as well as mental trauma. The brain was healing slowly as evidenced by her improvement in re-learning routine daily tasks. However, the mental acuity of this near genius lay buried in the blackness of a deep depression.

While Marita saw to Sandra's feminine hygiene, Jim Barnes assumed the responsibility of caring for all her other needs, continually providing affection, companionship and affirming assurance that she was safe and need not fear the reoccurrence of the dreadful collision. Still days droned on into months and no change was discernible.

Meanwhile, Marita, in studying the astronaut's physiological trend analysis, detected a slow deterioration in body mass and a decrease in the level of calcium in each astronaut.

Her son, Adam, did not show these symptoms. His body was growing at a normal rate for a young pre-teen. Taking into account that his bones were soft compared to youngsters on earth, the calcium level was higher than normal. Marita attributed this phenomenon to man's natural tendency to adapt and evolve in new environments. Not able to confer with Sandra, the other doctor on board, she notified NASA mission control. Two days later NASA responded.

"Venus X this is Kennedy Control. We advise that each crew member must drink at least a pint and a half of goat's milk per 24 hours. Do you copy?"

"Roger, Kennedy Control, we copy but we don't have that supply of milk due to the loss of some of the goats during the collision. We are getting less than a gallon per day. We'll share it equally unless advised differently," Marita replied.

"We understand. Medical staff will look at this and we'll keep you posted. In conjunction with the milk intake, the exercise regimen must be stepped up such that each person spends a minimum of three non-consecutive hours out of every twenty four on the body building machines. In addition, each of you must walk one continuous hour on the treadmill."

"Mission Control, please supply exercise programs tailored to the individuals since none of your instructions fit the exercise profiles we started with." Marita was not confident that the crew could or would want to live up to these last instructions.

"Roger Venus X. We'll supply this in a few days. Meanwhile send us daily physical exam data on all crew members and Adam as well. We have no explanation for his normal growth compared to the rest of you."

A week later, Mission control defined the milk rations based on a study of the up to date physical profiles of each crew member. It was not an equal share per person and this triggered jealousy in Nancy Flowers who saw it as one more case of gender bias. Though she was six inches taller than Marita and weighed twenty pounds more, the two women had the same allotment.

To add to the irritation, Sandra Meyers

was given the same amount as she and Marita while Barnes and Glen Ross were allocated much larger and personalized portions. Though mission control doctors were correct clinically and had taken into account race and genetic background data, the obvious disparity grated on Nancy's strong "equality for all" belief. She did not voice her displeasure but, as the weeks went by; her irritation manifested itself in sarcasm and curtness with the men. Life on board became more stressful day by day. The exercise program took most of the crew's free time. Only young Adam Ross remained impervious to the strained nerves of his fellow passengers. Adam never knew life in the freedom of mother earth. All his points of reference were within the confines of life on the ship. Tension was normal to him and he learned to flow with it as part of living. Adam did not rationalize this. Rather he thought,

"That's just the way it is."

Chapter 50

The prosecution decided to try Croft and Hershburg together but separate from the four conspirators. The jury trial lasted four days. The two could not mount any plausible defense because of their refusal to explain why they did not report the contacts with Venus X. The jury took only two hours to return a guilty verdict against both men.

In May of 2010 they came before the court for sentencing. Listening to the prosecution's recommendations and to Defense attorney Erich's plea for suspended sentences, Judge Adamanti looked into the faces of the defendants for a long two minutes.

"Mister Croft, (began the judge in sonorous tones that conveyed authority and the seriousness of the situation), you have deliberately set about to conceal the existence of a United States space vehicle; depriving the crew from proper assistance in their mission. Further you set about this unprecedented act while in the service of your government as a member of the United States Air Force assigned to duty with NASA."

Colin blushed as the judge continued to berate him. "I don't know why you were not tried before a military tribunal. Nevertheless, you presumed to take into your own hands the safety of these men and women without medical or technical support, a reprehensible display of egotism. I would like for you spend as much time in prison as the astronauts will spend in space."

Judge Adamanti paused a long thirty seconds to glare at the defendant before continuing. "However, the law has set a maximum sentence that I cannot override. I therefore sentence you to be confined for four years to be served at the Maryland minimum security facility. The law allows you time off for good behavior; but I would caution you to walk the straight and narrow. I don't want to see you in my court again."

At these words, Jane croft jumped to her feet shouting, "No! No! Colin. Tell them why you did it, tell them! "While the judge banged his gavel for order in the court, Colin turned to his wife and said, "Jane be still. We've come too far to change course now." Croft would keep secret the mutinous actions of the astronauts even at the cost of prison; rather than jeopardize their safety. Nothing must add to the stress of the crew trying to bring the damaged ship back to earth.

Turning to Sam the judge continued, "Mister Hershburg, you were not under military rules of conduct; but as a NASA employee your conduct comes under the umbrella of the agreement you signed in 1994. You are no less guilty than Mister Croft for not coming forth with information about the ship. I see your actions as subordinate to Croft. In some ways, though you did not voice it, you acted like the prison guards in death camps who hid behind 'I was only following orders.' I sentence you to two years in a minimum security facility to be selected by the Texas Department of Corrections. You are eligible for reduced time for good behavior."

Turning his attention to the prosecution and defense attorneys he spoke in a more polite tone. "Mister Erlich you have a week to file your appeals meanwhile the defendants are to be remanded to the court officers for incarceration in the county house of correction until final disposition of the appeals."

"Your Honor, if it please the court, my clients are not men who will flee and I believe it would serve no purpose to keep them incarcerated until the court acts on the appeals. Therefore, I request they be freed under their own recognizance until then."

"Your point may be well taken, counselor, but my ruling stands. This court is adjourned." At that moment in time the men, who had chosen to stand for their comrades in space, were wrenched from the women they loved and thrown into an environment completely foreign to their background and moral code. Once again, the gods of Venus X unintentionally caused dramatic changes in the lives of those on earth who cared most for them.

Chapter 51

At the news of the verdict, Owen Davis could hardly contain his joy. His dislike of Croft, spawned when the ex-Air Force Colonel had used the newspapers to pressure NASA into recognizing the existence of Venus X, had grown into acrid hate. He called June Landon immediately.

"June, did you hear the news? They just found Croft and Hershburg guilty."

"Yes, I just heard the news bulletin. That should keep them out of your hair for a while. I know how hard you've worked to even the score for them putting the screws to you in the papers when they first came to you."

June had listened to Davis rant about how he would teach Croft a lesson he wouldn't forget. Her lover's obsession with the matter taxed her feelings for him to the point that their sexual encounters became a tolerant action on her part. A far cry from the gusto she had brought to bed before the Venus X intrusion.

Oblivious to the subtle tone in her voice that said, "Can't we forget about this and get back to what we both have been working for all these years," Owen blustered on. "Listen, love, have the project manager, Styles, contact the astronauts and tell them of the verdict and what the charges were. That should get Ross off our backs with his weekly requests to talk to Croft. Oh, can we get together after work and do a little bit of celebrating?"

"I'll call you by four o'clock if I can make it or not." June was beginning to reevaluate her relationship with Davis. Her recent fortieth birthday had triggered a feeling of insecurity and uncertainty about her future, particularly as to what she would end up with from her liaison with the Welshman. She was not as easily available to him as before. The sense that he might never divorce his wife became a disturbing reality. She had never allowed herself to think this way until now. June struggled often with whether she should broach the subject or not. The possibility that he would respond by leaving her for his wife or some younger woman always discouraged her. She kept silent.

Chapter 52

The crew of Venus X was stunned at the news that Croft and Hershburg were going to prison. Dumbfounded, they slowly began to talk among themselves trying to understand what was going on earth side. Ross calmed them as best he could. Morale must not be affected by unknowns. The spirit of the crew was fragile at best. Glen could not afford to see them demoralized by events beyond their control with the mission only half completed.

"We don't know any details of the Croft situation so let's not jump to illogical conclusions," Glen began. "I'm going to contact NASA and see if we can get a reading on the charges and some background on the case."

Glen called NASA and project manager Styles' response was limited to, "Your two friends have been convicted of endangering the lives of military personnel and civilian employees, of a government agency, by not divulging the existence of a safe Venus X crew."

At that moment Ross knew what was happening. He tested his theory with Marita.

"Honey, I think we've hurt Croft and Sam Hershburg badly by not wanting them to divulge our existence. I believe the reason they're in jail is that we disobeyed orders to turn back and they are keeping silent about it. They must figure if it gets out we'll be tried for mutiny when we get back. If we don't get back; then we'll go down as heroes. I never would have believed that Colin and Sam cared for us that much or that they were that dedicated to seeing the mission completed. How do you see it?"

"What you say makes sense to me, Glen. You need to tell the crew what you think. It may restore their morale some."

The crew agreed with Glen's assessment and voted to tell NASA that it was their unanimous choice to insist upon the secrecy of the transmissions. That disclosure never reached the judge or the prosecution's ears; for Davis put a gag on Styles and any others who had received the transmissions. His explanation was, "Not releasing the information is in the best interest of the mission. We must not tarnish the reputation of the crew if we are to maintain the support of the American public." The antagonists had arrived at the same conclusion for markedly different reasons, one self-sacrificing the other self-serving.

The appellate courts turned down Erlich's appeal briefs. Sam and Colin were transferred to the prisons assigned. The astronauts were told that their insisting on secrecy did not excuse the criminal action of their friends. The clang of cell doors closing on Croft and Hershburg echoed through miles of space to imprison the crew of Venus X in a dark cloud of sadness. The gloom would dissolve when Hershburg and Croft would be freed.

Chapter 53

It took the astronauts a year to recover from the collision. The cleanup effort distracted the crew such that none observed that the speed of the craft was decreasing. It was Jim Barnes who first detected the phenomenon. Three days of extensive measurements and computations revealed the speed was 40% less than immediately after impact.

Jim called NASA to confirm the finding and told Glen Ross what was happening. Two days later Vernon Styles told the Communication Engineer on duty, "Wake up Venus X, I need to talk to them."

Ross answered the call, "What have you got for us, Styles?"

"We agree with your computations. If you stay at this speed you'll take 38 months longer to get back to earth orbit. We recommend you fire the booster rockets for 7 seconds and re-compute your air speed." "NASA, we depleted the fuel when we maneuvered to avoid the rogue star. We need an analysis on what we have for reserve, if any at all. Also, the External Gravity Sensor data has been reading max positive values since the accident. We have assumed that the sensors were slammed to the stops and are hung up."

"Roger Venus X. We did a fuel check already and you have no reserve. From now on we will ration your fuel to get you home on schedule. Our people calculate this firing is an acceptable part of the rest of the mission profile."

"OK Styles, we have to trust you guys on this. We'll fire in thirty minutes. Watch for our acceleration."

The ponderous space ship, resembling a large swamp turtle gliding through murky waters, shook and slowly accelerated through the dark vacuum. The calculations were correct and in a few minutes Venus X was soaring towards earth at 60 million miles per hour. The crew let out a unified sigh of relief knowing they had averted a sure disaster. All knew that the food supply could not have lasted an extra three months much less three years.

"That worked, Mission Control, we're back to normal speed. Incidentally, we must have jarred the Gravity Sensors loose for we are getting null readings now."

"We copy, Venus X. Suggest you monitor the external gravity readings daily to verify they remain stable."

"Will do, control."

Chapter 54

It was unseasonably cold and rainy in Tampa the day the appeals were denied. Jane and Sarah left the courtroom together wrapping their light raincoats about them as if they could ward off the icy inner gloom that gripped them. On the steps, lawyer Erlich was apologetic for his failure to win the case.

"That's alright, Mister Erlich. We know that you did the best you could. Thank you for taking the case. You gave us hope. We'll do the best we can to pay the rest of your fee. Bye now." Jane's voice was weak and wavering. The trial left her exhausted. "Is it really over?" she asked herself silently. Only the splat, splat, splat of their steps on the wet cement punctuated their slow walk to the parking lot. Jane fished through her handbag for her car keys. Fondling them unconsciously, she looked at Sarah's pale, drawn face.

"Have you decided what you will do, Sarah? Will you move to be close to Sam before the fall semester and the children start school?"

"I've thought a lot about it, Jane, and I've

decided to stay in Tampa. My family lives here now and the kids like the schools. Sam and I have been having lots of problems lately. I know that most of it is my fault, but I can't go on with the shame and people looking at me like I'm a criminal. I just can't. When Sam gets out; I'll see where we stand then."

"I'm sorry to hear that, Sarah. I've decided to move near Colin."

"Why would you leave everything behind? Why do this, Jane?"

"Because Colin is going to need me. He won't have any family or friends to visit him. He needs me."

"He doesn't need anybody. If he cared spit he would not have talked Sam into stone-walling this thing. It was pride and stubbornness that sucked him into this whole secret thing and it's cost me my marriage and your life besides. Now they're spending time in jail as felons. I don't know if I'll ever be able to forgive Colin for wrecking our lives. Sam should have known better and stood up to him, but oh no! The mission was more important than me or the children or our marriage. I'm sorry to leave you this way but sooner or later you had to know how I feel."

Jane turned away from the younger woman, unlocked the car door and slumped into the driver's seat. Her mind was functioning in slow motion. Maybe what she had just heard was a bad dream. When she got home she could not even remember starting the car or driving the 8 miles from the courthouse. Her mind raced over the accusing words with which Sarah had cold-bloodedly stabbed her.

The graying 55 year old woman sat at the Formica topped kitchen table stunned to have heard spoken the thoughts she had suppressed for many months. Jane could not cope with facing her real feelings about the situation. She went to the bedroom and crawled under the covers without undressing. She would not leave the security of her bed and blankets for three days and nights. She did not answer the phone or the door bell, rising only to go to the bathroom and returning to the darkened room.

On the fourth morning weak from hunger, with no tears left, Jane Croft got up. She showered, put on clean nylons and undergarments and slipped into a simple navy dress. After eating two pieces of wheat toast laden with orange marmalade, she cleared and washed the dishes. Taking her coffee cup into the bedroom she retrieved the luggage set from under the bed.

An hour later Jane locked the front door leaving behind her, the life she had loved for thirty years. It took her three days to get to Maryland where she rented a small kitchenette apartment. The following week she took a job as a hostess in a twenty table family restaurant. Only then did Jane call the prison to find out the rules governing phone calls and visitation times. Jane Croft was where she belonged. Stand by your man was not just a song title to this Air Force wife.

Chapter 55

Three months after the successful firing of the jets, Ross observed a change in data that pointed to the ship velocity increasing. He immediately contacted NASA.

"Mission Control, we seem to be experiencing an increase in speed. Can you verify for us? Also the External Gravity data are at negative 50% max and dropping steadily."

"Roger, Venus X, we copy. We are recording an increase in ship velocity. We will check this out and reply ASAP." A few hours of tracking revealed an acceleration rate which unimpeded, would cause the craft to reach too great a speed. The retro rockets would not be able to slow the vehicle to the safe re-entry velocity when they reached earth.

Styles as program manager had to come up with a quick solution. The staff brain-stormed a few to find the best option.

"We can let them continue accelerating until they get closer to earth, then fire a long retro burst. That way we hold off consuming the fuel as long as possible."

"How about changing the flight profile to

lengthen the distance to orbit intersect; so they can use less fuel to decelerate more slowly? Calculated correctly, the higher speed will offset the longer distance and still get them back to earth at the original time and angle." "Here's a third idea. Have them rotate the ship so that they use the booster jets to slow down. That way they'll conserve the retro rocket fuel for re-entry time." Styles asked, "What do you make of the external gravity readings? Are they accurate?"

"Mister Styles." The young electronic engineer from Hybrid Systems Incorporated, manufacturers of the gravity sensor systems, responded. "The accelerometers may have been jarred off the diamond mounts. That would have them flopping back and forth as the ship changes speed. However, I'm persuaded to believe the readings because the changes are steady and symmetrical. Not the erratic readings that we would expect if they were flopping around. I suspect that for the first time man has seen the 'gravity wave' phenomenon."

One of the senior physicists, irritated by the young man's observation, snapped, "Einstein was theorizing about exploding stars.

The crew described a scenario of a collapsing star or black hole effect. We can't be guessing about these things." As he spoke he was blaming himself for not recognizing the possibility of the existence of gravity waves.

"Well whether there are gravity waves or not I believe we have to keep the speed under crew control." Styles broke in to end the useless dispute. "This far into the mission they don't need to think they are being bounced around without the ability to control the situation. Crank out the numbers to rotate the ship and fire the boosters so that we get them back to optimum mission velocity. Be damn sure that you keep track of this when they arrive at re-entry time."

Mission Control transmitted the data to the space craft and Ross implemented them. First he triggered the directional jets to perform a slow 180 degree turn. As he ignited the boosters the astronauts waited silently. Each knew that this firing had not been part of Mission Control's calculations when the ship had to accelerate three months before.

For the next year the ship velocity would cyclically increase and then decrease with peaks and lulls at three month intervals. Each cycle diminished in change rate until the phenomenon finally disappeared.

With every acceleration or deceleration the ship had to turn 180 degrees; and boosters were fired to control the velocity within a safe range. By years end the Control Rocket fuel was depleted to 10% and the Booster Rocket supply was at 15%.

With confirmation from Mission Control that the ship velocity was holding constant, Commander Ross called the crew together.

"Well good people," Ross began trying to keep a light tone, "There are no rocket refueling stations out here so I believe we've reached the point where we can no longer deviate from maintaining a shortest distance to earth course. Unless someone comes up with some magic I don't know about; that will be our standing order."

There was no response. All but the injured Sandra were fully aware of the peril that a no fuel situation presaged.

"For the time being all external space walks will be limited to emergencies and food retrieval. Jim, you and Nancy set things up so we can use the Exit Pressure chamber as a food storage area. From now on when we do food retrieval let's bring in a month's supply and we'll keep that compartment at freezing temperature. We don't know how much we may need the power packs when we transfer to the recovery ship."

"Glen, how do we get out in an emergency situation to repair the outside or assess damages?" Nancy was concerned that Ross may be suggesting a solution without sufficiently considering the danger of sealing off the only way the crew could exit.

"Good point, Nancy. You two must do the best you can to set up the storage so that in an emergency we can open the outside hatch and push the food out ahead of us as we work our way out of the ship. Leave space for one of us to fit in the Pressure Chamber against the hatch opening to the inside of the ship." Ross waited for the others to consider his plan. When no one spoke, he continued. "Do this tomorrow. That will give you time to look at the chamber prints and plan the layout."

Chapter 56

While the space men and women struggled through the year of velocity corrections, Jane Croft settled into a routine of weekly Thursday visits with her husband. She chose that weekday because it was the day she had met Colin. Her roommate in her college freshman year had persuaded Jane to attend a dance sponsored by the Air Force Academy seniors.

The dance atmosphere was a heady thing for the small town girl from Wayne, Iowa. Colin approached her dressed in the formal Air Force Blues with white shirt and blue bow tie. His black low quarters, as the military dubbed the dress shoes, shined mirror-like. Something about him struck a chord in her and she knew this one was special.

Jane felt the blush creeping up her neck to color her face a light pinkish tone. The pink reddened as an inadvertent memory crept into her mind. The perfectly shined shoes reminded her of the old admonishment, "Never wear patent leather shoes because the boys can see up your dress." She almost laughed aloud at the thought and her impish smile and pink complexion captured the soon to graduate airman's heart. Three months later, on a Thursday night, he asked her to marry him.

She flew out to Nellis Air Force Base where he was assigned after graduating from the Academy. They were married at a Thursday night candle lit ceremony in the Officers Club. Thursday was indeed the best choice to see her husband.

At first the prison visits were too short as the conversations explored the details of their new lives. In a few months there was much less talk and few questions as both realized the dull, humdrum life the other was living. As much as Colin was a prisoner so too, was Jane trapped in a life of week piling onto week of sameness. She had no social life and her only acquaintances were her fellow workers.

It was four months before Jane realized that one of the waitresses was also a prisoner's wife. She had seen her in the prison visitors waiting room. The two chatted and the waitress revealed that she knew two other women who were there for their man. As their friendship grew the two decided to invite the other women to a cake and coffee get acquainted evening.

Soon the four were meeting on a twice a month basis and the sessions developed into support and sharing times. Jane, the only one of the four over thirty years old became, by deference, the facilitator. Realizing her inadequacies in counseling, Jane began attending evening courses at the local junior college. This new direction brought energy into her otherwise humdrum routine. By word of mouth other women came to join until a dozen participated regularly.

The group was too large for the small apartments the women rented so one day as she prepared to leave the restaurant, Jane approached the owner.

"Mister Sanborn, a support group for women in the area, meets at my home twice a month. At present there are twelve of us but others are inquiring into joining us. We don't have a place big enough to house the group. I wonder if you would consent to our using this dining room on Monday nights when the restaurant is closed. I would personally assure the orderliness of the meetings and the cleanliness of the room before we would leave." "What's the purpose of the group?" Sanborn asked.

"The women are wives or girlfriends who are here to support their men who are inmates at the prison. We share each other's burdens and needs. As best we can, we encourage each other in the common parts of our lives. We've nicknamed our group WOW for Women Outside the Walls."

"I don't know Missus Croft. I'm concerned that some of these women may be criminals themselves. The police might frown on my using the place for meetings that may really be planning sessions to help the women's partners to escape."

"We worried about that early on and made it a written rule that there will not be any conversations on this subject while in the meeting room, not before, nor during the official meeting, or after its close. Obviously, we can't monitor each person outside this time frame. Up until now we have no evidence that any of the girls are involved in illegal activities. We really need the room, Mister Sanborn. Give us a try for three months. You can always close us down if you are not satisfied with anything going on."

"I'll think about it and let you know."
Sanborn moved back to the kitchen. Jane
wrapped the light raincoat about her and slowly
walked into the North Carolina mist, unsure that
they would be able to use the restaurant dining
room. Sanborn approached her two days later
and said, "My wife and I talked about it and
we'll let you use the room on a trial basis.
Understand that if we see anything that doesn't
look right we'll have to stop your meetings."

"Thank you so much, Mister Sanborn. We
won't let you down. We will come in after 7 and
leave before 9:30 every Monday. OK?"

"OK".

Jane could not have foreseen the results
of this small support group. Soon other women,
waiting for their men imprisoned in various
parts of the country, heard of the sessions from
some of the attendees or their friends and
began inquiring into starting their own group.
Responding to requests, Jane, with the
financial support of the Sanborns, visited small
groups to help them in forming independent
chapters of WOW.

Colin Croft was proud of his wife's new

found interest. It relieved his worries concerning Jane's loneliness and lack of friends in this new city. He told other prisoners of the group and they in turn, encouraged by the outside support, wrote to friends in other institutions who told their women, encouraging new groups to form.

Chapter 57

At the Kennedy Space Center, the concerns about young Adam Ross's calcium level and metabolism triggered a series of tests resulting in Mission Control instructing Marita to examine the boy in a more critical way. It became evident that her son's skeletal structure was markedly different than expected. She had always known that his bones were not hard but rather more like solid plastic foam. Marita had allocated this to his growing up in a weightless atmosphere.

Further tests revealed that his skeleton was normal as far as the interconnections of bones. The center of the bones had marrow and the spinal column marrow was generating the blood as it should. Why was there no hard shell to protect the inner core? How were the ligaments and muscles interacting with the more porous and softer bones? What differences existed that permitted the teeth to be normal while other bones were not? The finger nails were also normal.

Marita transmitted a blood sample profile specifically designated for DNA testing. The results showed no perceptible abnormalities. After a yearlong study, NASA publicly requested world medical community assistance in diagnosing this situation. The results were inconclusive at best and bordered on conjecture and un-provable hypotheses. Scientists were forced, by default since no other proof was available, to admit that the body of Adam Ross, the first extra-terrestrial earthling, had, or was, evolving in response to its birth and life in a weightless atmosphere.

The concept of a slow evolutionary process as animal forms adapted to their environment was now challenged. Was it possible that the adaptation was much quicker than first believed? Could only man make such dramatic change in its physiology in one generation? What would happen to Adam Ross when brought to earth with its powerful gravity force and atmospheric pressure? Would it crush him or would his body find some magnificent way of adapting?

Chapter 58

The monotony of life on board Venus X took its toll on the astronauts. Daily, each withdrew further into his or her own thought world. The conversations were no longer interesting and the little irritating habits that were tolerated for the first twelve years were now major sources of disagreements. Commander Ross spent considerable time patching differences among the crew. He queried Mission Control. "Styles, I need help in regards to crew morale. I've tried all I can think of but things keep deteriorating. It's taking all of our energy just to garner food and prepare it. Our ingenuity in preparing appetizing meals was exhausted long ago. In some cases, it's taking constant pressure on my part to maintain personal hygiene. Our clothes are worn out and we have just enough to cover our private parts. We need something to help us see the light at the end of the tunnel. Some are very doubtful we'll make it back to earth. What can the Psych majors propose to help us?"

"Venus X, we understand the problem is severe. Ross, we'll do the best we can to get you the help you need." A week later Styles contacted the ship. "Venus X, this is Styles at Mission Control put Commander Ross on the mike."

"This is Ross. What did you come up with?"

"Glen, the gurus recommend that we supply your data base with current world news, transcripts of major sporting events which your crew will choose and some academy award movies of the last ten years. You need to look at what you and your people are willing to scrub off the present entertainment data base. Supply us a list of what you plan to erase from it and your choices of amusement."

"Roger, Styles. It sounds encouraging."

"In addition, and this is the best news, we are contacting your next of kin and making arrangements to allow them to talk to each of your people one at a time on a regular basis until we get you people back here safe and sound."

"That is a great idea. Let's do that real soon."

"Try to convey to the crew that we are very optimistic about your safe return and your welfare is of paramount concern to everyone in the country. Bring them on home to us Ross. We know you're the man for the job."

The encouraging, complimentary words were from a deep sense of admiration and respect which Styles had gained for Glen Ross over the two years he had supervised Mission Control for the Venus X mission.

"Those are great suggestions and we'll gin up the lists pronto."

The news they would be able to speak to loved ones on earth had a marked effect on the crew. A renewed sense of survival and surety of return to earth permeated the ship. The anticipation was as if each one was preparing to go to the high school prom with the girl or the guy of their dreams.

It became important to be well groomed and to be optimistic for the people at home. They had a "Raison d'etre". The people in the good old U S of A were waiting for them to come home. They felt important to their families on earth, and of the mission. Their individual responsibilities for its success were rekindled.

Chapter 59

June Landon took over all the details of contacting the relatives and arranged for communication hook-ups from residences to the Kennedy Space Center. She orchestrated the schedule such that Marita's mother and father would be the first to speak to their daughter.

This would satisfy the women of the country by placing the spotlight on the Yaqui female doctor. The American public would empathize with the pride and joy the parents would have as they spoke to their daughter for the first time since she had rocketed into space. In the same way, the dreams and aspirations of countless young women and teenage girls would appear more achievable as they related to Marita and her leadership role in space travel.

The next conversation must be between Ross and his son. This would capture the bulk of the male citizenry as they related to the major league baseball hero and the pioneer space conqueror. June Landon had learned the power of the media and positive publicity. She was the consummate PR person for the mission and the space center.

As she became more of a public figure and busier with work; her relationship with Owen Davis faded in importance. She spent less and less time with him and preferred the company of Stuart Latham, a local TV newscaster she had met at various news briefings.

Davis, never one to let emotions interfere with career goals, turned his sexual attentions to Lily Longtree, the young, attractive secretary he had hired to replace June when she had taken the Public Relations position at Mission Control.

In two short months after she came to work for him, Owen had bedded the Kansas farm girl. However this Wichita lass, with the milk white complexion and high pale-rose cheek bones was no naive, country bumpkin. She knew exactly what men like Owen Davis needed. Most work days ended with the two rutting like moose in heat on the same couch where Colin Croft and Sam Hershburg had sat waiting to meet with Davis four long years ago.

Davis continued in close

communications with June to stay abreast of the media popular Venus X project. Now, however, his thoughts were taken with overtures which some of the influential State Republicans had made regarding his running for congress in Washington.

Chapter 60

The Yaqui Pueblo was abuzz like a drone of bees as the up-coming talk between their "dimunita Marita" and her parents dominated most conversations. Juan and Consuelo Gonzalez were very concerned. As Juan repeated frequently each day, "We must be very careful of our words for we must say nothing that will embarrass Marita or our nation. The Anglos will get much joy at pointing out any mistakes we make."

The day finally came and the news media turned the Gonzalez home into a quagmire of cables, cameras, fax modems and more people than should ever be allowed in any home much less this small five room ranch.

To the dismay of the fourth estate, Marita insisted that the conversation be private and not made available to the news media unless she and her parents agreed after the talk was finished. She knew full well the importance her tribe placed on propriety and confidentiality. She would not allow the media to disparage or sensationalize this special moment in her tribe's history.

Fitted with headsets and throat mikes, the chubby round faced mother and her stocky vaquero husband waited for everyone, except one NASA communications engineer to leave their home. He monitored operations in case of an electronic failure. The others were escorted to the street, 50 feet away, by four swarthy tribal police officers. The Anglos were not in control on Yaqui nation territory.

Consuelo let tears of joy and relief dimple her white cotton blouse. She knew these were not tears to be wiped away or hidden. No, these were tears only mothers know about. The conversation quickly drifted into a mixture of Spanish and Yaqui dialects. "How are you Mama? How are my brothers and sisters? Make sure the young ones stay in school." "Marita, we miss you so. The tribe needs your doctoring. Talk to Papa, I can't speak anymore." "Is Mama OK, Papa?" "Don't worry for us, Marita. Take care of yourself and come home safely." "What's new in the pueblo?" "We have a casino now and profits have paid for a new clinic and they named it the Marita Gonzalez Medical center because they said you were dead. We are all proud of you." "Bye, bye Papa.

I love you and miss you. Tell Mama I love her
and can't wait for her to hug me against her
bosom." "Bye, bye mi niña, Marita." It ended so
quickly. There was so much that had not been
said, it would have to wait.

The media returned to the house and
Juan and Consuelo Gonzalez had their fifteen
minutes of fame. The questions were inane as
usual. "Did she sound well? Have you always
had a good relationship with your daughter?
Are you afraid she will die before they get back
to earth? Do you think some of your other
children will become astronauts? Is it true you
have a brother in prison for murder?"

Then it was over.

The national television crews and
reporters rolled up the cables, packed cameras,
jumped into rented vehicles and raced to the
air-conditioned comfort of their respective hotel
lounges. "Why the hell would you want to live
in that desert with no AC?"

Empty crumpled cigarette packs,
hundreds of butts carelessly strewn about the
dry desert grass, pop bottles, some half drunk,
some broken, left their telltale rings on tables
and shelves, the refuse gave silent witness to

the behavior of insensitive persons devoid of respect for those less educated or affluent than they. The Anglos had come again to pollute the Indian's land, leaving squalor behind. The Yaquis wondered if the white man would ever learn respect for others and for nature.

On board Venus X, Marita left the control room and secluded herself in her sleeping bag. A loneliness chilled her as if it came from the very marrow of her bones. A hunger for her people and the simple life of the pueblo gripped the depth of her soul. It would not go away until she could walk onto Yaqui land.

Chapter 61

"Handy Andy" Ross, first baseman for the Atlanta Braves and son of Glen Ross world famous astronaut, pulled out of the stadium parking lot in his fire-engine-red MG. The season was over. He had batted .305 and was considered a shoe-in for the golden glove award. No world series this year. The pitching had not held up. Still he had a good year and his new contract would no doubt reflect it.

Andrew's wife, Marlene, was waiting at the house with Todd their three year old and the family luggage. All summer they had planned this two week vacation to Disney World. Todd would see Mickey Mouse and she and Andrew would have time for each other.

As he had done from the first day he owned his prized sports car, Andrew pushed the radio power button before the transmission was in second gear. He ignored the news broadcast as he thought about the way Marlene reacted when he told her that he would have to drive to the Kennedy Space Center while at Disney World. NASA had arranged for him to talk to his dad.

At first she was quite irritated that something would interfere with their time together. Later as she reflected, she realized it was very important for her husband to speak to his father.

"One last news item that just came over the wire..." the voice from the radio announced. The Federal Grand Jury in Tallahassee has just returned a "no cause for indictment" verdict in the case of former Senator Birdwell, former white house chief of staff Conrad Smith, retired General Casey Morgan, and ex-head of NASA Ray Rhino. A member of the jury said the government had no witnesses or tapes of conversations which were conclusive enough for an indictment. So we see an end to charges that, at best, seemed out of character for these four, respected, public officials. We now return to the regularly scheduled program."

It was the only segment of the news report Andrew heard. "Now the bastards will write their exclusive stories and travel the rubber chicken circuits while making more money out of this crap," he thought.

News of the grand jury results did not have much effect on Colin Croft or his wife.

They both knew that the imprisonment of others would never change the guilty verdict against Colin. Sam Hershburg was not interested in anything but counting the next 90 days when he would be eligible for early release, based on good behavior. Eighteen months in jail was eighteen months too many. His estranged wife saw it as one more injustice in this bizarre set of circumstances in which she found herself. She was distraught that this whole thing had cost her a happy marriage and her love for Sam.

Chapter 62

As they lounged poolside watching Todd splash about in the wading pool, Andrew broke the peaceful silence. "Well, I've got to drive over to the Space Center tomorrow to talk to my dad."

"Are you worried or anxious about it, sweetheart?"

"As a matter of fact I'm really nervous about it. It's like the first time I batted in the majors."

"When did you last speak with your dad?"

"I talked to him on the phone the day before they took off. I don't remember much of what we said. I remember more the last couple of days we had before he started training for this mission."

"What was so important about those days, Hon?"

"I guess it's 'cause it was the first time I liked my dad."

"Can Todd and I come with you tomorrow? I'd like to be with you."

"Thanks, Hon, I didn't want to ask you to

give up your vacation but it would mean a lot to me to have you there so you can hear his voice and he yours. He doesn't even know we're married. I wonder how he'll feel when he hears he's a grandfather."

"Don't fret, sweetheart. The first time he sees Todd, he'll love him. All grandpas are proud of their grandsons."

The drive from Orlando to the space center was in silence, Andrew wrapped in thoughts of what to say in five short minutes and Marlene respecting his need to be alone with his thoughts.

June Landon-dressed for the press, met Andrew and his family at the reception desk. She rescued them from the handful of security personnel who had heard that the sports figure was to arrive that day. Andrew never minded the attention. In fact he was always surprised that people were interested in him just because he played baseball.

"First stop," June said, "Is a short news conference. The press is taken up with the story of a nationally known athlete speaking into space with his equally famous astronaut father. They may ask stupid questions about your private lives. You don't need to answer, just move on to the next question."

Andrew laughed. "I'm used to those type questions. They do it all the time to us win or lose."

"This conference is very important to NASA. It will keep the mission in the public eye. We hope it will ease the funding out of Washington for this and other missions."

"Are you saying this is just a publicity stunt for NASA's welfare?" interrupted Marlene.

"Not at all, Missus Ross. Be assured that the main focus of all our personnel is to bring the crew home safely. We are prepared to do anything to assure its success, even pander to the media if it will help to supply the finances we need to do the job."

"Oh, I guess you may be right-I never thought of it that way." Marlene was embarrassed at Landon's quick explanation.

"Right now the crew is suffering from serious morale problems. Depression seems to be affecting most of them, and Commander Ross has explicitly agreed for these talks to take place as quickly as possible before things get out of control spirits wise. Your father,

Mister Ross, is one hell of a fighter. All indications are that without his bulldog tenacity the mission would have failed long ago. You can be fiercely proud of him."

Andrew was touched by such praise for his dad. He had heard only negative things from his mother for the first few years after his parents had divorced. The news conference was no more difficult than the many he had seen or been part of in the locker room of the Atlanta Braves.

June cut it off after ten minutes and led the trio into the control center. The timing was perfect. Voice communications were established and Andrew was instructed there would be delays between responses due to the great distance of the space ship.

"Commander Ross, Styles announced, we have your son, Andrew, on the mike. Do you or he want the conversation secured like the Gonzalez family requested or do you want it public?"

"I've got no problem with public if it's ok with Andrew."

"It's fine with me Dad. You sound great, just like you were in the next room. How are you doing?"

"Not too bad, but we're all anxious to get home. How about you, son?"

"Just great. I made it to the majors. Those tips you gave me the last time I saw you made the difference. I'm playing for Atlanta. We both achieved our dreams like you told me we would."

"That's good stuff, kid; I knew you could do it. I'm sure you know that I married Marita up here and you have a fourteen year old half-brother named Adam."

"Yeah, I'm anxious to meet them. I'm married too and we have a three year old named Todd. Now you're a grandpa in space."

"What's your wife's name?"

"Marlene, Marlene Goetz. She's beautiful. You'll like her."

"I'm sure. Is she there with you?"

"Yes, dad, do you want to say hello?"

"Roger. Put her on."

"Hello Mister Ross, this is Marlene. I hope you can hear me? I'm so nervous my voice is shaking."

"You sound just fine. Take care of my boy and my grandson till I get home."

"I will sir. Here's Andrew again."

"Dad, they just gave me the cut off sign so I'll say goodbye. I love you dad. Come home to us soon."

"I understand. I love you too. Say hello to your mom when you see her. Goodbye."

Styles took the mike. "Do we have any business to take care of, Commander? If not we'll sign off."

"Roger, we understand, voice comm going off the air."

Chapter 63

Navy Commander Glen Ross, combat hardened top gun out of Miramar fighter pilot school, rated the best helicopter pilot in the Navy allowed only a single tear to escape from each eye. He had never experienced such loving admiration for anyone as he did for Andrew at this moment. Before the drops reached his cheeks he reverted to the man with ice in his veins.

"This is no time for weak sentimentality; can't jeopardize the mission by wallowing in loneliness and self-pity. Pull yourself together and start acting like a man." Andrew's words played on the tape of his mind. His stoic response to the conversation reinforced the perception the crew had of their leader. In the words of Nancy Flowers, "He's a cold unfeeling man without compassion or empathy. So how can we expect him to understand our loneliness and depression?"

Later, Glen lay rigid, unmoving, staring up at the ceiling with unseeing eyes. Marita came to him wrapping her arms around him, consoling the man she loved. She looked at him with tender love as he silently allowed tears of loneliness and sadness to run out of the sides of his eyes across the temples into his ears. The rest of the crew would never know his pain. Only the trusted Marita was allowed this glimpse of his soul.

Andrew had turned to his wife and embracing each other they sobbed and comforted each other. After a few minutes June Landon asked if they were up to another short session with the media. Andrew declined and she ushered them out a back entrance after having arranged for their car to be moved there, out of sight of the press. The return to the fantasy land of Disney World was silent until the innocent one broke through with, "Mommy, Daddy fighting? I gotta peepee." Andrew and Marlene burst out laughing releasing the pent up emotions. The vacation was back on track.

Chapter 64

Colin Croft listened to the radio broadcast of the conversation. Hearing the strength in Ross's voice gave Colin a shot of encouragement. It raised his hopes for the success of the mission and the safe return of the men and women he had relegated to twenty years of isolation in space. His imprisonment was a small price to pay compared to their sacrifice. The warrior he had chosen would lead them back.

Three months later Sam Hershburg was released from prison and took a train to Tampa. It would take six months for Sarah to get over her anger and accept him back into her life. The day they remarried was Adam Ross's 15th birthday.

As best they could, the crew celebrated with Adam. There was no Sean to concoct an alcoholic brew and tell wild Irish stories. The awareness that Pennington was still strapped to the side of the ship instead of quietly enjoying the celebration as he had always done went unspoken. Soon the festivities droned to a quiet time with the astronauts turning to their own reveries as they slowly drifted to their normal activities.

Nancy Flowers took Adam's hand and softly said, "Come with me, I have a present for you." She led the boy to her cubicle and with the tenderness of an experienced woman she took him into her sleeping bag and introduced him to the wonder of sexual intimacy. Adam responded with all the virility of a young man approaching his sexual peak.

When it became evident to Glen and Marita what was going on between their son and Flowers, Marita confronted Nancy.

"Nancy, what is it with you and Adam? He's only 15 and your 43. You're not thinking of pursuing this affair any longer, I hope." Her irritation with Flowers' bossy arrogant self-confidence fed her protective mother's need to defend her son from predator females.

"I don't intend anything more than to give him a chance at knowing a woman and learning how to express love intimately. There are no young girls here with whom he can fall in puppy love. No drive in movies where he can learn how to make out. No back seats of cars where the passion steams the windows. He needs to have a chance at living that phase of his life. If we don't get back to earth I'm the only chance he has. Sandra can't do it for him in her mental state."

"I want it to stop right now. You're just using him to satisfy your own needs. You don't love him. You've always resented him. What will happen when you tire of him or you get too weak to lay for him?" Marita was in a rage. Her dislike of Nancy had grown deeper and deeper as the years passed. Now this sexual activity with her teenage son unleashed hatred that she would never control completely for the rest of the Mission.

"Don't worry about your baby. The worst that can happen; will be as if he were in high school rejected by the girl he thought would love him forever. Don't sweat it, I'll end it before we get back to earth and your little boy will have become a man."

"I'll talk to Glen. He'll put an end to this fiasco."

"Don't bet on it. He can't control everything we do up here. We may all be dead in a minute. Give the boy a chance to experience life a little."

"On earth this would be statuary rape and you know it. Nothing good can come of this."

"Grow up! He's the only one up here who has no peers to relate to. I told you not to have him in the first place. Now you'll see that he's going to make decisions for himself; and you won't control him anymore."

"I knew from the first time I met you that you couldn't be trusted. Now you're so jealous of me and my family that you'll do anything to hurt me, even foul up my son. I'll find a way to stop this, you'll see."

"You'll be wasting your time and your energy. Goodbye," as she floated off leaving Marita and her anger.

All of Marita's efforts to convince Adam to stop meeting with Nancy fell on deaf ears. Glen ordered Nancy to end it but she ignored him. As with all the other astronauts Nancy's strength and stamina diminished until she could no longer respond sexually. By then Adam felt no lust for the emaciated woman who now looked so old to him. With an unspoken agreement he stopped going to her cubicle. Nancy had satisfied his needs for two years.

Chapter 65

She paced the floor of the well-appointed office, puffing nonstop on her menthol cigarette. After five smoking free years the tension had the best of her and in two short weeks she was back to a pack and a half a day. The bronze decorated inner door opened and the tall, handsome, brown haired lawyer with the machine-tanned face beckoned her to come in.

"Please Come in Ms. Davis. Can we get you a coffee or soda, maybe a tea?" He closed the door behind them.

"No thank you but some water would be nice." In a minute the secretary came in with a glass of clinking ice cubes floating in Perrier water.

"Please make yourself comfortable and tell me how I can help you."

"Thank you. What do I have to do to divorce my husband?"

In a half hour the lawyer had learned of the husband's infidelities and his view of the marriage as politically advantageous. She had not had relations with him since the new secretary had come on the scene. She did not want to live the charade of a politician's dutiful wife. With every new conquest he made she feared he would contract AIDS and bring it home to her. The lawyer had her sign the necessary papers and assured her that in less than a year the divorce would be final. He escorted her out of the office.

As she walked by the secretary's desk, Roxanne Davis jabbed the freshly lit cigarette into the sand filled container, crumpled a half full pack and threw it into the waste basket. She walked out of the building free of her smoking habit and a philandering husband of twenty years. She had not imagined how good it felt to be free, relieved of living with the burden of betrayal and deceit.

The irony of life was never more evident than the day Owen Davis was served divorce papers; while miles away, Colin Croft was released from prison. Davis immediately called his lawyer and instructed him to do whatever he had to do to prevent his "bitch wife" from getting a dime of his money. Too late, she would get half of everything.

Colin walked into the arms of his faithful

life companion. The suit he had worn when entering the prison two years before was a size too big, the trousers pleated in the back by the necessary belt without which the pants would not stay up. The jacket hung like a big brother's hand me down. He was almost totally gray and his pale complexion was a far cry from the healthy tan he had always sported.

To Jane Croft he was the most beautiful sight in the world. They had made all the arrangements, when told of his early release, to move back to Tampa. Jane had shipped their belongings to Florida the same way she had handled things when Colin was serving in the Air Force. They took two weeks to drive to Tampa savoring every precious moment together.

Colin approached the personnel manager of the company where he had worked before the trial. The president of the company had admired Croft's integrity and loyalty to the astronauts during the hearings. Men of this caliber are rare and a company is fortunate to have them on their staff, he told the personnel manager. Colin was hired at a thirty percent increase in salary as Assistant Marketing

Manager to the Aerospace Industry.

The Crofts and the Hershburgs resumed their friendship and Sarah Hershburg's defection was never mentioned.

Chapter 66

The first contact Sandra Meyers had with her mother was tenuous. Sandra was slow at realizing that it was not a dream. When she asked about her dad there was a long pause. "Oh darlin, your Poppa died two years ago. He had an unexpected heart attack and died in my arms while we waited for the emergency medics to get here. I'm sorry but I had no way of letting you know. NASA said they were censoring all information that may hurt your morale."

The image of her mother cradling her dead husband in her arms triggered the horrific memory of being trapped against Pennington as he died. Somehow the awareness that her mother could endure this trauma and resume living a normal life stirred an acceptance of her own pain. In an unfeeling, matter of fact way, which stunned the crew members who were at her side, Sandra said, "I'm sorry to hear that Mama. We lost our Mission Commander. He died in my arms too. He reminded me so much of Poppa and he was smart and wise like Poppa. I miss him. Do you miss Poppa?"

"Darlin, sweet darlin, yes I miss him very much and I can't wait for you to get back home so we can be together. They tell me I have to go now. I love you."

"Goodbye, mama, I love you too and we'll be home soon." Turning to Jim Barnes she asked, "We will be home soon won't we?"

He took her in his arms and held her close re-assuring her they would be home soon. He would be very gentle with her for as long as it took for the brilliant doctor to heal completely.

Day by day Sandra improved. The physical trauma to the brain had healed long ago but the terror that had gripped her in a deep depression masked it. Now the dark cloud was slowly lifting and with it her fellow crew member's morale.

Chapter 67

Nancy Flowers awaited the call from her father with trepidation. When she was fifteen her parents divorced. Nancy chose to live with her father as she blamed her mother's drinking for the breakup. By the time she was a freshman in college, Nancy was much less condemning of her mother. She came to know the autocratic, pompous, self-centered man for what he was. Soon she could not live with him anymore. Nothing was as good as what he had. No one knew as much as he about anything. Every conversation was a teaching monologue on his part.

Would he be the same over the air waves? Would he dominate the conversation, keeping it centered on him? Would he care what her feelings were or what was happening to them in space?

Her apprehension was well founded. They spent the time with her listening while her father rambled about everything he was doing. When she broke in with, "How's Mom doing Dad? Have you heard from her lately?" His reply was curt.

"No. By the way Pauline and I"
(neglecting to tell Nancy that Pauline was the
lady of the moment) "Are going to vacation in
Florida next February. I'll try to duck into the
space center and check out their operation."

Nancy wasn't sure NASA could survive
his bombast. "Well, Goodbye Dad; call again
when NASA can arrange it." She did not wait
for his answer. Flowers went to her cubicle to
lie down with the loneliness that gripped her.
"No family, no husband, no child, screw-it. I'm
still one hell of an astronaut. The best there is."
The demon melancholy was stuffed back into
the bottle to ferment until someday the cork
would pop because of some unexplainable
trigger and depression would engulf her.

NASA established a schedule such that
each month one of the crew would get to speak
with his or her family on earth.

Chapter 68

Two weeks after Jim Barnes spoke with his Mom and Dad for the first time, he sat at his monitor watching a video of Super Bowl XV. As the announcer interviewed the black super star who had been named MVP, Barnes was moved to tears. He had not shown a great deal of emotion after speaking to his parents but now seeing the black athlete wrenched the loneliness loose from the cellar of his soul.

A few moments later, Adam floated by and saw Jim sitting, rigidly staring at the screen, tears streaming down his cheeks. The boy sensed he should not speak to Barnes. Instead, he went to his mother and told what he had seen.

"Adam, you stay around and if anyone is looking for Jim tell them he's with the doctor and can't be disturbed, I'll go see what's going on. You were right in not speaking to him." With that Marita hastened to Jim Barnes's side.

She approached him and gently touched his shoulder. "Can I help you, Jim? Do you want to talk about it?" Barnes looked up at her and then put his head in his hands.

"I think maybe you're the only one who can understand what's happening. Since I heard my folk's voices I've been so lonely for the company of black people. I'm the only one on board who has left his culture and his color behind, except you, Marita. Do you miss your people?" Before she would have a chance to tell him of her feelings; Jim continued, "You know, I never thought it would be so difficult to have only white people around me. Only now do I realize how different we are. I miss the jargon and the music. I miss hearing the brothers telling the funny inside jokes the whites don't understand. I long for the feel of a black skin other than mine and the smell of a black woman. God, I pray I can make it home. When I do, I'm moving back to Georgia near my folks; and I'll go to the black only bar and sit and listen to my people. I'll dance and hold a black woman tight against me and smell her hair and know I'm where I belong. Never again will I take my Dad's loud laughter for granted; nor be embarrassed by the crude language my old friends use. I'll be home with my own kind."

"I know, Jim, I know." With that she took his hand and placed it against her cheek. She moved his hand slowly over her chin to let him know it was alright to touch her. Slowly, he touched her forehead and ran his fingers over her eyebrows. The feel of the dark Indian skin stirred memories of tender moments with his mother when he was the only child not old enough to go to school and he had her all to himself.

With their eyes closed Marita allowed Jim to feel the smoothness of her shoulders, the roundness of her breasts, her soft arms and stomach. She touched his face and felt his arms, the hair on his chest, the hard stomach and straight back. This was not a moment of lust or sex. This was man and woman touching their roots, reaching for their ancestry, trying to recapture their identities as Black man and Indian woman.

They knew when they had satisfied the longing for their people. He held her hands in his. "Thank you, Marita; I hope you are not insulted by my touching you. I'll always be indebted to you for allowing me to reach home."

"I understand Jim. I thought I was the only one different and isolated from their culture. I thank you for letting me reach my people for a moment." She withdrew her hands and went to her cubicle.

For the rest of the voyage they would have a reverence for each other that transcended friendship. They had achieved an oneness without sexual intercourse, an oneness of soul.

Chapter 69

For two years, after NASA took over communications with Venus X, Styles, under the orders of Owen Davis, supervised the building of a vehicle to perform the recovery of the astronauts. Styles assembled a team of experts in the space mission field. After broadly defining the specifications the team sent out bid requests. They settled on two teams of avionic companies to compete for the design phase and now it was time to award the build contract. Davis signed off on the choice of a team consisting of Hughes, Raytheon, and Lockheed. Lockheed would be responsible for the vehicle, Raytheon for the guidance system and Hughes for the control avionics.

Styles contacted Venus X to inform the crew of the progress. "Styles," Ross asked, "Can you give us copies of the proposal or a synopsis of what the ship will look like?"

"We'll transmit an overall write up when we see the final design prints. For now I can tell you that we have chosen a design that will make the move from Venus X to Retriever 1, which is the name of the new recovery ship, as simple as possible. The concept is that you will exit through the usual port but you will not have to suit up because Retriever 1 will pressurize the lock chamber. This will eliminate using your ship's power."

Ross interrupted, "How many of us will Retriever 1 transport on one recovery mission?"

"You're jumping ahead of me, Glen," Styles continued. "We are bringing all of you back at the same time. Retriever 1 is designed similar to a revolver with seven chambers that look like torpedo tubes. These will be synchronously rotated to accept one of you at a time. The chambers will contain breathing apparatus and communications gear but must be sealed until you return to earth."

"Why must you seal the chambers? We're anxious to see other humans."

"We realize you're anxious but we must keep you in a controlled pressurized environment because you've been in zero G space for so long that atmospheric pressure and gravity may be more than your bodies can handle. Also the chambers will be lead lined to isolate any radiation problem you or the outside world might encounter. The chambers will be felt lined and cushioned so your return flight will be as comfortable as possible."

"OK, you guys are in control and may know best. In case it slipped your minds, Diaz will update you on our physical dimensions. The last thing I want is for any of my people to be left up here while you redesign some lead lined chamber."

"Roger, Glen, we will want a last minute update when the chambers are on the drawing board. That's all for now."

Every other month Marita transmitted the size of the individuals on board. After a year of reporting, there were no longer any significant changes. The astronauts had stretched in height from the smallest change of 2 1/2 inches for Marita to 4 inches for Jim Barnes. The cylinder length design was frozen at 6 feet 6 inches with an inside diameter of 36 inches.

To counter balance the weight of the cylinders when occupied; all heavy engine parts were designed to be forward of the center of the ship. The first test flight was conducted in the sixteenth year of the Venus X mission. To the dismay of the designers and mission control, the first time that the MSC's, the acronym for the Man Storage Chambers, were rotated, Retriever 1 went into a spin. Only the immediate action of the pilot halted the rotation before the crew became too dizzy and disoriented to control the ship and return to earth.

The ship was redesigned to carry small rockets mounted perpendicular to the revolver chambers. These were synchronized to fire when rotation of the cylinders was initiated supplying a force in opposition to the rotation of the ship.

The second test flight was successful but the pilots found the tail section of the ship too heavy making the landing extremely difficult. The crew seats were moved forward six inches. This made things somewhat tight for the front seat leg space but the compromise was the best to be had this late in the design.

The third test flight was completely successful and included moving three men from a second space craft, designed to simulate Venus X, into the chambers. All systems were go. Now, the wait for Venus X to reach earth orbit.

Chapter 70

Two months after Styles had proudly announced to the astronauts of Venus X that Retriever 1 was ready and waiting for them to reach earth orbit, Ross contacted Mission Control. "We have a real problem up here. The main electric generator just crapped out. The windings have shorted out. We are going to shut down everything we can and try to supply the garden area as normal as possible."

"Roger Venus X, we copy. The main generator has malfunctioned. What's your plan for repair?"

"First thing you should understand is that it did not malfunction, it burned when the windings shorted together!" Ross was in no mood for clever words that couched the severity of the problem. "It means we will have no lighting anywhere else. We are going to shut down all comm gear. We must set up a schedule to report to mission control on a monthly basis like we did with Croft and Hershburg."

"What will you do for temperature control and for oxygen supply?"

"I'm setting up a short tour schedule to have only one person on the Control Deck for a one hour shift. Jim Barnes is looking into running some tubing from the garden area to supply some heat to the pilot seat area. We're looking for ideas from Mission Control to help us around this problem. In the meantime we will use the portable oxygen tanks at the control console."

"We understand the severity of the problem and the complete staff will work to find some help for you and your crew."

Glen Ross uncharacteristically thought aloud. "What have I done? Did I convince this crew to continue the space mission only to die in a powerless craft floating in space forever?"

"Glen, my love, don't be so hard on yourself we all agreed to continue the mission against NASA orders. You did not force us and you are the only one who has kept us going with any semblance of hope. We came because we wanted to and we will see it to the end whatever it may be. It was all worth it to have our love and a son. It's worth every struggle to get him home to earth."

"I didn't know you were listening.

Thanks. With you I'm sure we'll make it." Glen Ross was back in control of his emotions. The mission must be completed at any cost.

The crew moved their sleeping bags into the garden area and prepared to ride out the next 30 months under the most austere of conditions. None of them had paid attention to the steady drone of the main generator until now. The only noise to be heard in the garden was the few surviving birds singing in competition with the roiling of the treatment vat waters.

By means of pressure pumps designed to run off a small auxiliary generator outside the gardens, these waters were continually agitated. This noise became an almost unbearable source of irritation to the crew as they struggled to survive. They lived in darkness waiting for the ship to come close enough to the Sun so that solar power could be used to power the Control Deck area.

After seventeen years of living with the steady hum of the main generator, the silence lent an eerie feeling in the darkened garden area. Depression enveloped the astronauts as their confidence in the reliability of Venus X waned. It was Sandra, almost fully recovered from her depression, who raised the hopes of all by reminding them, "We're on course and on schedule. The ship will carry us in range of sunlight and the Solar Energy Panels will work like they did before. Don't worry we'll have electricity again. It's only six months until we get into sun range. What's six months? We've already done more than seventeen years. We should be able to do it standing on our heads."

The response was not raucous shouts of agreement but rather a quiet ascent as they steeled themselves to face the coming months. Until the sun shone again brightly on their ship, the gods of Venus X could focus only on surviving with their sanity intact. Through it all the giant craft soared silently in the infinite vacuum of the universe. Oblivious to the precious cargo it carried; Venus X pursued its destiny as if it had a soul of its own.

Mission control had no solution to the loss of power. Styles reviewed the tapes from Colin Croft and Sam Hershburg to learn what the astronauts had devised as a monthly communication schedule. Meanwhile NASA continued tracking the course of the space craft. When Ross transmitted to earth they briefed him on status and then waited another month hoping to hear from him again.

The communication blackout ended the family radio transmissions before a second round of talks were completed. The space voyagers were left to deal with the realization that they were at the mercy of who knows what; an expanding universe that would prevent them from reaching earth orbit or a collision with meteor showers or asteroids. Perhaps the loss of remaining power sources, maybe nuclear radiation leaks they no longer could detect would be the assailants. If the gardens stopped producing starvation would defeat them in the end. Were there unknown forces, against which they would have no defense, seeking to destroy them?

Their minds played tricks on them. Awake they imagined danger and asleep the nightmares gave them no rest. Marita prayed. Nancy Flowers angrily willed she would not be defeated by anything nature threw at her. Sandra Meyers stayed joyfully optimistic believing that if she had survived the years of depression surely she would complete the mission.

Jim Barnes hung on to an obsessive desire to be among his people again. Adam continually talked about Sean Murphy and how he would not give up on the mission; even dying rather than causing it to fail.

And what of Glen Ross? Glen Ross knew, in the deepest recesses of his being, that destiny had called him to succeed in this mission. He would not consider failure as an option. He would bring them home!

Chapter 71

At the eighteen year mark the solar panels began to store energy. In one week the storage cells were fully charged and Glen Ross activated the Control Deck systems. Communications with NASA resumed on a daily basis and the crew was elated to return to their normal sleeping areas.

Mission Control transmitted the news worldwide. Soon they would have two way television transmissions. This did not escape the President's press secretary. He suggested that the first TV contact should be with the President. You can never have too much positive publicity if you want to be re-elected. The Commander-in-chief agreed and NASA was notified. Owen Davis could not have been happier. This would be great publicity for his future campaign for a senate seat. The crew received the news with great joy. Now the people at home would see that they could make it. With all the logistics in place the women astronauts primped and helped each other with hair styling. The men shaved as best they could and went so far as to press Marita into playing barber for them. They gathered around the observation deck where they would all be in camera range.

At mission control, Owen Davis stood behind Styles. It was the first time in three months that Davis had come to the control room. Busy with his campaign for a seat in the House of Representative, Owen had progressively turned over day to day operations of the Space Center; but this day was different. This would be a great opportunity to garner votes for everyone in his district would see him speaking to the President.

When the first video picture reached Mission Control the ground personnel were stunned. The sight of the scantily dressed, emaciated astronauts was horrific. Styles and his staff had not envisioned a disheveled, bug-eyed, space crew.

The happy astronaut's smiles could not hide the sagging skin of their faces from the years in a weightless environment. Dominated by wild looking, staring eyes, the distended faces told in a stark manner what price the gods of Venus X were paying for their space exploration. Yet these pioneer men and women seemed inured to the changes they had undergone.

"Cut that picture off the monitors," Styles ordered. Davis responded sharply. "What the hell are you doing, Styles? This is big news with the American public. Get that back on line for the President's conversation with the crew."

Over the years, Styles had developed deep admiration for the crew members. No way would he allow the world to see them in such a demeaning state.

"Don't you touch those controls," he barked. "Owen, I'm in charge of this project and until I'm relieved of duty those pictures will never be shown to the public, only to the President." Keying the intercom, he ordered, "Attention all mission staff. As of this moment TV pictures of the crew are classified Top Secret. You are to reveal to no one what you have seen and will see during the President's talk with the crew of Venus X. This order also applies to any and all observers who are not Mission Control Staff members."

"You're missing a great opportunity to touch the hearts of the American people and rally their financial support for the project, don't you agree, June?" Davis would not give up the chance for publicity without a fight.

"Yes. The people have a right to see what their dollars are doing," Landon suggested. Her public relations mind blocked out Styles' compassion for the space travelers.

Styles ignored them. He had his technicians disable all outside TV lines except the one to the White House. He advised the President's press secretary that no pictures of the crew would be made public under any circumstance. The world would hear that that the television transmissions had failed.

"Please advise the President that he should prepare himself for a sight similar to the pictures taken of prisoners of war in concentration camps. We will allow the two way conversations but only the video of the President to be transmitted to the nation. I'm sure when he sees the astronauts he will agree that we have made a wise choice. Tell him we are ready for the interview as soon as he can get in front of the cameras."

Styles did not let Davis handle the microphones. He positioned himself so Owen Davis, perennial publicity hound, could not have access to open mikes.

"Venus X the President of the United States would like to speak to you."

"We're ready Mission Control."

"Go ahead Mister President," Styles cued the Commander-in-Chief.

"Hello. Congratulations, men and women of Venus X." The words he had rehearsed were buried deeply in his mind as he stared at the depressing image on the TV monitor before him. He continued hesitatingly. "The country is, uh, most proud of what you have accomplished. We are, uh, enthusiastically awaiting your return." The President barely heard Ross reply.

"We are anxious to get home. There's no place like earth, believe me."

The forewarning had been insufficient to prepare the tough ex-dock-worker for the picture before him. He did not know what to say to the crew now that he had seen them.

"I, uh, commend you all for the, uh, sacrifices you've made so that man may reach the stars someday." Now he regained his composure. "I want you to know that I will personally see to it that you have every facility at your disposal to assure your safe return. If there is anything you want that needs my support now or any time during the rest of the mission just sing out and you'll get it."

Ross was ready for such a statement. "Mister President the crew would feel much safer if Colin Croft and Sam Hershburg were at Mission Control as our communication links. They know more about our space craft than anyone on earth and push comes to shove they would be invaluable in analyzing any problems we may encounter up here."

Ever the consummate politician the President replied, "I am not familiar with these names but if that's what you want then you've got it."

"Thank you sir, it will be a relief to hear their voices talking us home. You can't know what a great morale booster this will be for us. Thank you again, sir."

"If you have any other needs, tell Mister Styles and if he can't make it happen then I'm instructing him to come directly to me and it will happen. Good luck and happy landing."

With the interview over, the President turned to Press Secretary Foley. "Did you see those poor creatures? I don't see how they can last another two years. What do you know about those two men they asked for?"

"As I remember, sir, they were convicted of some wrong doing in regards to this mission. I'll get you the details by tomorrow."

"While you're getting that info, contact Styles and tell him I want those two, what's their names, at the Kennedy Space Center within a week.

"I'll see to it, sir."

Chapter 72

The next day Foley reported that Croft and Hershburg were convicted criminals and could not be employed by NASA. President Canteleone; raised in the little Italy section of New York and ex-dock- worker, had maneuvered his way up the executive ladder of the AFL/CIO union. He came into political prominence at a time when the large majority of voters realized that they were in the low income bracket and could not aspire to a middle income since such a group no longer existed. The time was ripe for a blue collar president.

Canteleone knew politics and knew how to wage a bare-knuckles campaign. He won handily. In just his second year in office, the President was still very much the dock worker.

"What the hell do you mean they can't hire them? Didn't I say for Styles to get them over there? Is he bigger than the President?"

"It's not Styles but Owen Davis, the head of the center. He says the fed regs prevent him from hiring known convicted felons and unless congress changes the laws his hands are tied. He finished by telling me that he was sure you would not want him to break the laws in case something went wrong and the two men were responsible for the failure of the mission."

Canteleone knew a threat when he heard one. "Who is that son-of-a-bitch? I'll fire the bastard and put in somebody who will obey orders from the President."

"He's a long time government employee and could make a lot of noise about our black mailing him into breaking the law. Well, there is one alternative, sir."

"What is it?"

"You could issue an official President's pardon for the two men based on your review of their cases, sir. Then they could work for the government and Davis would have no choice but to obey your orders."

Rolling up his shirt sleeves Canteleone stood up and paced around the office weighing this option. "By God, let's do it and then get me a complete FBI dossier on this guy Davis, I want to take real good care of him in the near future." Canteleone was back at the union hall taking care of trouble makers who wouldn't toe the line.

Chapter 73

When Croft received Styles' phone call requesting him to come to work at the center he had not yet heard of the Presidential pardon.

"Are you sure you can hire me with my prison record?"

"Oh, you haven't heard, Mister Croft. The President has pardoned you and Mister Hershburg. He is requesting that you both come to the center immediately and take over the communications with Venus X. I don't see how you can refuse the President and the direct request of Glen Ross and the crew of Venus X."

"Fax me all these details and an official job offer and I'll come."

"Great! I'm looking forward to meeting you. The fax is as good as in your hands."

Croft could not wait to tell Jane about the pardon. He left work immediately and sped home. When he got there, Jane was on the phone trying to reach him for she had just heard it on the news. They called Sam and Sarah to meet them at the steak house for a celebration. Now they could finish the job they had started 18 years ago.

The next day the fax was on Colin's desk and he took it with him to show the company president and request a leave of absence. It was granted, for the company management knew full well the prestige and publicity Croft's NASA assignment would bring to the firm.

Sam had no trouble achieving the same cooperation from his employer. Within four days Colin and Sam went from ex-cons to key employees at the Kennedy Space Center-the power of the presidency at work.

The first morning they drove to the center brought back memories of eight years ago. As they sat in the lobby waiting for an escort to Styles' office they reflected silently on the events that had started here and so dramatically impacted their lives.

The clack, clack, clack of high heels coming from the long corridor woke them from their reveries. They looked at each other and burst out laughing at the possibility that this was just a dream. But it was real. When the high heels went silent June Landon stood before them.

"Welcome Mister Croft and Mister Hershburg. It's indeed a pleasure to have you

join the Venus X team. My name is June
Landon and I'm the Public Relations Manager
for the Project. If you'll come with me we'll meet
Mister Styles in his conference room. We've
arranged for a media session to give them a
chance to meet you and get your reactions to
the events of the past week. Mister Styles and I
agreed that it would be less distracting, long
term wise, if you got this out of the way, then
you'll be freer to concentrate on bringing the
astronauts home safely."

June had chosen to divorce the new
work arrangement from the previous Davis
encounters. As they followed her to Styles'
office, Colin prodded her. "Do I understand that
you are no longer Davis's secretary? How did
you manage to move into this position?"

June had entrenched herself solidly
enough in her new position that she no longer
felt that she owed Croft or anyone
explanations. June was excellent at her work
and was confident that she would always be
able to earn a living at PR work.

"When NASA took over the Venus X
project from you two, an opening came up for a
public relations person and I applied. My years

with the center gave me credibility and I haven't disappointed management yet. I hope that you will look past the unfortunate events of the past so we can get on with the task at hand. I will do my best to make your stay comfortable and pleasant."

"How much is Davis involved in the project? Are we going to have to go through him for anything?" Sam wished he had asked that question before accepting the assignment.

"Very, very little... Mister Davis is more involved with other projects and his contact consists of receiving update memos every other week. Other than the day the President spoke to the astronauts, he has not been in the control center in months. Mister Styles runs the whole show."

When they reached the room, Styles was at the door waiting to greet them. Croft scrutinized the tall, handsome man as he accepted his strong handshake. Colin never trusted a man with a limp grip. As he gazed into the dark-blue eyes crowned by a full head of tousled blond hair he sensed that Styles was a man he could trust. Croft's instinct in such things seldom failed him. "Welcome Mr. Croft,

Mr. Hershburg. We feel very fortunate to have you as part of the Venus X mission once again. You've met Ms. Landon and I believe you know Mr. Davis." Owen had purposely stayed in the midst of the news people so he might size up his two long term adversaries. Now he stepped forward and offered his hand to welcome the new staff members. Neither accepted.

Colin glared at his nemesis with a hardness in his eyes which told Davis all the anger and bitterness prison can bring to an innocent man.

"I should have known that you couldn't miss a chance to be in the limelight. Understand this, Davis. I don't want you anywhere near me. You want to say something to me you go through Styles or your little miss public relations. When the space crew is back on earth you and I will take care of unfinished business."

Croft had spoken so softly that only Hershburg, Styles and Davis heard what he said. Owen Davis turned to the news media and said, "Ladies and gentlemen, I welcome you all and introduce to you, Mr. Colin Croft and Mr. Sam Hershburg, two welcomed additions to the

Venus X program. I leave them at your mercy. Treat them gently, we don't want to discourage them their first day back." He turned, motioned to June Landon to follow him and left the conference room.

Once out of hearing range he told June to monitor all activities of the two and to fill him in on everything at the end of each day. Landon was incensed at the thought that Davis still believed he could control her and use her whenever he chose. Appreciating the fact that he could possibly have her fired or laid off, she nevertheless made her stand.

"Look Owen, I'm not going to stooge for you any longer. You will have to live with Styles' reports as you have in the past. Your problem with those two is not my concern. I've got a job to do making sure the public and Washington stay fully committed to saving the crew on this mission. I will not get involved in tactics that could jeopardize their safety."

"Are you forgetting who runs this center? If you want to keep working here you damn well better do as you're told." He played the trump card of authority.

"Owen, if you try to get me fired or laid

off, you'll find yourself facing charges of sexual harassment and prejudicial conduct because I will no longer sleep with you. If you don't think I can make this stick keep in mind everything I know about your wheeling and dealing here at NASA and your sexual conduct with every skirt you've lifted including that Wichita Witch you call a secretary. If I have to leave this job or the center, then you are going down with me. Go back to running the center and leave this project and me alone."

She turned and walked into the conference room where Croft and Hershburg were stone-walling every question about the past with a standard, "We're not at liberty to discuss that but we're pleased to be here," while repeating they were only here to help their friends get back home safely. June grasped the situation and announced the end of the interview. "That will be all for today, ladies and gentlemen. I'm sure you can see that Mr. Croft and Mr. Hershburg are anxious to get on board and up to speed on the present status of the project. Thank you and please follow the security guard's instructions as you leave the center."

Chapter 74

Styles led Croft, Hershburg and June
Landon into his office adjoining the conference
room. Unlike Owen Davis's plush
appointments; this office was starkly
functional. Every piece of furniture served a
purpose. Even the wall hangings were stellar
constellation maps or detailed drawings
pertaining to the project. No frills here, only
necessities.

The project manager asked his secretary
to bring in the coffee cart. "We will have a long
session so I had a day's supply sent up from
the commissary. That will limit interruptions. I
took the liberty of ordering some sandwiches.
We can have a working lunch. I hope this is ok
with you all?"

Sam and Colin were impressed by the no
nonsense attitude of their new supervisor. They
nodded ascent and Styles continued.

"Mr. Croft, I want you to know that your
previous position as program manager of
Venus X brings a welcomed history to our
team. I assure you that we will be looking to
you for all that you feel is pertinent to our

mission. I'm naming you Assistant to the Program Manager. This puts you as my right hand man and grants you free hand to pursue whatever is necessary to bring the crew home. Is that satisfactory to you?"

"You're very kind and I'm looking forward to working with you. By the way, call me Colin. Mr. Croft may not wear well with your other staff members."

"Fine, Colin. Please call me Vernon. "For you Mr. Hershburg..."

"Make it Sam, please."

"Good. I would like you to work closely with the Psychologists on the staff because you probably know the crew members better than anyone. We need to keep them as mentally well as possible and you can give insights no one else has. Also, I want you be the primary voice contact for the rest of the mission, if its ok with both of you?"

"Fine," they responded as one voice. For the next 6 hours, the foursome listened to presentations from a dozen key persons. The two new men were bombarded with technical data on every aspect of the mission. What was most astonishing to Croft and Hershburg was the advancement in the communications hardware fostered by breakthroughs in miniaturization and the use of multiple satellite relay systems.

When the briefing turned to the health of the crew, Styles ran the video tapes of the crew's talk with the President. Colin and Sam sat stunned. They were unable to reconcile the memories of their healthy teammates with the emaciated, hollow eyed creatures on the TV screen.

"Vernon," broke in Croft, "Could we send a rendezvous ship with fresh food supplies. They don't look like they can last another two years."

"We've struggled with that possibility but the consensus is that it would consume too much of the Venus X fuel and would really jeopardize any chances they have of reaching earth orbit. The low fuel situation will be reviewed by the next presenter. The maneuvering to recover from the encounter with the collapsing star sucked up more than the reserve; such that they probably have just enough fuel for the necessary course corrections at earth orbit time. Why don't we

break for 15 minutes?"

Chapter 75

"Mission Control, this is Venus X. We need a reading on our remaining fuel and what kind of corrections we will have to make when we reach earth orbit intersect." Glen Ross was responding to Nancy Flowers' concern that the course they were tracking would take the ship much too far from the original point of earth intercept.

"Roger Venus X we will crunch the numbers if you think necessary. The last calculations did show a slight drift off course but nothing alarming. Give us a few minutes and we'll get the real time data."

"Roger, Mission Control. We'll wait on your call."

The new calculations showed a larger deviation off course than the previous data. The Duty officer immediately sent for Styles. Vernon stopped the briefing. "Well, gentlemen, it looks like you are going to work. I've been called to the control center. You might as well come along and get your feet wet right off."

The elevator ride up to the top floor took only a few minutes and, for Sam and Colin, stepping out of the lift into the control center was a moment of mixed feelings. Joy and elation at being back where they belonged yet anxious and uncertain as to their ability to be of help to the space voyagers.

Styles listened to the update status with increasing concern. He asked the Mission Control Navigation Engineer for his assessment of the problem. Then, they conferred with the resident field representative from the manufacturer of the power plants aboard Venus X. All agreed that a course correction had to be made.

"Colin I want you and Sam to get on the mikes. You need to let the crew know that you're on board and in positions of authority. Get the firing sequence and duration of firing. When you have established contact and are ready, give those orders."

"Commander Ross, This is Colin Croft advising you that Sam Hershburg and I have been assigned as primary communication personnel with Venus X and its crew until all of you are back safely."

"Croft, it's great to hear your same stuffy voice. You should have been up here with us then you would have become less "Air Force Academy" and more human." Ross could not resist needling the Air Force Colonel but his voice betrayed the joy he felt at hearing the man most responsible for encouraging and supporting the mission from the very start.

"It's great to hear you. Say hello to the rest of the crew. I'm sure we'll get to talk to them as days go by. Sam has been assigned as the prime comm officer so most of the contacts will be with him. If you need to talk to me or Vernon Styles, Sam will get us on the horn. I'll turn it over to him now. Take care and bring it on home Ross."

"We'll give it a hell of a shot, Croft."

"Roger Venus X. This is Sam here at your disposal. I want to set up a video shot of the whole crew the next time we communicate. For now say hello for me and let's get down to the business of a course correction. Our gurus down here tell us that you need to change course by 2 degrees clockwise. The present course would miss your earth intercept point by twenty thousand miles. Does this jive with your calculations up there?"

"Glad you two are back on board. You

must tell me all about it someday when you and Croft are buying the drinks."

"OK Glen, you need to fire the left steering rockets for a 75 second burst. We will transmit to you an updated course program. Once it's installed in the Nav Computer the sequence should activate automatically. The screen should countdown 30 seconds before the firing and count up to 75 seconds. You'll have nothing to do but go along for the ride."

"Roger, Sam. We copy 30 seconds to ignition and 75 seconds to shut down. Let's do it."

Twenty minutes later Mission Control verified that the new program was loaded correctly and the sequence was under way. The ignition was on time. As most of the crew watched; the massive ship slowly turned; although imperceptible to the occupants save for the vibration felt as the rockets fired.

"Mission Control did we have an error in firing time? We thought it shut down prematurely at the 71 second mark."

"You observed correctly, Venus X. We are checking why the premature shut down. It might just be a transmission error of one bit changing the 5 to a 1. At any rate it was not an over correction which would have to be rectified. The next course correction will take care of it."

"If you say so, Sam. we'll wait on your analysis. Venus X signing off for now."

Inconceivably no one on board or at Mission Control observed that the Fuel Available and Fuel Consumed numbers in the data file were not changing. The automatic update system had not registered any changes since the power generator failure. The computer did not report that the rocket nuclear fuel supply was exhausted. The ship was without navigational power and the astronauts oblivious to their plight.

Chapter 76

The night the course correction was made, June Landon stayed with Stuart Latham as she had been doing for six weeks. During the night as they lay next to each other sharing the events of each other's day, Latham asked, in an innocuous way, why the TV transmissions had failed when the President had spoken to the Astronauts two weeks before.

When he held her in his arms after making love, June never thought of Stuart as being first and foremost a TV Newscaster. She trusted him. Without thinking June answered, "The communications didn't fail. Styles chose not to let the networks have it." She caught herself and knew she had already said too much.

"Does he always censor everything?"

"No, but this time he thought he had reason. He even went against Davis's orders. I can't talk about this anymore It's classified."

Stuart Latham had heard enough to convince him that there was a story here. Tomorrow he would follow it up. He turned to June and gave her a long goodnight kiss and lay quietly as both feigned sleep. She bashed herself mentally for having said too much hoping he would not pursue what he had heard because he loved her. He planned to meet with Owen Davis and get the full story out of him. June learned the hard way that reporters may not be trustworthy bedroom playmates.

"It's six thirty, Kitten. I have to leave for the station." Latham, already dressed in one of his four tan gabardine suits, light blue tie and brown deck shoes, had made sure to get up earlier than usual so he wouldn't have to talk with June. He knew that when the story broke, she would be incensed and their relationship would never be the same.

As she heard the door close behind him, June turned over to nap a little longer only to bolt upright as she suddenly remembered her gaff of the night before. She jumped out of bed and raced to the bathroom not wasting time to cover her naked body.

"If anyone saw me through the bedroom window, I hope it makes his day 'cause mine is sure going to be the first of many lousy ones if Stuart breaks this story. How could I have been so stupid? That will teach me to lay off that second Margarita." She must get to Stuart and make him promise not to pursue the story. She didn't take time to go to her apartment for a fresh change of clothes.

Latham was not available to take her phone call so she drove to the station to speak to him personally. The receptionist told her that Stuart was out of the building, at a meeting with Owen Davis.

"Damn, I'm sure Owen will know who leaked the information to Latham. That bastard is going to use this against me as payback for my not reporting on Croft and what's his name. Damn, damn, damn!" She saw her career going down the drain. If she got fired who would hire a PR who could not keep silent with Top Secret information?

Davis relished anytime a TV newscaster wanted to interview him. "You can never get too much publicity when you're running for office," he would tell his secretary, Lila.

"Miss West, show Mr. Latham in please." "Have a seat Mr. Latham; do you care for coffee or something?" Davis had seen the newscaster on TV. He could see now what attracted June Landon to him. He was more handsome in person than on the tube.

"Nothing for me, sir, I had breakfast already."

"What can I do for you Mr. Latham?"

"Please call me Stuart. Sir, I have unconfirmed rumors that NASA prohibited the transmission of the pictures of the crew of Venus X during the conversation with the President. Could you verify or deny these rumors?"

In one short sentence Davis had the weapon that would let him get rid of Landon and put Styles in his place for countermanding his orders to let the public see the pictures.

"Obviously, we cannot give credence to unconfirmed rumors. Where did you hear this story, Stuart?"

"Mr. Davis, I can't divulge my source but It has been very reliable in the past. I think the public who is paying the freight for this mission has a right to know why the censorship and who authorized it."

"Off the record, who leaked this to you?"

"I can't say, Mr. Davis."

"Are you free for the rest of the morning?"

"I'm at your disposal, sir."

Davis triggered the intercom and asked his secretary what appointments he had for the rest of the morning. None seemed politically important so he had her re-schedule them and told her he would be out until after lunch.

"Let's you and I go for a ride. You like pleasant drives in the country, don't you Stuart?"

"I'm your man."

Chapter 77

The data analyst walked into Croft's office looking like he'd seen his dead mother-in-law resurrected.

"Mr. Croft, excuse me but I think you need to know this right away."

"What is it, Schmears?

"I believe I found the reason the firing ended prematurely. I've reviewed the last few firings for similar mishaps and found no problems but then I noticed that the Fuel Available and Fuel Consumption files have not changed since the generator failure. That was before you came aboard, sir. I showed this to our programmers and they said there's no data coming in from the fuel sensors."

"Good work. If you haven't told Styles about this do it now. I'm going up to Mission Control, meet me back there." As Colin raced by her desk he told his secretary, "Get a hold of Hershburg and tell him to get to Mission Control right now."

Within two elevator rides to the top floor the three men were questioning the data experts and the fuel control consultant.

"There are no back-up sensors and no fault indicators associated with them because these are simple devices with only one wire connected to the sensor PC board," they heard the latter say as he continued. "We ran a diagnostic on the board and no flags showed up. Either the sensors are dead or the input gate is open."

Sam jumped in. "Can we swap the input to another gate?"

"That will take a physical wiring change. I don't know if they have the strength or the dexterity to do it without scorching the board and causing more damage."

"What about rewiring the harness?

"No way. That's flirting with a real disaster." Croft broke in. "Those were port rockets we fired. What's the data on the starboard side?"

"It's the same sensor because they work off the same nuclear pile," the harried consultant replied.

"I haven't heard one good word about this design. Styles, I suggest we initiate a short firing, first port side than starboard to see if either side is working or if they're both disabled."

"That's a real gamble, Colin. If the left malfunctions but the right side fires we will be driving the ship further off course."

"I thought of that Vern, but I don't see too many other options right now. We need to find out if they have any Directional Rocket fuel left or if it's just a failed sensor.

"Alright, Colin. Let's talk to Ross up there and see if any of his people have a better idea or if they want to try this. Meanwhile have the Navigation Engineers prepare a scenario to fire the shortest burst possible. If the crew agrees we want to be ready to implement ASAP."

Colin turned to Hershburg. "Sam, find out how soon we can contact the ship."

"I'm ahead of you. The next window of opportunity is two days from now at 14:30. We've got 48 hours to get ready with a workable solution."

Chapter 78

Vernon Styles was nervous as he forced down the scrambled eggs and toast his wife had prepared. He kept going over in his mind the alternatives they had; to steer the space ship. Make the wrong choice this afternoon and he could doom Venus X and its occupants to an eternity in space.

The voice of the news caster on TV broke through his thoughts. "This morning we have a film clip of utmost importance to not only the citizens of the United States but of the world. This station has received the first and unedited television transmission from the Venus X space ship. We must warn you that the contents may not be proper viewing for young children. Stuart Latham is at the Kennedy Space Center following this story. Stuart."

"Good Morning. This rare footage is of the crew of Venus X as they had assembled to speak to the President. We have not been able to confirm, why these pictures were not released to any TV stations at the time President Canteleone spoke to the astronauts. We repeat our warning that the pictures you will see are extremely depressing and this station suggests you send the children out of the room."

Styles jumped to his feet and raced into the den. On the screen were the images he had fought to keep from the public eye. He grabbed the phone and called Croft. "Did you release that tape to the TV station? Turn to channel 7 and see for yourself."

Croft caught the last four seconds of the clip but it was enough to fill him in on what Styles was asking.

"Why would you think that I would give this out? Damn it, I agreed with you when you showed us the tape. You had better check with little miss Public Relations. Maybe she knows. I can assure you that neither I nor Sam Hershburg would be part of this. I'll see you at the office as soon as we can get there." Croft did not wait for an answer. He jammed the phone into its cradle, grabbed his suit jacket and bounded out the door as "Emergency. I've got to run, Hon" trailed behind him.

Styles could not reach June Landon as she was on the phone trying to talk to Latham at the station. How did he get that tape she wanted to know? How dare he use their love and intimacy to further his career? She had feared the worse when he had not returned her call for two days and the station would not reveal his whereabouts. She gave up and drove to the center.

June barely had time to drop her handbag into the desk drawer that Styles was confronting her with questions about the leak to the TV people.

"I did not give out that tape to anyone. I'm not the only one with access to it. It never got out of our hands until your two fair haired boys, Croft and Hershburg, showed up." She would never admit to telling Latham about it but she had not given him the tape.

"June, you had better find Latham. You know him very well so get to him and find out who gave him the tape."

"He hasn't returned my call in two days and the people at the station won't let me in to see him."

"Find him! I don't care how but I want to know who gave him that tape." It was the first time she had seen Styles so angry.

At that moment Croft and Hershburg

burst into the room. June Landon took advantage of the opportunity to slip out of the office and pursue her effort to find Stuart Latham.

"Vernon, control center just informed us that the President's press secretary is on the phone. They're transferring his call to your office. You'd better get in there."

Styles picked up the phone before the first ring was finished. "Vernon Styles here, how can I help you?"

"Mister Styles this is Jack Foley, President Canteleone's press secretary. The President is very upset that you changed your mind and released that video. The American people are going to raise a stink as to why we've sent people into such a mess. They'll want to know why we can't get them home immediately. The President wants to know what you are doing about accelerating the flight home before they die up there."

"I understand, Mister Foley. We're investigating all avenues to hasten the recovery date. As soon as we have the plan with the best chance of success we will notify the White House with a synopsis of the schema and the

President can then announce it to the public.
Please assure President Canteleone that we did
not release the tape to the media. It was
obtained covertly and we are making every
effort to find the source of the leak and deal
with it."

"Fine, keep on top of this and make sure
my office is kept abreast of all developments."

"Yes sir, we'll keep you posted. Thank
you for calling." Styles had not noticed that
Owen Davis had slipped into the office.

"Well Styles," Davis sneered, "Which one
of your two convicts sold the tape to the
media? How are you going to explain this to the
President? You've got a security system that
can't even keep track of a video tape. How
secure are real sensitive documents. When you
let those two guys have access to the whole
project you invited the fox into the hen house."

"Morning Owen, I don't believe for one
minute that they're responsible for this leak.
No, I think somebody wanted to make an easy
few hundred bucks and sold the tape to
Latham."

Croft walked in on the conversation with
the news that the tape was still in the Secret

File; so someone with access to the combination must have made a copy and returned the original to the file. Only ten people knew the combination to the file drawer. They were: Five Control Center Shift Supervisors, and Styles, Landon, Davis, Hershburg, and Croft.

Chapter 79

Colin Croft pulled Styles aside and quietly reminded him that they must contact the crew and resolve the fuel shortage situation. The program manager responded immediately.

"Gentlemen we can't get bogged down about this security leak problem, we have a job to do. Let's get up to Mission Control Center and clear up the low fuel problem."

Davis heard these last words as he was at the door. He wheeled on his heels and forced his way abruptly through the other men and stood inches away from Vernon Styles. "What's this about a low fuel problem? Why wasn't I brought in on this?" His survival instincts had triggered a possible career threatening situation and he was not about to be kept in the dark about it.

"Owen, we're not sure. The problem may only be a faulty enunciator. We're running some checks and should have a handle on it shortly. I did not think it sufficiently serious to talk to you about it until we knew something more solid." Styles did not want Davis barging in and forcing decisions on matters that were beyond his technical knowledge of the Venus X space ship.

"Let me know the extent of the problem as soon as you have all the facts. The people in this country are going to be upset enough at the TV pictures without adding a fuel shortage problem to their concerns and, damn-it-all, get to the bottom of this security leak in a hurry."

"Will do, Owen, I'm calling security in on it right now." As he watched the back of Owen Davis disappear from the doorway, Styles picked up the phone and punched in the number of Kennedy Security. As he waited for the chief of security to come to his office, Vernon turned to Croft. "Colin, you and Sam get to Control Center and get things moving to try the short course correction bursts we discussed yesterday. I'll get up there as soon as I brief security and we get all the classified lock combinations changed."

At the White House, the President's office had notified the FBI; and the Florida office was already dispatching two agents to the Space Center.

The elevator ride to the Control Center seemed endless as Sam and Colin mentally reviewed the firing sequence and the dangers involved. As they walked into the center they looked at each other and each knew that the other was fully aware of the risk they were taking with the lives of their comrades on board Venus X. As with one voice they said, "It's the only choice."

Colin gave the order to program the firing sequence the Navigational Engineer had developed. In a half hour the sequence was checked out. By that time Vernon Styles had made his way to the center and he gave the order to contact the space ship.

"NASA Mission Control this is Venus X do you read us?" Glen Ross's voice came crackling through the speakers.

"Roger, Venus X. Your transmission is noisy but we can understand you well enough. We have a short firing sequence we want to download into your Nav Computer. The game plan is to fire port rockets for two seconds then fire the starboard rockets for two seconds. This will isolate the malfunction for us. Is this alright with you?"

"I don't feel too solid on this one, Sam. If only one of them fires we are going to be driven off course. Can't we shut off the fuel supply and go through the ignition sequence? This way we'll hold course and still check the electronics." Glen knew that a wrong course correction could result in Venus X missing the orbital re-entry point. Ross's intuition was troubling him. He knew that every time he had this feeling in the past that the premonition had proved valid.

"We understand your suggestion, Glen. We've discussed this approach but it doesn't tell us if there is a blockage in one or both of the fuel lines."

"Well, I want to do it in two steps. If the ignition sequence checks fail then we can assume we have an electronic failure. If they give us a green light then maybe we can find a way to check the fuel flow without firing. I don't want to fire the rockets unless we have to make a course correction." Ross was adamant. Styles, Croft and Hershburg agreed to do it his way. Styles ordered the navigational engineers to program the two phase test; and to coordinate with Commander Ross, when ready to down load it to the space ship. They were to notify him, or Croft or Hershburg, before contacting Venus X.

On board the ship, the crew was struggling with depression at the realization that they may be powerless to steer their craft into earth orbit. The prospect of soaring closer and closer to earth for the next six months only to miss earth orbit and skip off into space to die from hunger demoralized every one.

Sandra Meyers, who was joyful as she slowly recovered from her depression, began to slip into melancholia. No one spoke unless it was necessary for the performance of mission tasks. Nancy Flowers become more and more sarcastic toward anyone who came near her which prompted the others to shun her. This added to her sense of being alone against the world. Jim Barnes turned almost catatonic.

The poor diet of the past few years had robbed them of their strength and energy. It left them unable to fight against the mental stress of powerlessness. Adam, now seventeen, grew bitter at the prospect of never seeing what earth life was like as he saw himself living in space forever.

As for Marita and Glen, they could only cling to each other in the darkness of their cubicle. There was no love making or passionate sex. This had been lost long ago as their bodies slowly wasted away. Now their love for each other was expressed by tenderly holding each other; drawing strength from the feeling that together they could surmount the crisis and live to return home. The gods of Venus X would now wait for the God of gods to show them a way to get back home.

Chapter 80

The FBI agents interviewed the ten persons who had access to the combination of the security file. None were declared as suspects. Croft and Hershburg were interrogated more than the others; but the agents did not find any cause to be suspicious of them. Despite the pressure of these interviews the two men and Styles continued their efforts to test the low fuel situation on Venus X.

NASA loaded the new software into the spaceship's Nav Computer. A week later, when the communication window was favorable, Glen ran the firing sequence. All systems functioned properly. Even the igniters triggered the test circuit indicating that current had flowed properly.

"Mission Control, we read a Go system here, can you confirm?" Ross did not know whether he wanted a confirmation or not; for either way they were in trouble. If they had received the same data as he had on board it meant they would have to attempt a real firing sequence. If not, it meant he and his crew could not rely on the fault isolation hardware or software.

Meanwhile the agents interviewed Stuart Latham and applied great pressure to get him to reveal his source but the reporter hid behind his First Amendment rights. Latham refused to meet or talk with anyone from the Space Center and only spoke to the FBI with his lawyer present.

On board the space biosphere, morale was deteriorating at an exponential rate. Every confrontation between two of the space voyagers seemed to precipitate more problems between others. The day of the test firing was at hand and as they secured themselves for the ignition thrust. None could speak. It was left in Glen Ross's hands to communicate with Mission Control and to initiate the sequence.

Believer or atheist the lesser gods of Venus X had a prayer in their minds that both ports would fire simultaneously; for that is what Ross had suggested. If both ignited, the ship would stay on course and the problem was simply a faulty alarm signal. If only one fired, they would go off course. If neither fired, the navigational fuel pile had been fully consumed and they could no longer control the ship's direction.

As the computer screens printed out that the igniters were on, the crew stopped breathing for a full thirty seconds. Then all knew they had no fuel to make course corrections. No one un-strapped their safety belts, no one spoke. Finally Glen Ross keyed the transmitter.

"Mission Control, we did not achieve ignition. I repeat we did not achieve ignition. Please confirm." His voice was strong and decisive. His face was as stone, no emotions, jaw set, eyes steely, fixed. He refused to accept the possibility that he would not bring the ship home. For the first time in his life he was angry at his flying machine. In his mind he cursed the rockets for consuming all the fuel. He hated the rogue star that caused the extra firings. And, he swore at God for not caring that they might all die, lost in space. Glen Ross, the ice man, melted into an everyday human frustrated by circumstances he could not control.

"Roger Venus X, telemetry confirms no ignition. Glen, we have called in all the talent available to come up with a fix for this malfunction. Meanwhile tell us what we can do to help you to continue with the mission as planned."

"There's not much you can do. We'll just have to bite the bullet until the brains find a fix. I think its best we sign off now and I'll get back to you during the next communication window."

"Roger Glen, Mission Control signing off."

Chapter 81

Two weeks later, as happens so often in criminal investigations, lady-luck stepped into the picture. While enjoying one too many martinis with a good friend and colleague, whom he trusted completely, Latham let it slip out, that a certain busty PR gal had tipped him off. The friend worried that more serious security leaks were involved, made an anonymous phone call to the FBI. It was not too difficult for the agents to identify to whom Latham was referring.

They brought June Landon in for questioning. The interrogation was rigged to imply the TV newsman had accused her of supplying the tape. She denied it vehemently but did admit that she had spoken to Stuart about the condition of the astronauts.

With no real evidence against her the government did not file charges. The NASA officials in the persons of Owen Davis and Vernon Styles asked for her resignation. The Welshman, Davis, had his vengeance on the woman who had done so much for him yet had dared to refuse to obey his instructions.

One month after the video tape was run by Latham. June Landon left Kennedy Space Center. Styles assigned the task of holding press conferences to Colin Croft.

June went into seclusion to avoid the tabloid reporters; who were unrelenting in pursuit of an exclusive interview. After two weeks of camping in the north woods of Maine, she was ready to return to her apartment. The early October foliage had calmed her while enervating a desire to find out who had given Stuart the video tape. To her surprise, Latham had left a message on her telephone answering machine. He was sorry she had lost her job and wanted to see her. June mulled over the pros and cons of seeing him and decided it could be the way to find out who had leaked the tape. She left a message with the TV station receptionist for him to call her.

Two nights later June prepared for his visit by taking a scented bubble bath. She perfumed with his favorite cologne and dressed in a teal sheath dress that he found particularly attractive. She clipped on the pendant earrings he had enjoyed removing many times as the beginning of their sexual ritual. Her effort did not go unrewarded. When she opened the door after letting him ring a half dozen times, Latham was struck by her sensual beauty.

"Wow, you look ravishing," he blurted. "Can I come in? I took the liberty of bringing you a white rose as a peace offering."

"Certainly Stuart, Thank you for the flower, it was very thoughtful of you." The sparring match was on. He would apologize profusely and once she forgave him, he would try to get her into bed. She was, after all the most voluptuous woman he had ever known. Self-serving though it may be, Stuart loved her. June made small talk and feigned forgiveness. At the right time she would try to get him to reveal his source.

They were on their guard, parrying and thrusting with polite words, skirting the real issue they both knew would have to be faced sooner or later. After two glasses of sherry and a tray of stuffed mushrooms and crackers and cheese, Stuart apologized again and asked her forgiveness.

"I'm so sorry, Love. I had no idea Davis would ever put the blame on you when you had meant so much to him. Has he come to hate you that much that he would throw you to the media wolves knowing it would ruin your career and maybe your whole life?"

"Are you telling me that Owen gave you that tape? You owe it to me to tell me who gave it to you. Was it Owen?"

"You know I can't answer that question. If you go to the press and make accusations, they won't believe you. They won't believe that anyone else was involved but you."

"I don't want to go to the press I just want to know whom you bribed to get that tape. I know I don't have a chance to prove anyone else did it. It's for my own peace of mind. If you're not willing to tell me then your words of remorse are lies. How can I trust you're not wearing a wire to record our conversation so that you and your source can edit it and make it sound like I supplied that miserable tape?"

"I swear that's not what's going on. If I thought, if I could believe, that what I tell you will never leave this room then it might be different. Now you've got me wondering if this room is bugged."

"Stuart, we can't get anywhere if we don't trust each other. We can pat each other down to assure ourselves the other is not wearing a wire and then let's take a walk on the beach where no one will hear us. I'll believe you're really sorry and that your loving me is not just a lie, when you tell me who gave you the tape. If you are not willing do this, then leave right now and don't ever come to see me or I'll file a restraining order against you." "Alright, let's talk."

Chapter 82

The astronauts on board Venus X had been chosen, among other reasons, for their proven abilities to respond positively under the most trying and dangerous conditions. Faced with the lack of steering fuel, their resiliency and mental toughness was taxed to the limit. Glen Ross had to pull the crew out of its depression. They must work to find a solution to the fuel crisis. He called a meeting on the control deck. Glen spoke slowly but with as much confidence as he could project in his weakened condition.

"We all know there's a good chance we're not getting back to earth. However, there has to be a solution to this problem. I'm asking you to help me find it. We know this ship better than anyone on earth. They may find a fix but we can't wait for that. We need to resolve it ourselves. Let's brainstorm, and no idea is too far out."

The crew sat in quiet as each searched his or her mind for possibilities. Jim Barnes asked, "Can we use the retro rockets to guide us by firing only one side or the other as needed?" Nancy Flowers suggested, "How about finding a way to transfer some of the ship's operating fuel to the directional control pile?" Though she seemed in a daze and unaware of why they were meeting, Sandra Myers spoke with uncommon certainty,

"We have to slow down. We are going too fast."

Marita jumped in, "Of course. Any correction to the system we come up with will be very slow and at our present speed we could over correct so badly that we might never recover. Sandra has hit on a crucial point."

"I had considered using the last four Asteroid Deflector nuclear rockets as controllers," Glen offered, "But the more I think of it, they cause too severe a back thrust and we would be zigzagging all over the place. I suggest we don't fire these rockets even if a meteor or asteroid is on a collision course for the earth."

Barnes reminded Glen, "This is our primary objective, to destroy or at least change the course of any object large enough to cause extensive damage or great loss of life, if it could strike the earth."

"Yes Jim, I know but the odds of our intercepting any such object without directional controls is out of the question. We will fire these rockets only if the object is endangering our ship." No one protested his suggestion. Saving the lives on earth took a back seat to self-preservation.

Glen broke a long silence asking, "What other sources of propulsion do we have, Jim? You're the most familiar with our nuclear system."

"Well, we could use the water evacuation ports for some thrust; but I don't think they would generate enough force to change our course significantly. Besides we've got another three months to survive and if we lose the water we won't need to get back to earth because we'll all be dead of dehydration."

Once more Sandra broke her silence, "The spacewalk packs have fuel left." Though locked in surface depression, Myers was still the brilliant engineer whose forte was problem solving. It was as if this part of her brain was unaware of her emotions and functioned as it would in a laboratory setting on earth.

Barnes responded immediately, "This

may be our best chance. What do you say Glen. Shall we run through some numbers and see what we can do with the packs?"

"It's the best we've got. Let's crunch the numbers with the assumption that we will fire the retro rockets to slow us down before we try any course corrections. Nancy, you and Jim get to work on whether the man packs could redirect the ship in some way." Glen continued, "Marita, you and Sandra crank out some data using a 'best straight line approximation' course rather than a 'curved orbital entry' course. Keep in mind we could enter the atmosphere outside the seven degree safety window. Let's not skip out into space or burn up on re-entry."

"Glen," Nancy suggested, "If we can control the course with the man packs then we might be able to make a flare out correction when we approach earth orbit intercept."

"Good thinking, Nancy. Meanwhile I'm going to contact Mission Control and have them assign a team to duplicate our work. They have more facilities at their disposal and could confirm or shoot down some of our findings."

A new enthusiasm filled the room.

Encouraged by Sandra Meyers's lucid response; the crew moved with resolve, hopeful that the problem could be solved. They would find a way!   They would survive!

Chapter 83

As they walked the beach, Latham confided, "It was Owen Davis who gave me a copy of the tape. I don't know how he managed to put the blame on you. I never intended for you to suffer from this. In my enthusiasm to break a story of nationwide interest I acted hastily. I would love to find a way to pay Davis back for what he's done to you." He could not admit he was the one who leaked her involvement to his co-worker.

"If we could get Owen to admit to witnesses that he was the leak then his empire would crumble," June added.

"June, he's too clever to admit that to anyone. He would have to be taped without his suspecting anything."

"How can we tape him? Could you wear a recorder, Stuart? You could meet with him, and make believe you are about to reveal his part in this thing."

"I can't do that because it would destroy any opportunity in the future for me to get informants to trust me. My career as a newsman would be over."

"Well, Stuart Latham, my career is down the toilet and I'm not ready to give up on pinning the blame on the right donkey. Please think about it and see if you can help me with this. Let's call it a night and talk about it in a few days."

When they got back to the apartment Latham asked to stay the night. Landon was not naive enough to believe his great declaration of love so readily. She put him off with, "I'm sorry, Stuart, but I'm not ready to start up with you yet. Give me time. Call me if you come up with any, anything. Good Night."

When Stuart showed up at her place later that week he had no new ideas but June had decided. She would try to get Davis to slip and admit his guilt while she recorded their conversation.

"Stuart, do you know anyone who knows how to bug a room? I think if I get him into my apartment he'll probably brag about how I need him even though he framed me."

"That's too risky, June. I think this guy can be very dangerous; if he thinks he's being double crossed. There must be some other way."

"Well you won't risk your precious career to see justice done so it's up to me. Find an expert on covert bugging and I'll do the rest."

"There is a technician down at the station who moonlights as a surveillance agent. I'll get his number for you and you can call him. Be damn sure you don't tell him what you are doing and I don't want my name mentioned with any of this."

"Thanks. I hope he can help." She did not say what she really felt; for fear Latham would not continue to help. She thought, "You're some hero you weasel. You say you love me and want to bed me down but you're just a rat, no not even a rat, you're barely a mouse. How I ever thought I could love you and not see this side of you is beyond me. I'll thank the day I can get you out of my life forever."

"Stuart, you have to go now because I've got lots of work sending out resumes." "Why don't I mix us a drink, June, and see if I can light some of the old fire you had for me. I think it's still there and only needs a little coaxing to get the embers glowing again."

"No, Stuart, go home. I told you I needed time and I mean it. Goodnight," as she ushered him out of the apartment. "A lifetime won't be enough, you coward," she whispered under her breath as he walked down the stairs to the street below.

Ten days went by with no word from the newscaster. Then he left a phone number on her answering machine making sure he did not identify himself. She called immediately "Hello, Conway Belcher Investigative Services; how may we be of service?"

"My employer has asked me to coordinate this project and I'm conversant with all the details. I'm free this afternoon. Since confidentiality is of the utmost importance, perhaps we could meet at the Turquoise Oasis lounge at two o'clock. Just ask for Peggy, the bartender will know me."

"Two o'clock it is." He hung up.

June had decided to act as if she were a co-worker so the technician would not tie her to the bugging. After lunch she donned a black wig and dark glasses. She wore a simple cotton dress that camouflaged her figure and she would not be easily remembered since many women at the cape wore this style and coloring.

Once at the bar she told the bartender

that she was meeting a man she had met through a TV dating system and he would be asking for Peggy.

"Could you stall him a bit when he gets here? I want to size him up before I go through with the date. This is the first time I've done anything like this and I don't know what kinds of men use these dating services."

"Ok, Peggy. What will you have while you're waiting?"

"A Tom Collins will do." She turned to scan the room. There were three men at the far end of the bar. Four women seated in a booth talking and laughing a little too loudly; revealing that they perhaps had sipped a brandy too many after their lunch. She wondered what their husbands were doing and what they would say if they saw their wives in this situation.

A man reading a racetrack journal engrossed in picking the horse that would bring him wealth and fortune was seated at the table nearest the door. The half-drunk glass of tap beer had left circles on the table top suggesting he had been there a while and was a sipper not a guzzler.

Oblivious to the customers, the waitress on duty was sitting, at a table-for-two, eating her lunch. A party of business men was waiting at the register to pay their bill. Someone's expense account was about to be padded because no one was treating any of the others as a customer.

"I'll sit in the far booth over there." June walked in small steps clutching her purse the way she imagined a nervous woman on her first blind date would.

The beer sipper folded his handicapper's sheet. Bracing himself with one hand on the chair and one on the table, he rose slowly out of the chair. The pained look on his face implied either knee problems or a sprained back. The middle aged man with graying temples and a stomach that preceded the rest of him by a good ten inches walked to the bar.

"Barkeep can you point me to some broad named Peggy, she said you'd know her."

"Listen, Mac, I don't run a pick-up joint for pros. You'll have to take your business elsewhere."

"This is no pick-up. She's from out of town and her brother asked me to keep an eye out for her."

"Let me serve this drink and I'll ask around." When he got to June's table he told her the guy had been here all along and asked "Did she want to meet him."

"Yes, send him over."

The bar tender nodded toward June and said, "there's your Peggy, I'll act like I believe your stories but don't come in here again for a pick-up."

Belcher returned to where he had been sitting, picked up his beer and ambled to June's table. "Hi, Peggy? I'm Conway Belcher. My expertise is in electronic surveillance. My fee, if we agree on working together, is one hundred dollars per day, in advance, for a stake out job. Otherwise, one hundred dollars up front for installing a listening device in a home and two hundred when I turn over the taped recording after removing the device.
Do we go on or do I leave now?"

Chapter 84

The power experts at Mission Control were not enthusiastic with the fix the crew was considering. They preferred something more reliable and predictable though it might mean sophisticated modifications to the space ship. Despite their protests, Vernon Styles insisted that a separate team investigate Commander Ross's suggestion while the rest of the navigational and power experts would search for a safer method of steering.

Three days later the main team had no solution and the ancillary team came to Styles with their findings. Vernon called in Croft and Hershburg to listen to the report. The lead engineer sounded discouraged as he began his presentation.

"Mister Styles, the possibility of guiding such a large mass using the man packs is very questionable. By our calculations, it would take twenty percent of the fuel from two packs to move the ship enough to correct the course by a quarter of a degree. The packs would have to be an integral part of the ship at that time. If they could lash them securely enough and found a way to fire them simultaneously they may effect slight directional changes."

"That's not going to cut it, will it?" asked Sam Hershburg. "Fill us in. Will it work?" said Croft.

"Well gentlemen, if the corrections are made early enough and accurately we might get them on collision course with earth. This means we must fire the retro rockets immediately to slow the ship enough so it will not veer too far off course with the first firing."

Styles spoke quickly. "We'll do that." The engineer continued. "Then we have to find a way to make the man packs an integral part of the ship in order that the rocket thrust has a full impact on the direction of the spacecraft. Most importantly, we need the most accurate course correction on the first firing so that we don't have to make more than one or two before flare out."

"I'm waiting for the rest," said Styles, the impatience in his voice stabbing through the tension in the room. "That's all we have right now. We haven't found a source of power to cause flare-out. I'm sorry. Maybe the other team will have a solution."

Colin Croft broke a short silence. "We all agree the ship must be slowed down or we'll have to make large corrections. Vernon, I suggest we talk with Ross and his crew to see if they agree and are willing to make this significant change in the flight plan."

"I am with you, Colin. You and Sam get on the air with Commander Ross and decide when he would be ready to do it. Meanwhile you control experts come up with the data for the optimum firing duration that will reduce their speed to allow for direction changes using the man packs. If the other team comes up with a better course control idea then we will be ready for it. Let's do it gentlemen."

On board Venus X, Glen Ross was proposing a flare-out plan to the other astronauts. "I would like you to break up into two teams and run some data as to the feasibility of affecting a safe flare-out by using the four remaining ADR's, the nuclear Asteroid Deflector Rockets. I want to tilt the two front rockets nose up and the two aft rockets nose down and fire them simultaneously. The ship should pancake and we might be able to slip into earth orbit. I realize this is pretty iffy.

Obviously, we need to decide what speed we want before we calculate the effects of such a firing." Glen was interrupted by Sam's voice.

"Venus X, this is Kennedy Mission Control do you read me?"

"Roger, Kennedy, this is Venus X. What have you got for us?"

"Glen, Sam here. We recommend deceleration as soon as possible. Our people are looking at data to choose the optimum speed you should have before we attempt any course corrections. How does that play with you and your people?"

"That is pretty much our consensus. How soon can we have the data and what do you have in mind for navigational power?"

"Our experts are still looking at it. As soon as we have a best solution you'll be the first to know. Do you have a first choice of velocity before you try navigating?"

"Not yet. We are crunching data ourselves up here. Right now we are toying with the possibility of using the last four nuclear ADR's for power to pancake us into earth orbit. Have your staff look at what the ship would do if we point the two forward

Asteroid Deflector Rockets up and the two aft down, then fire all four at once. If Mission Control has a better idea we'd like to hear it."

"Roger, Commander, we read you and will get back to you as soon as we have any answers. Mission Control out." "Venus X out."

Sam looked up from the monitor screen and tried to interpret the look on the faces of his two superiors. Did they think any of this would work or did they share his deep fear that after twenty years in space it would all be for nothing? Venus X and its doomed crew could race by the earth in an endless glide; perhaps ending in the gravity field of some planet or star until it burned like a Viking funeral ship of old. They would even have dogs at their feet if any of them still existed. Through some quirk of memory Sam remembered Gary Cooper in the movie Beau Geste. He thought, "It would be the way Glen Ross would have it given no way back to earth."

The concern blanching their faces told him he was not alone in his fear.

Chapter 85

Belcher slid his six foot three two hundred and fifty pounds into the booth with some difficulty as his stomach creased around the edge of the table.

"First, let's be up front with each other, Miz Landon."

"How do you know my name?" she blurted in disappointment.

"It's part of my job to know everything about my clients and their situation before I buy into an assignment. That way I don't get surprised or suckered into bad situations. It was easy to trace your number when you called. I thought you got a raw deal at NASA so maybe I can help you out."

"Can you bug more than one room at a time? I have a four room Condo on the second floor of a four unit complex."

"Yes, I can. I have a new device I've built whereby you can have some music playing to drown out the voices and I can still decipher the conversation. It costs a little more, fifty bucks per day. If you think that the other party or parties will be suspicious then by your turning on the music it disarms them. It may be worth your while."

"Yes, yes, I think that would be a good idea."

"I'll need access to your stereo or hi-fi or whatever you would be playing music with. And I need an hour in the place to set up the volume controls etc. When do you need to have this done?"

"I'll make my apartment available anytime. When can you do it?"

"Thursday night would be good for me. OK for you?"

"Yes. Seven o'clock would suit me best."

"You've got it."

June gave him the address. She dropped a dollar tip on the table and they left together. June strode out confidently not like the shy, demure, lonely heart she had tried to portray earlier. The bartender promised to remember her the next time she came in to pick up a John. The fake wig and the dark glasses would not fool him next time.

At exactly seven o'clock that Thursday night, Belcher pressed the button to June Landon's apartment. Once he identified himself over the intercom she buzzed him in. He deftly connected an amplifier to the audio output jack of the stereo system and an inverter amplifier to the receiver which would pick up the sound from the miniature microphones which he strategically located in the four rooms.

He ran all the wires under the living room rug and hid the amplifiers, the receiver and a transmitter under the sofa. He hid the recorder, which would receive the processed sounds from the transmitter, on a shelf in the kitchen broom closet. It took Belcher forty minutes to adjust the gain of the amplifiers and the delays from the four microphones to effect a full cancellation of the music from the stereo thus recording only the small talk conversation he and June carried while he made his adjustments.

"OK, Miz Landon. You'll record everything in your apartment until you tell me to disconnect. The system turns on when you turn on the stereo. If you don't want to listen to the music just turn down the volume but don't shut it off or you won't record."

"I will call you when I want it disconnected. It may be a few days. Here's the one hundred and fifty dollars for the installation. Contact me when I can pick up the tapes."

"Thanks. Goodnight."

The web was spun now she must lure the fly into her parlor.

Chapter 86

"Mr. Styles, Mr. Davis wants you to come to his office. He asked that you bring what you need to brief him on the status of the Venus X project." The secretary's voice, over the intercom, burst into Vernon Styles' somber thoughts. The flimsy chance that the astronauts could be saved had cost him two long, sleepless nights. His eyes roved around the room looking at the charts and photographs of space shots without seeing them. With his mind so preoccupied, it took all his energy to focus on what he would have to tell the Kennedy Space Center Manager. Davis would expect another easy solution to a difficult problem. Styles realized this might be the one to cost him his job.

As he approached the door to Davis's outer office Vernon straightened his shoulders, lifted his head. He was ready now. "Mr. Davis sent for me?"

"Yes, Mr. Styles. He said for you to go right in."

"Good morning Vernon. Make yourself comfortable and tell me where we sit on your project."

As always; Styles chose to sit on the sofa, though it was the furthest from Davis. Somehow this gave Vernon a feeling of distancing himself from the man whose ethics he disapproved. Little did he know that he was sitting where Davis and his secretary frequently had sex.

"Owen, the flight is progressing on schedule and on course. The health of the crew is deteriorating rapidly. I believe keeping them alive for the next three months will be the most difficult part of the mission. From what we can determine, they stopped exercising a few years back and the food is sparse since the collision with the magnetic field of the collapsing star."

Davis turned his chair at a ninety degree angle to his desk. His eyes darkened with irritation at the thought that this project may turn into the biggest disaster in the annals of NASA. He did not want this on his watch, particularly now, as he was launching his campaign for congressman of the district.

"Is there any way we can ferry some food to them. I don't have to tell you what it would mean to everyone to lose them now that the whole country is counting down to their safe return."

"There's something else, Owen."

"Dammit, I want an unexplained success here, not a well-documented failure," as he spun around to face the man who was turning his day into one big headache. "What else has gone wrong?"

"If you remember there was some question as to the fuel supply for the control system. It turns out the worse we feared is true. As it stands they cannot steer the ship."

The concern on Styles' face told Davis that things were worse than the tone of voice had conveyed. "What are you doing to fix this problem?"

For the ensuing fifteen minutes, Vernon detailed all the steps that had been taken and what they would be doing next. "Bottom line, Owen, what we are doing is to forego the original flight plan which had the ship follow a prescribed spiral course until a gradual entry into earth's outer magnetic field. As you know, they were to affect an orbital pattern where the pickup ship would engage it and disembark the crew."

"I know all that, Styles," Davis snapped at the harried program manager. Tell me what the hell you're going to do that's going to get their asses back here safely."

"We are setting the ship on a crash course for earth and we'll make last minute corrections to get them into orbit."

Davis accepted the explanations. However, he berated the Project Manager for not detecting this problem and resolving it sooner. "Your project is the biggest headache of all the projects we have here at Kennedy. Fix the problems, Styles. Go get the job done and don't miss anymore failure messages. I don't want you in here with more bad news. If you can't handle the project; tell me and I'll get someone who can."

Vernon walked out, shamed like he had the time the Principal at the high school had chewed him out for cutting classes and suspended him for two days.

Meanwhile, at Mission Control Center, the preparations were in progress to fire the retro rockets. The new program to initiate and control the firing time was downloaded on the onboard computer. In the darkness of space, the ship's crew slowly moved into their respective positions and fastened the hold down harnesses waiting for the ship to reach the optimum position for firing.

Chapter 87

As the door closed behind Styles, the secretary's voice startled Davis with, "Mr. Davis, Miz Landon is on the phone."

"Hello June. What can I do for you?" There was no exchange of pleasantries on his part. He spoke the question that filled his thoughts. What could she possibly want of him? Did she find out that he had framed her? No, of course not. There was no way she knew. No one could trace it to him. He had left it on the backseat of a taxicab. When he left the cab Latham got in.

"Hi Owen. I haven't heard from anyone at the center and I wondered how things were going. Would you meet me at Donnely's for dinner sometime, for old times' sake?" She silently prayed that his ego would rise to the bait.

Davis did not answer immediately. He remembered how those dinners invariably led to lusty sex that would leave them both breathless and exhausted. His memories, of the many sexual pleasures they had shared, stirred his desire to have her once again, even if there was no love between them. The timing was perfect since his secretary was on vacation. In a casual voice that belied his excitement Owen answered, "I guess it would be good to let by-gones be by-gones. Would tomorrow night be good for you?" No sense in missing a good lay he thought.

"Yes, that would work for me. Why don't you make the reservations and I'll meet you there at 8 o'clock." June tried to sound as sensual as she had in their telephone conversations during their affair.

"Fine. I'm looking forward to seeing you." Davis had taken the bait. June made sure she would arrive later then Owen so she could make an entrance that would impress him. As she walked into the foyer, all eyes were riveted on her. She wore a lavender, knee length, sheath dress. The matching spider silk stockings were decorated with arrow cut outs that pointed up away from the ankles toward the thighs. Balanced on three inch heels and her face framed by long dangling gold earrings her voluptuous figure seemed almost fashion model slim. The plunging neckline revealed a gold heart pendant trapped between her firm, ample breasts.

As she walked to Owen Davis's table she drew the envious eyes of every woman and the lustful admiration of every man. Owen was stunned by her beauty. He had forgotten she had such a sensual walk and bearing. The room was shrunk to the place she stood as she waited for Owen to awkwardly scramble out of his chair tipping it backwards so that he had to grab it before it hit the floor.

"Hello Owen."

"June, my god you look absolutely radiant. I can't remember you ever looking more beautiful. Vacationing seems to suit you well."

"In case you forgot, I'm not vacationing. I'm unemployed looking for work." She caught herself from speaking acidly and resumed with a pleasant, "You look well, Owen."

"Yes, yes, I'm very well but I miss you around the center. Maybe we could get to see each other once in a while when you get settled in your new work. Do you have any hot prospects for jobs?" Seeing her tonight convinced him that it could be a great arrangement if she were available to him now and then. Her replacement; his secretary, was becoming too possessive and talking of making their relationship more permanent, as in married.

June saw through the scheme but decided it might be to her advantage to play along with it for the time being hoping he would be less guarded with her and admit to his part in the tape release.

"That might be nice and as far as job prospects; I hope that you will give my prospective employers a good word about me. Maybe you have some info on positions that are open which may fit my qualifications." Davis heard her words but his mind was on getting through the meal and taking her back to her place for more intimate activity. He made sure the wine did not run out and he acted as perfect a date as possible. As they walked out, satiated with seafood and a digestive of Drambuie on the rocks, he felt like cock of the roost. All men envied him the pleasures they fantasized she could give.

June suggested they walk back on the beach. He agreed, wanting to please her so she might be more amenable to his advances once they were in her apartment.

Before stepping into the sand she bent over and took off her shoes. Exposing her thighs she slowly rolled down her stockings and shoved them into the shoes. She got the effect she wanted.

"You've still got great legs, June," as Davis relished the sight of the slim white legs contrasted against the dark of the night. He followed her lead, got bare footed and rolled up his trousers to calf length. With shoes in hand and his jacket slung over his arm they strolled the half mile to her condo complex feeling the cool water and wet sand oozing through their toes and squishing under their feet. By the time they reached the steps to her apartment the sea fog had rolled in and the damp air seeped through her dress and his shirt.

Chapter 88

Strapped in the seat originally assigned to Sean Murphy, Adam reached to hold his mother's hand. With the confidence and naivety of a seventeen year old boy, who has yet to realize he's not immortal, Adam comforted his mother.

"Don't worry Mama, everything will be alright. Papa will get us home. Besides you always say that Jesus will protect us."

Marita squeezed his hand and in the most assuring voice she could muster she replied, "Yes, Adam, I'm sure we'll be OK." But she and none of the other adults were as sure as the space boy. Each one kept silent, lost in his or her thought. The possibility, the ship would come apart if the deceleration was too severe, haunted their confidence.

Suddenly, it happened. The firing of the retro rockets shook them out of their reveries. The deceleration forced them against their padded seats. Objects such as pencils, note pads, monitor mouse controls and headsets began to float around the crew members like leaves on a cool fall day. Reaching out to catch the floating items distracted the crew from their fears and one by one they began to laugh.

The game and the laughter it triggered opened the gates and relieved the tension that had enveloped the ship. Venus X had not come apart. They would have the chance to try to orbit earth and be rescued. Rescued was the word they acknowledged. No retrieval or disembarking or other fancy space jargon. Rescue, that was their hope.

"Venus X, Venus X, this is Mission Control. We had a green light on the firing, what's your status?" Sam waited for the response. The few seconds of delay due to the distance of the ship seemed interminable. Finally Glen Ross's voice blared over the Center speakers.

"Roger, Mission Control, we also lit the green. The computer velocity number is decreasing. We would appreciate continual update from your end to verify our numbers and to confirm when we have stabilized to re-entry velocity."

Glen's voice was tinged with near giddiness triggered by the crew laughing and joking as they pursued the elusive floating objects. Sam Hershburg detected this and, looking toward Colin and Vernon, he said, "Did I hear laughter or giggling in his voice or am I imagining things?"

"That's what it sounded like to me. Ask him what's going on," was Croft's reply.

"Venus X, is there a party going on up there? You sound almost jubilant."

"We'll try to describe it to you when we get home. For now I can tell you that something finally broke the icy tension we've been in for the last few months. We're seeing a flicker of light at the end of the space tunnel to earth."

"That's great news, Glen. We'll keep you advised to velocity status and Mr. Styles recommends you prepare for a course correction maneuver as soon as possible."

"Roger, starting preparations now. Adam Ross will handle communications while I monitor the suiting up." Glen signaled the four other astronauts and they slowly assembled their gear for the upcoming spacewalk.

"I'll go over the plan to make sure we're all on the same page. Marita, you and Nancy position yourselves starboard at stanchion 135. Jim, you and Sandra are to use starboard stanchion 45." The four voyagers continued to get into their suits not seeming to hear Ross but in actuality their attention was on his every word.

He continued. "We will not fire the backpacks until you each have verified your pack and your partner's are secured flat against the main beam of the ship. It's imperative you all fire simultaneously or we won't get the thrust we need. I will countdown from ten and you will fire on zero for two minutes. I will give the order to shut down the packs. If you're not ready to fire we must hold the count. Are we all clear? This is the last briefing we can have before you exit the ship."

All four acknowledged they understood with a thumbs-up. They were ready. Over and over, they had rehearsed their part in their mind, since the plan was defined and agreed to by Mission Control. Now they nervously waited for the moment that would either put them on course for a safe return to earth or doom them to extinction in space.

Chapter 89

June unlocked the door and entered the apartment. Davis followed her without waiting to be invited. As she walked by the stereo she casually switched it on activating the recording devices. Turning her head back toward Owen she said, "You had better take that wet shirt off and pour us a drink while I change these wet clothes for something more comfortable."

When she returned to the living room Davis was standing bare chested holding two glasses of champagne poured from a bottle June had placed unobtrusively in an ice bucket behind other bottles.

"Here's to old times, June."

"It has been a lovely evening, Owen. I wish it were not clouded by my having been forced out of NASA for something I didn't do. Why did you believe I would give out those tapes?"

"Let's not hash this out again. You leaked the info to Latham. How he got the tapes is not important since he would not have known about them otherwise." His irritation fueled more by the possibility she might not want to have sex than by any guilt he felt for betraying her.

"Did you give the tapes to Latham," she asked abruptly?

"Now why would I do that? Would I go against Styles' decision not to go public?" The sarcasm in his voice and the smile on his face would not register on the tapes, she would need more. June decided to let it go for the moment and see how the champagne might lower his guard. Instead it made him more amorous and confused her thinking.

The alcohol triggered the lustful attraction she had for him, which had dominated their relationship. Now her original reason for their meeting was clouded by her sexual desires. Soon she found herself naked, in bed, responding to his kisses and caresses.

The sensation of his forcing himself into her broke through June's hazy mind. "This is all wrong! It's not supposed to happen this way!" her mind screamed silently. The more frenetic his passion the more she hated what she was doing. June could stand it no longer! She raked her finger nails across his back, ripping skin. Enraged, she bit his lip fiercely until it popped and the blood spurted like a cherry tomato.

"Ow, you horny bitch!" He leaned back and punched her full force in the eye splitting her left eyebrow. June fainted from the combined force of the blow and the effects of the wine. Davis finished what he had started and left the bed thinking smugly that he had aroused her to such a peak that she had turned animal. "Old stud Davis still has what it takes" he told himself.

He went to the bathroom and tried to wash the scratches and his puffed lip. When he put on his still damp shirt it stuck to his back as each fingernail cut burned painfully. Davis returned to the bedroom where June was now conscious. The blood from her cut eye was beginning to coagulate as she had dabbed it with the pillow case.

"Look, Honey, next time, tell me you want to play rough and I'll bring handcuffs and a whip. Call me when you need some good loving again." As he walked away picking up his jacket off the living room sofa she called to him.

"Owen, tell me, how did you pull it off getting the tapes from the security files. I think you owe me that much," as she held the pillow against her damaged eye.

He shuffled back to the bedroom door. As he went by he turned the stereo off unconsciously ending the recording.

"Now why would I tell you that? So you can try to prove that you're innocent? Look, I don't want to hear any more about the tape. What's done is done. Don't bother to get up, I can let myself out. Besides, I want to remember how depraved you look after rough sex." He walked out of the room to the front door.

"You bastard!" The angry words were but a shadow of the hatred and shame she felt. He turned the knob and looking back he said, "You know, there's no reason why we can't get together like this every now and then. I can find time for you and my secretary the same way I used to be able to satisfy you and my wife before she got jealous."

June did not have time to answer before she heard the door close. She got up and hurried to the bathroom. She had never felt so violated. Always, sex had been part of a deep affection for the man.

"My God," she said to the anguished face

staring at her from the mirror, "I feel like a raped whore. I've got to get out of here!" She stepped into a pair of black, jogging shorts. Pulled on an oversized tee shirt and stooped over to put on a raggedy pair of white deck sneakers. Grabbing the fanny pack she used as a purse, she raced out of the apartment not even taking time to lock the door behind her.

"I've got to run. I need to feel the wind in my face and sweat the stench of him off of me." A half mile of running on the sandy beach did not cleanse her shame. Tears salted the perspiration on her cheeks. She dropped the fanny pack, kicked off the deck shoes and ran into the fog shrouded water.

June was a strong swimmer, on the varsity team in high school. The choppy waves did not impede her as she dove through first one then two waves; then again and again until she reached deeper waters. Now she effortlessly did the Australian crawl, slicing through the undulating waves. The cool Atlantic water soothed her emotions. A quarter mile later she became conscious of the taste of the salty ocean. She continued until fatigue sapped all angry emotions.

"I've got to rest a bit if I want to be able to swim back," she thought as she turned over on her back to float and regain her strength. In the darkness June did not see the water soaked plank half submerged on the crest of the wave. Driven by the surface current of the incoming tide it smashed into the left side of her face knocking her out.

No gasping for air. No struggling just a filling of the lungs with each unconscious inhalation. As her body lost its buoyancy, June Landon slowly sank to the bottom. The under tow of the high tide gently carried her lifeless body out to sea. No more shame.

---No more guilt---

Sometime during the night, a vagrant, walking the beach in search of a place to sleep, stumbled onto the fanny pack and the deck shoes. He stripped the pack and stuffed its contents into a black garbage bag with the rest of his meager belongings. He salvaged the canvas shoes sticking one in each of his back pockets. He threw the empty fanny pack into the first refuse container he found. Later, in Miami, he would sell the credit cards and trade the shoes for a quart of Chianti.

Chapter 90

"Venus X, Mission Control here, are you ready for Course Correction activity?" Glen looked at the four friends and saw them lining up to leave the ship.

"Roger Sam, we are as ready as we'll ever be."

"We copy Glen. The ship is approaching desired velocity. We recommend your people get into position now."

"You heard him crew, let's do it." His voice exuded confidence, but as he watched Marita enter the pressure lock chamber and close the hatch behind her, a deep fear gripped him. The realization that she may be too weak to return to the ship drew an uncontrollable gut wrenching moan heard only by the boy at his side. For the first time Glen Ross, pilot extraordinaire, the man always in control of his emotions, the man with ice in his veins, knew what the loss of his wife meant. Doubts about the plan wormed their way through the labyrinth of his brain.

Silent thoughts... "Why did I push so hard to continue this mission years ago? Now

Sean is lost in space. Pennington's a frozen cadaver tied to the ship like a deer carcass on the roof of a pick-up truck. Sandra's mind is still screwed up. The rest of us are like walking zombies, so weak we can barely do the simple things like eating and bathing. God, why did I work so hard at convincing the others the mission was more important than the life of any individual? Too late, too late, it's almost over... can't look back. I've got to bring the ship home. I'm the warrior. I'm the only one who can pull it all together. No time for second thoughts...gotta see it to the end...can't let the others down. No place for fear. Get with it Ross. You're the man."

Glen turned his attention to reporting to Mission Control that the four crew members were outside and attaching the back packs to the ship.

"Roger Glen. We're clear down here. When you're people are ready you can proceed with the firing at your discretion. You've got a two minute window from this time mark now."

"Sandra and I have secured the packs, we're ready." On hearing Barnes' voice Glen shook off all feelings of uncertainty and returned to complete control of the situation.

"How are you coming along, Marita and Nancy?"

"We've just finished securing and are ready to depress the firing switch when you are." Marita's confident voice added to his reassurance that all would be well.

"Barnes and Meyers here, we're ready when you give the word, Glen"

"OK good people; let's push this big whale of a ship on the road home. The countdown begins now. Remember we fire on zero and only cease when I give the command to shut down.

Ten, --nine, --eight, --seven, --six, --five, --four, --three, --two, --one, --zero."

The four astronauts were flawless in depressing the switches. Each pack fired. For what seemed like forever the ship did nothing. Then ever so slowly Venus X responded to the thrusts of the rockets. The ship inched away from the tethered astronauts. Only the fact that they were grasping the control switch lines dragged them along close to their only source of survival.

Focused on the ship's motion, Jim

Barnes did not notice his tether line float into the path of the rocket exhaust. After twenty years in cold outer space, the contrast of the heat on the frozen line frayed the cord.

"Cease firing!" Glen shouted into the microphone. "Get back in here troops and let's see how close we've come to getting this baby on course." The exhilaration in his voice was contagious as the four moved quickly to the entrance hatch.

They floated about at the hatch and finally Sandra entered first followed by Marita then Nancy. Jim had allowed himself to drift to the end of the tether. On seeing Nancy secured inside the vacuum lock chamber he gave as strong a pull as he could on the line. The sudden whip like jerk pulled the shredded section apart. Jim saw the ship drifting away from him and no means to catch up. His back pack was still secured to the stanchion.

"Ross! Ross! I'm in trouble. My tether line broke. You're drifting away from me." The desperation in his voice engulfed the exuberant mood being shared by Sandra, Marita, Adam and Glen as they awaited the re-entry of Nancy and Jim.

"My line can bring us both back in."
Nancy was already opening the hatch and
threading the line out ahead of her to allow
herself the freedom to push off from the ship as
soon as she located Barnes.

"Stay cool out there Flowers. We can't
afford to lose two of you." Through the
observation window, Glen watched Jim drift
slowly out of range.

"I'll give it my best shot." Catching a
glimpse of her fellow crew member she pushed
herself in his direction as if off a diving board.
At the end of the line she was jerked back like a
running dog at the end of a leash. Barnes was a
mere three yards from her. She pulled herself
back to the ship and disconnected Barnes'
broken line. She fastened one end to her line
and once again pushed off toward the receding
space man. As she approached him she tried to
twirl the loose line over her head as you would
a lasso and release it towards Jim.

In the weightless firmament the cord
floated like a snake. Barnes flailed about trying
to reach the lifeline. Everything seemed in slow
motion as if time was standing still, waiting to
see how the drama would play out. In the end

the cosmos claimed one more of the gods of Venus X.

"No! No!" Nancy screamed. "It's not fair. We're too close to lose you now." Her words floated out into the vast expanse of the universe, unheard by anyone.

"Nancy, get back in the ship there's nothing you can do." Glen's voice was soft now, and gentle for he was as devastated by the irony of losing their comrade so near the end of the mission as the rest of the crew.

From that time on none on board could escape the specter of death snatching one of them before they reached earth.

"Mission Control, Venus X here, we just lost Jim Barnes. His tether line sheared and, before we could get to him, he drifted out of range. Nancy Flowers made a valiant life risking effort." Glen's tremulous voice and somber tone expressed the despondency in the hearts of each one on board Venus X.

"Ross, did we copy correctly? Did you say you lost Jim Barnes in space?" Sam Hershburg voiced the disbelief of Styles and Croft standing behind him.

"Dammit, Sam, you heard right! We're

signing off for now, until we pull ourselves together. We'll accept your info regarding the accuracy of our trajectory towards earth. Venus X out!"

"What in god's name is going on up there?" Croft asked no one in particular. "How can we be losing only men on this mission?" No answer from Sam or Styles. They would have to wait until the ship landed to ask the questions that were on their minds.

Chapter 91

Conway Belcher hung up the phone. "This is the third day she doesn't answer. I better go over and see if my gear is still there," he muttered to himself. He had waited two weeks expecting June Landon to call but no word had come. Now she was not returning his calls. He cleared the stale slice of pizza from the kitchen table sticking it into the refrigerator. It might do for a midnight snack later. He locked the studio apartment door behind him and hurried to his Chevy wagon.

The ride to June's apartment was brief. As he got out of the car he looked around hoping no one would see him. No response to the buzzer. He tried the door knob and to his surprise the door opened. He was not prepared for the scene before him. The disheveled bed with blood on the pillow and the crimson blots on the bathroom towel told him this was not a place to be found with his bugging system.

He hurriedly retrieved all the microphones, stuffing them into his pockets. Then he pulled out the recorder from the closet. Belcher rushed out the door with his gear storing everything in the back of the wagon. Returning to the apartment he wiped his finger prints from everything he remembered touching, unintentionally destroying many of the prints left behind by Davis and June Landon. When he got back home he called Latham.

"I just found a mess in your old girlfriend's apartment. It looks like somebody might've got hurt bad. You may want to get an exclusive on this story." The phone clicked in Latham's ear as Belcher hung up without identifying himself but Latham knew who it was.

The newscaster could not resist the chance for publicity. He raced to June's place. He had left messages on her answering machine but she had not acknowledged any of them. What he saw alarmed him. Latham called the station and told his program producer to keep a three minute segment open on the ten o'clock news for a late breaking scoop. Then he called the county Sheriff's office to report what he had found.

While the investigators poured over every inch of June's apartment, Belcher sat at home munching on the cold pizza and listening to the tapes he had retrieved. The system had worked flawlessly and even the heavy breathing and noises that people make when having sex came through clearly. To his dismay the tape was blank at the critical moment when she had asked Davis to confess his part in the leakage of the NASA tape.

Belcher tested his equipment and found it in perfect running order. "I'll be damned," he muttered, "Either she shut off the stereo or someone erased the tape. I wish I had installed a video system; then I'd know what really went on." As he always did, Belcher reached over and turned on the TV for the ten o'clock news.

The weather girl with the high pitched voice droned on and on about highs and lows, jet stream omega patterns, and finally the week's forecast. Conway was about to go to the refrigerator for a beer when the station shifted to a remote telecast from June Landon's condo. There was Stuart Latham, in his glory, reporting the mysterious situation of the missing woman and the blood stained apartment. Latham would have no trouble following the investigation since he would become a prime suspect in

Landon's disappearance.

The next morning Belcher decided the tapes were too hot to peddle to magazines. He might alienate some of his close associates on the police force or even become a suspected accomplice in whatever the investigation uncovered. He phoned Charley Wade his friend in the county detective bureau.

"Charley, Conway here. I've got some tapes I think you need to hear. They're from that missing woman's apartment. You've got to make sure I'm not implicated in any of this. I don't want to lose my private investigator's license."

"How did you get involved in this thing?" The irritation in Wade's voice told Belcher the police were finding more unanswered questions then they wanted. Conway had made the right decision. This was too big for him to meddle in.

"When can I hear what you've got?" Wade barked.

"Stop by my place any time today. You can listen to them and decide whether they're of any value to you. They'll sell real high on the open market if you can't use them."

Wade and his partner Donovan were assigned as primary investigators in what was believed to be a routine case of a lover's quarrel; or perhaps a rape. As they listened to the tapes they realized that things may get complicated if the security break at Kennedy center was involved.

They had to find answers. "Who had shut off or tampered with the tapes? How come only Latham's fingerprints were on the door knob yet they had two other sets of prints all over the apartment and a third single thumb print on the door jamb in the kitchen closet? What happened to the woman?" The finger prints were easy to trace.

June Landon's prints were as expected in her own dwelling. Identifying Davis as the man on the tape was obvious. She had called him by name and his prints were traced through the FBI. Evidently he had done nothing to hide his presence in the apartment. Belcher clarified the doorknob and kitchen door jamb print.

Now they must find the woman. Also, who edited or shut off the tapes and why? Wade called Davis to arrange a meeting at the space center. At eight am the exact time agreed upon, Davis ushered the detective and his partner into the plush office.

"Welcome to the center gentlemen. Please sit down. My secretary will be bringing in coffee shortly. What can I do for you this morning?"

"We understand that a Ms. June Landon worked for you here at the center. Is that correct?" Wade asked the question in a tone of voice that conveyed boredom with the situation. He let his eyes roam the office not looking at the man behind the desk.

Meanwhile, Donovan's role was to focus on Davis; with a congenial disarming smile, all the while paying close attention to the NASA chief's body language and facial expressions. Wade and Donovan had played these roles many times when questioning suspects and Davis was on the verge of becoming one.

"Yes, she worked here more recently as the Public Relations person on the Venus X project. She resigned under the cloud of some security breaches." Davis was on his guard. Was it possible that June was pressing assault charges against him? That bitch. I'm the one who should have pressed charges for her biting and scratching, he thought.

"Do you know where she lives?" More monotone.

"I'm sure we have her address on file. My secretary will give it to you as you leave." No sense in telling them any more than they seemed to know.

"When was the last time you saw her, Mr. Davis?" Wade turned in his chair gazing at the pictures on the wall of some previous space shots. Davis was irritated by Wade's attitude. He addressed his answer to the smiling detective who seemed in awe that he was interviewing the NASA chief.

"It's interesting you should ask. A couple of weeks ago she invited me to dinner to discuss some business opportunities she was considering. June always respected my opinions in such matters and I felt a fatherly responsibility for her welfare. Is she in trouble?" The Welshman was growing impatient at not knowing why these two cops were questioning him.

"Would you know what day that was?" Wade asked taking a pad and pencil from his shirt pocket prepared to write down the information.

"I'm not sure. It was a few weeks ago. My secretary may have it on my calendar. It was not NASA business so I'm not sure she will be able to give you that date. What's the problem?"

It was Donovan's turn to reply. "Well sir, we have been asked to investigate the possibility that she is missing. We are talking to anyone who may be able to tell us of her whereabouts."

Wade turned a nonchalant gaze toward the NASA chief as Davis picked up one of the memos from the desk. Owen seemed to be scanning the memo as if to convey that he was too busy to continue the meeting.

"How long has she been missing? I heard that she had gone to Maine for a few weeks when she left NASA. Maybe she's gone back there or is gone out of state for job interviews." Davis got up and walked to the window. With his back to the questioners he continued. "How come two detectives are doing leg work on a missing person case? Don't they usually assign these cases to lower ranking officers?"

"Well sir," Donovan ever the polite one explained, "There were signs in her apartment of some blood perhaps due to an altercation with an acquaintance. The department is concerned that she may have suffered foul play. That is why we have been asked to do some investigating."

"Why did you come to me? Why would you think that I would be able help you find her? At any rate I've told you all I know and I do have a heavy work load today. If that is all, my secretary can escort you to the lobby. You obviously know June's address if you've been in her apartment. I don't appreciate your wasting my time with questions when you already know the answers. Ask my secretary if she has the date of my meeting with Ms. Landon." Davis returned to his desk and began shuffling the papers, dismissing the two detectives by ignoring them.

Wade and Donovan were ready to leave. When they had the lab reports on the blood samples they would come back to the arrogant Davis if some of the blood was his.

Chapter 92

Walking to their car through the sun drenched parking lot, Wade and Donovan should have felt at peace but no sunny day could break through the feeling they shared. Davis had lied in response to their questions and was definitely hiding something.

"What do you think he's hiding, Charley?" Donovan asked, having his own perceptions yet deferring to the senior officer.

"Well, we know he's lying. We don't know where the woman is, alive or dead. He may just be hiding that he beat her. She could have left town." As Donovan got into the driver's seat, Wade continued. "Until we find her we need to interview Latham. He's already told us they were going together. He may know more than he's told us. I'll talk to him; meanwhile you put the squeeze on Belcher. He's covering his ass pretty good for a simple taping job between two lovers. We can't miss any leads on this one. If the head of Kennedy Center is involved in beating women and possibly security violations, we'll be up to our asses in outside agencies."

"You're right. I think he killed her. Maybe he found out she was recording their conversation. Then he erased the part that might have implicated him and dumped the body somewhere. We need to look at his car and see if there's any evidence she was in it." Donovan was more ready to believe his hunches than Wade was. It made them an effective investigative team.

Latham had an airtight alibi for the night of the taping. Stuart had been on an assignment out of state with a camera crew.

Belcher was at work at the TV station with plenty of co-workers to verify his presence there throughout the night.

Wade did not rule out the possibility that she may have disappeared a few days later and that Latham or Belcher or both could still be involved in whatever happened to her. It was time to bring in Owen Davis and find out why he was lying.

Chapter 93

On board Venus X, tension was ripping apart any semblance of cooperative teamwork. The frayed lanyard that was all that remained of Jim Barnes's last spacewalk became the catalyst for distrust and anger to erupt. Nancy Flowers was the first to question why the strap had broken. Filled with frustration at not having been able to save her fellow astronaut, she spit out her venom at Glen Ross.

"Ross, I think someone cut that strap wanting to kill Jim or one of us. Who do you suppose would want to kill off the only black man on board? Or did he die because that leaves you the only male survivor. You would be the center of attraction once we're back on earth. Maybe your little squaw rigged it so you are the only conquering hero to go back."

Before Glen could respond she spat back at him. "Maybe Sandra and I are going to have an unfortunate accident so only you, Marita and Adam return as the glory family from space."

"What the hell's the matter with you. We loved Jim as much as any of you. We needed him for his expertise in the power source area.

Now we have to rely on Mission Control to dictate the flare out maneuver with no check and balance up here. We have nothing to gain by wishing him or you harm."

"Bull shit. We die and the rest of you divvy up the little bit of food that's left. Is that why you killed Jim?"

Sandra, who had been listening to the argument, burst out. "Oh my god! Is that what you intend to do? After all this time you want to kill us so you can have more food. I hate you! I hate all of you!" she screamed. "Don't any of you come near me, I don't trust any of you." Her fragile state of mind prevented her from rationalizing what was truth. Fear of dying so close to getting back to earth triggered her paranoid reaction. She pushed herself to float to her quarters.

Marita burst into the fray like a tigress protecting her cubs. "You damn fool. Your stupid babbling flipped her out. Where do you get off accusing Glen of murder? He's the only one who's kept us going for the last five years. At some point or other we all took turns at wanting to give up. He was always the one who picked us up and promised we'd get back to earth."

"How typical, Ross hiding behind his little missy's skirt. When did you cut the lanyard? As Jim was entering the pressure lock chamber?" Nancy spewed her long smoldering dislike and disdain for the Yaqui Indian woman.

Glen Ross tried to step in and defuse the squabble. "Hold on now this is getting us nowhere..." but Marita cut him off.

"Listen bitch, you were the one who was supposed to check his equipment. How come, if the strap was cut, you didn't see it and report it. Did you want him dead because years ago he didn't screw you but preferred Sandra even when she was addle-brained?"

"That's enough!" Ross shouted. "We've got one more month to survive and we can't do it fighting each other. Nancy, you can think what you want but from now on keep your accusations to yourself until we get home." Turning to his wife he gave her a stern warning. "You too Marita, if you can't tolerate each other any longer, then stay away from one another except when you have joint tasks to perform. At those times I expect you both to behave professionally. Make no mistake. If I have to, I'll tie you both in your quarters rather than jeopardize the rest of this mission." The anger in his voice cut through their irrational thinking. Sandra moved off to perform data logging of the space walk. Marita, with a few tears forming in her eyes, could not believe what her husband had threatened. She was his wife. How could he treat her so rudely in front of the woman she disliked most of all? Like a little school girl being reprimanded by the teacher, she felt totally humiliated.

"How dare you talk to me like I was a serf on your plantation? I'm your wife. I deserve better than that. You didn't defend me or agree when I said she may have cut the lanyard. If you loved me you would have sided with me." Her woundedness floated on every trembling syllable.

"You were out of line as much as she was and my job is to bring this ship home. I don't have the luxury of coddling two women who jealously hate each other. It has nothing to do with how much I love you and respect you. It's about trying to maintain some discipline and teamwork until we hit the ground. I'm sorry if I hurt your feelings but try to see it from my perspective."

Marita turned her back on her husband. The perceived betrayal was too much to forgive. Marita would never understand the compulsions of duty and honor that drove her husband to an "even-to-death" commitment to any task he undertook. The last month of flight would see the crew enveloped in the silence and distrust of one another. Adam however felt disappointment in his parent's estrangement and refused to believe that his Dad could even consider killing one of his crew.

Chapter 94

Wade called Davis. He politely invited him to come to the station to clear up some information they had about June Landon's disappearance. Owen balked at the invitation until the detective made it clear that; if necessary, they would come to the center to escort him.

The next morning Davis showed up at Wade's office in a belligerent mood. "Why did you get me here? I've told you all I know about my ex secretary."

"We have some very good proof you were in her apartment the night she was last seen by anyone. Would you clarify why you didn't tell us about that when we first talked with you?" This time Wade kept his eyes on Davis's face every moment. The hardness in the detective's face could not be mistaken.

Owen realized he was not being questioned for background information. He wondered how they had found out he had been with June that night, "I didn't think it was important since I only stopped in for a nightcap and to finish our talk about her job search. Did she tell you I was there?" Owen wanted them to reveal how they knew he had been there.

"We know that you had more than a drink. In fact you quarreled didn't you? Why don't you talk straight with us Mr. Davis? That way we can clear up this situation and get back to work on more serious cases."

"I think I should have a lawyer present. If you have no objections I will contact one and we'll come in and talk with you." Owen got up and moved toward the door.

"If you insist, Sir, but if you have nothing to hide why don't you tell us what went on and we can wrap things up now." Wade knew he could not detain Davis yet he wanted to get the truth before a lawyer came in and clouded everything with legal mumbo-jumbo.

Davis did not answer nor break stride as he walked out. Donovan, who had sat in silence stood up and slammed the door shut. "He's hiding something more than an argument or else why does he think he needs a lawyer? We've got to find her dead or alive."

"Let's not panic. Wait till we hear what he has to say with his lawyer present. I agree that something smells in this case."

While Owen Davis made a quiet search for an experienced counsel; the ever opportunistic Conway Belcher, who had made a duplicate of the recording, contacted three prominent tabloids and put the tape up for auction. The high bidder gave the private investigator fifty thousand dollars cash. Two days later, Ray Welch, A.K.A. Conway Belcher, his fifty thousand dollars and false passport and I.D. in hand, was flying over the Atlantic bound for Murren, Switzerland.

The next week's issue of Peephole, the tabloid that had purchased the Belcher tapes, featured the allegations that a high placed official at the Kennedy Space center was under investigation in the beating of a missing fellow employee. Wade was livid at Belcher for leaking the information. Now he had no ace to play in interviewing Davis.

Under the advice of the Assistant District Attorney, Wade played the Landon tape for Davis and his lawyer. With no June Landon to confirm the validity of the tape it was easy for the lawyer to stonewall any interrogation. Davis went back to work confident that he was in the clear.

The local newspapers, following the tabloid leads, jumped on Davis's police visits. It was a slow news week and the possible scandal at the center became one of the lead stories on the six o'clock TV news across the country. At a news conference, the President was asked to comment on the situation.

"I did not read that article but I'll look into this and act on it accordingly." President Canteleone did not like surprise questions at his press conferences. "That will be all today, ladies and gentlemen." Barging into his office followed by his Press Secretary, Foley, Canteleone growled, "What the hell is going on at the cape? Fill me in. I don't appreciate being questioned on things I know nothing about."

"I didn't think it was of any importance, Sir, the media has blown it all out of proportion. It seems that Owen Davis, the Center Manager is one of the people being investigated in regards to beating a June Landon with whom he had or was having an affair. She's not been seen since."

"Is he the manager who tried to buck my orders when we sent those two guys in at the request of the space ship crew?"

"One and the same, Sir."

"Get someone down there and if he's mixed up in beating some woman, than make it clear to him, he needs to resign before it gets into the courts. Give him a chance to resign or by God I'll fire him, civil service or no civil service."

It took one week for the two FBI agents to confirm the validity of the allegations and to present Owen with the President's message. Foley called the head of NASA. "Mr. Davis, the President understands you are involved in a messy situation and hopes things will work out for you. However, it is in the best interest of NASA that you resign immediately. The President is quite firm on this. Please take care of this matter this week."

Davis was livid. "I haven't done anything wrong. A lover's quarrel is not enough reason to request my resignation. I'm ready to go public with this if the President pushes it."

"Davis, I'm telling you straight out, resign or he'll fire you for conduct which violates the agreement you signed when you went to work at NASA. The President wants your resignation on his desk by Friday or else."

"We'll see who wins out in this," Davis said as he slammed the phone in its cradle. Owen's campaign for a congressional seat was not moving well. He saw an opportunity to turn a bad situation into a boost for his candidacy. He met with his campaign manager and his three top aides. As a result of their brainstorming session, Davis called a press conference.

"Ladies and gentlemen, I've called you here to announce my decision to resign my position here at Kennedy Center so that I might devote all my time and energy to campaigning for the congressional seat of this district." He did not wait for any interruption. "I believe I can best serve my country and the citizens of the district by influencing a strong, robust financial support of the space program in Washington. I have submitted my resignation to the President and after listening to my reasons he accepted it. It is effective immediately."

"Mr. Davis, Mr. Davis. Has the recent publicity regarding your involvement with June Landon influenced your sudden decision to resign?" The reporter went for the jugular with the first question.

"No. I have cleared up everything with the police regarding that matter. The truth is that I have been putting off this decision from the beginning of the campaign. Now I must convince the voters that I'm the ideal man to represent them in Washington. My campaign manager will pass out a weekly schedule so that you can follow my efforts until we win in November. Thank you for coming and feel free to quote me often but quote me accurately. That's all I ask." Davis turned his back to the media people and walked out of the conference room and into his office.

He had the secretary bring in a cardboard box from the shipping area. Seething with anger at being forced to resign, he threw everything from his desk into the box. Then he called a mill wright crew to come in and pack all other personal effects and load them in his car. In less than forty five minutes Owen Davis was walking out of the NASA building for the last time.

The next day, the President assigned Vernon Styles as Manager of the Kennedy Space Center. Vernon's first official act was to name Colin Croft as his replacement as Venus

X Program Manager. Two weeks later the mail at June Landon's address contained a bill from her credit card company with many purchases from the Miami area. The police took it as a sign that June had gone there without telling anyone. She must have intended to return to her apartment since she had not asked for mail forwarding at the Post Office. Also she had not canceled her rent, telephone or cable TV. Despite Wade and Donovan's heated objections, the investigation was closed.

Chapter 95

"Venus X, this is Mission Control. We have data for you. Do you copy?" Glen took the microphone floating near his chair. "Roger, Mission Control, we hear you fine. What do you have for us?"

"Sam here, Ross. First we want to advise you that Vernon Styles has been promoted to Space Center Manager. He moved Colin into his old job as Venus X Program Manager so the chess pieces are where they were when you took off twenty years ago."

"Sounds great to us, everyone up here is giving a thumbs up. How does our trajectory look for earth intercept?"

"Our calculations show your track to be on a course that would miss optimum entry angle. The navigation staff would like you to make a slight correction using the man packs as before."

Glen looked into the sunken eyes that punctuated the swollen faces of his space companions. He stared at their starving frail bodies and knew there was not enough strength in any of them to accomplish another extra vehicular activity. He could try it but he doubted one man pack would move the ship enough to make a measurable course correction.

"Sam, I don't think we have the strength to go out of the ship again. How big a correction do we have to make and how many man packs will have to fire for how long?"

Sam reread the advisory report the Nav Engineers had given him. "Three man packs firing for ten seconds should move Venus X two and half degrees for an optimum intercept track. How does that sound? Could you do it?"

"Could one man pack firing for a longer duration get it done?" Glen waited anxiously for he saw this as the only way they could change their course.

"We are going to check this out and will call you ASAP. Mission Control out."

An hour later Ross received the word that one man pack might do it if fired for one minute. The critical point was the location of the single pack for if the thrust were set at the wrong place the ship could be driven into a slow rotation on its center axis with minimal effect on the course direction. Ross would try it.

It took all of Glen's strength to suit up. As he moved toward the pressure lock chamber, a cold clammy sensation swept over his body. Glen began to doubt that he could make it but he would respond to the call of duty even if it meant death. At least the rest of them might make it back. With a second pack hooked in his right elbow he worked his way to the center stanchion. Ross had decided that if the first pack malfunctioned or ran out of fuel he would use the second one; for this was their last chance to get on course.

While Glen positioned himself and the packs, Marita spoke to her two female companions. "Each of us has said things out of anger that were unacceptable. Could we put it behind us and work to make sure we don't lose Glen out there? Sandra you must trust Nancy and I, we mean you no harm. We want you to get home as much as we do ourselves."

Nancy looked at her hands and saw them for the first time as they really were. Long bones held together with skin drawn tight from dehydration and starvation. The once well-manicured finger nails now yellowed and cracked. She spoke the words in a monotone; her mind locked on what her eyes were forcing her to accept.

"You're right Marita. I lost it completely when I couldn't get Jim back to the ship. If you can, we'll let it go." They worked the rest of the activity in silence save the necessary technical phrases to control Glen's proper firing sequence. The first pack performed flawlessly and Glenn slowly worked his way back.

As he reached the hatch, he noticed Jim Barnes's lanyard which Nancy had tied to the nearest stanchion. He inspected the frayed end and realized it had not been cut but showed signs of heat stress. Guessing it must have been in the path of the rocket exhaust during the previous firing, Glen brought it into the ship.

All inspected the faulty cord and agreed to bring it back to earth for analysis so other astronauts may not suffer their comrade's fate. A quiet reserve came over each of them. They realized how over sensitive they had become to any criticism or disagreement amongst them; and that it had brought them to a point of nearly destroying each other and the mission. From

then on, they would guard their words and respect each other's space.

Chapter 96

On the ground, all preparations were underway to launch Retriever 1 on the 28th of October 2015. The ship would have one week of check out flight as it orbited to the intercept point. Then one week of stationary orbit as they awaited the appearance of Venus X.

Colin Croft, in his usual methodical manner, made the crew of Retriever I go over the rescue sequence every two hours, twelve hours per day, and seven days a week. They could rest when they came back with the pioneers of Venus X. He seemed oblivious to the crew's grumbling and he was tireless in seeing to every detail. He had lived the last twenty years for this time and any failure would not be due to sloppiness or lack of preparation.

In the darkened, predawn sky of the 28th of October; Retriever 1 lifted off majestically. The trail of fire from its rockets flamed like a meteorite, as the hope of rescue climbed into the stratosphere, now only a faint dot only perceivable by those with binoculars, then gone on its search for the beautiful Venus X of space. The twenty year pioneer mission of space survival must end at the congruence of two tiny man made space ships in the infinity of the God made firmament. The gods of Venus X were coming home.

Chapter 97

That same morning a woman's body, clad only in bikini briefs, washed ashore at Eldora fifty miles north of the Cape Canaveral. The county sheriff's office was notified. No one in town could identify the body. The mysterious appearance of the once beautiful nude was the most exciting happening in twenty years.

Newlyweds, on their honeymoon, had discovered the body at sunrise. Their memories of sex under the stars would pale but they would always remember the woman lying in the shallow water with two garlands of seaweeds draped around her neck covering one of her breasts...nature's feeble effort at preserving her dignity. The two were sought after celebrities until their honeymoon ended three days later and they returned to their Chicago apartment.

Meanwhile the sheriff's office sent finger prints and photographs of the body to the FBI in Washington for possible identification. The county coroner reported that the woman had severe contusions on the left side of her face but they were not the cause of death. He listed drowning as the cause on the death certificate. The woman had signs of having had sexual intercourse less than an hour before her death.

At Cocoa Beach where he had set up his campaign headquarters, Owen Davis was preparing for one last whirlwind tour through the district. The November elections threatened to arrive before he could turn the polls in his favor. The impending return of the astronauts from their twenty year space mission was predominant in the news and most people's minds. It was difficult to get the voters interested in the usual "less taxes and more benefits" issues.

Owen decided to use the awaited landing as the focal point of his speeches, stressing his ability and background as key attributes toward pushing more space programs through Congress. Davis made sure the voters knew he would be there at the landing as their representative. With a few well placed phone calls to friends at the center, he obtained a full schedule of the landing and the movement of the returning astronauts to the ICU section of Brevard County Hospital.

Croft had arranged for a floor of the

hospital to be used exclusively for the care and rehabilitation of the Venus X Crew.

"Jack," Owen shouted to his aide, "Make sure the press knows that I'm going to be at the loading dock of the hospital when they bring the crew in. It's the only entrance that can handle things the size of the Life Support Canisters. Don't leak this out until we're sure Retriever 1 is about to land. I don't want non press people swarming all over the place interfering with our ability to get close to the gurneys when they come in."

Chapter 98

Two weeks later, as Retriever 1 stood motionless 250 miles above the earth; Glen Ross received the order from Mission Control and activated the firing sequence of the four nuclear rockets. The massive space vehicle shuddered as it changed attitude.

At three hundred miles from earth Sam told Glen to activate the retro rocket firing sequence. Like setting the brakes on a runaway semi-truck the firing seemed to have no perceptible effect but ever so slowly the magnificent lady of space decreased velocity and achieved its proper speed to meet with its long awaited mate.

"Mission Control, this is Retriever 1, we have Venus X in sight and it will be in our grasp soon." A loud cheer rose in Mission Control but Colin Croft quickly restored order, for seeing the ship, was not getting the crew home. The rendezvous must be perfect for the crew of Venus X had no way to maneuver Venus X to help dock the ships together.

"Venus X, this is Retriever 1. We have you in sight. Unless you see a problem we don't see, we'll initiate chase maneuver. Do you read? Over."

"We copy Retriever 1. We can't see you but you can chase us down. We've waited a long time for this transmission."

"Glen, Glen, I can see them, I can see them! They're on the starboard side at two o'clock." It was Sandra who had first caught sight. The others floated to the observation window where she had stationed herself for hours hoping to catch a glimpse of the rescue ship.

"Retriever 1, we have spotted you, two o'clock starboard. Confirm and tell us what your data reads as to distance."

"Roger, Venus X. The computer sets us at fifty miles from your position. We are on course to come to the adit. When we get to you, do not, I repeat, do not pressurize the lock chamber. We will do it when we have engaged and secured to your ship."

"Roger, Retriever 1, we're hands off the pressure chamber."

As the ships edged ever closer to each other; the most dangerous part of the mission was at hand. Each ship traveling at forty five hundred miles per hour had to come together at precisely the correct angle and direction. In this case Venus X; with no directional capability became an unpredictable, moving target for Retriever 1.

All the practice paid off as Commander Bertram Bryant, pilot of Retriever 1, made the nexus so smoothly that the crew of Venus X was not sure they were attached to their rescue ship.

"Mission Control, we have link up. I repeat, we have link up. All systems are go. We will proceed with disembarking of the Venus crew when you give the order."

On board Venus X, the enthusiasm was only tempered by the lack of physical strength. Even after months of limited water intake tears formed in their eyes.

"Venus X, we are starting pressure equalization procedure. Release the pressure seals of the lock chamber at this time. We will try to keep our pressure slightly lower to assist your people in moving into the LSC's, the life support chambers. You've been briefed that these chambers will be your individual autonomous canisters until we have landed and you are safely moved into hospital quarters. You'll have all you need in nourishment and water as well as oxygen for the trip home."

"Roger Retriever 1, we have set pressure release into motion." Slowly the pressure between the two ships diminished. Both crews knew that too high a difference in cabin pressures would result in the lock chamber acting as a wind tunnel. When near equilibrium was achieved Retriever 1 Commander Bryant asked, "Venus X, Retriever 1 personnel request permission to come on board?" It was one Navy Commander showing respect to another.

Ross acknowledged as a ship's Captain would, "Permission granted."

The odor of twenty years of stale re-cycled air and the sight of the near dead astronauts caused a shiver to course through Bryant's body. My God, he thought, they may not make it back alive. We've got to get them into the life support chambers right now.

"Commander Ross, I'm Commander Bryant and this is Army Captain Wright. With your permission, Wright will stay here and assist your crew in getting secured in the LSC's. I would like not to delay one moment in getting your crew in place."

"Whatever you say Bryant, but I must remind you that we don't go back unless you retrieve Colonel Pennington's body from outside our ship. He's wrapped in his sleeping bag and fastened to a rear starboard stanchion."

"Right Commander, we'll get him after we get all you people tucked away safely. Do you have a boarding order you prefer?"

"Yes, Nancy Flowers first, then Sandra Meyers followed by Marita and Adam. I'll secure all systems and come last."

"OK. Let's do it." Bryant returned to Retriever 1 and commenced the turret rotation as the astronauts slid into their respective canisters. With Wright back on board Retriever 1, Bryant slowly disengaged his ship from Venus X.

Wright suited up for an EVA to recover Pennington's body. Once he reached the body, he could not unlash the cords that had solidified after years in the cold of space.

"Bert, I can't untie this mess. I'm going to slit the bag and just bring the body back unless you have a better idea."

"Do it, I'm contacting Mission Control now to see what we can do about returning to earth immediately. The Venus crew may not all live another day."

Wright was stunned when he slit the bag and found the nude cadaver. Somehow he had expected the body to be in burial uniform. Wright's mind took a cute turn as he thought well, you came into the world bare assed and you sure left it that way. He stuffed the rigid body into the canister and returned aboard Retriever 1.

Chapter 99

"Mission Control, we have success. The Venus crew is securely on board. We request a sequence to return to earth immediately. The health status of the rescued is precarious at best and I question if some of them can last another day." Sam looked at Colin Croft for direction. They both knew that alternative landing sites could not handle the deployment of the turret nor could they handle the medical needs of the starved crew.

"Tell them we'll run the data immediately. We need an hour." Sam relayed the message.

The Flight Dynamics Officer reported "The weather does not favor an early return, Mr. Croft. The forecast is for a very low ceiling and heavy rain over the next forty eight hours due to a tropical storm south of us."

Croft made the most trying decision of his life.

"Give Retriever 1 the earliest re-entry plan that will get them here. Sam, give your back up the mike and contact Jacksonville Naval Air Station. If we're too socked in to have them land here we'll divert them to

Jacksonville. We'll convoy the special Canister Ambulances from there. One of these two airports better be open or I may have destroyed the only chance of a successful mission."

The FDO's weather forecasters were too accurate to suit the Mission Control staff. Over the next four hours a cloud bank carrying heavy rains moved on shore and enveloped the cape area. All flights were grounded. Meanwhile Retriever 1 was piercing the atmosphere and beginning its orbital descent.

At 06:00 AM November 10th, 2015; Retriever 1 requested clearance to land at the Kennedy Space Center. The traffic controller answered, "Retriever 1, we are at present below field minimums with a ceiling of fifty feet and a visibility of an eighth of a mile. We recommend you divert to Jacksonville NAS, their weather is much better."

"Kennedy Center, clear the area and get us on your Landing Radar control. Tell them we're coming in no matter what the weather is." Wright looked at Bryant and saw a determination which could not be swayed.

"You know that this cockpit is above sixty feet. If the ceiling is at fifty we won't see the ground even when the wheels are on the deck."

"Well, Wright, when the wheels touch; be ready for one hell of a braking job because we won't know if we're in the middle of the runway or not and we'd best get stopped pronto. This is why we're making the big bucks, remember?"

Chapter 100

Newly elected Congressman, Owen Davis, relished his two day old victory despite a champagne headache. He watched the news channel with interest for he wanted to be well informed on any subjects that might be of use to him when he went to Washington in January. The newscaster broke in with the announcement that NASA was attempting to land Retriever 1 at the Center despite the weather. Seeing the opportunity to get some free press coverage; he called his former campaign manager now promoted to Aide.

"Jack, spread the word that we'll be at the hospital in a half hour, then come pick me up so we can drive there before anyone else."

The phone jangling stopped Vernon Styles as he walked out of his office on his way to the flight line to meet the incoming Retriever 1 and its precious cargo.

"Styles here, what can I do for you?" The caller sensed the hurry up; I'm busy, tone in Vernon's words.

"This is agent Stanley of the Washington bureau of the FBI. We have evidence that one of your employees has drowned in a suspicious manner. The corpse is in the morgue at Daytona Beach. We identified her as June Landon. Could you check your personnel files to verify she works at Kennedy Space Center and any next of kin we could contact to identify the body and take charge of interment?"

"I can tell you she was employed here until a month or so ago. I'll have personnel check for relatives. In the meantime I'll contact the local police who were investigating the report that she had been missing. Give me a phone number and fax number where you can be reached. Someone here will send you the info."

"Thanks. We appreciate your help. Goodbye."

Vernon called in his secretary. "I've got to get to the flight line now. Call Inspector Wade or Donovan and tell them to call FBI agent Stanley at this number immediately, they've found June Landon's body at Eldoro. Also get her personnel file and fax the name of the person to be contacted, from June's records to this fax address." Styles ran out of the office to the elevator. "Come on, come on. I don't want to miss the landing," he ordered as if the elevator would obey his words. Once on the tarmac he ran to Croft's side.

"What's the latest? Can they land in this weather?"

Colin took the cellular phone from his ear and turned to face Styles. "That cowboy Bryant says he's coming in no matter what the weather is. We can only hope and pray he pulls it off or else we will spend the rest of our lives trying to explain why we killed the Venus X astronauts by attempting to land them here instead of Jacksonville NAS as we had planned. You may have the shortest career as Center Manager in NASA's history."

"Why do you suppose he's insisting on landing below minimums?"

"He doesn't think they'll survive the drive down from Jacksonville."

The Landing Controller was expertly guiding the ship down until 100 feet from touchdown when a wind gust blew the ship off course. "Pull up. Pull up. You are off the runway. We'll bring you around one more time." All Croft and Styles knew was that suddenly a loud roar of jet engines, screaming to gain altitude, came crashing on them as they felt the heat of the jet exhaust on their heads.

They waited. --- Silence. --- No crash. Croft called Hershburg at Mission Control.

"What happened Sam?"

"They were blown off course almost at touchdown, they're coming around again. It better be right this time 'cause they might not have the fuel to get to Jacksonville."

"Right." Croft depressed the off button and told Styles what was happening. Ten minutes later, they saw a faint outline of Retriever 1 as it rolled by them on the runway. Then they heard the high pitch scream of the jets followed by the roar as the reverse thrust kicked in. They never saw the brake chute deploy in the fog.

Commander Bryant shut off the engines and waited for a tow vehicle to pull them off the runway to the unloading area. Wright looked at him with an admiring grin. "I can't believe you pulled that off Commander. I'm glad I was here to see it. My grandchildren will hear this story when I'm old and gray."

"Thanks, Wright. I'll buy the first two bottles of champagne after debriefing. I think this calls for getting drunk."

"I'm with you and have no fear we won't run out of champagne as long as I'm standing." Colin and Vernon jumped on the electric cart and raced to the site. They waited as the ground crew secured the ship and proceeded with the unloading of the turret. The twenty minute procedure taxed the nerves of everyone watching.

ter 101

Donovan took the call from Styles' secretary. He dialed the Washington number while yelling to Wade to pick up on his line. Yes, the FBI had identified the drowning victim as June Landon. Yes, there were signs of physical injury. Yes, dead for two weeks. The body would arrive at Cocoa Beach funeral home in two hours.

"We've got the sonofabitch. Wade, we've got the body, now let's go get him."

"You better believe it."

They called Davis's office and were told that he was at the hospital. As they pulled up, the TV crews were setting up and a dozen news people were milling about awaiting the arrival of the Life Support Canisters carrying the astronauts to the recovery area.

On the tarmac the ground crew loaded the LSC's onto gurneys one at a time. At each gurney Croft spoke to the space pioneers looking at them through the clear face window.

"Thank you Nancy Flowers. You are a true heroine and we're all proud of you."

"Nice to be home, Colonel."

"Sandra Meyers, welcome home. You're a wonderful sight to these old eyes."

"I made it didn't I. Thank God I'm alive."

"Marita, you have brought a son home from space. You are envied by all women. Thank you."

"Adam Ross welcome to mother earth. Everyone is anxious to know you and learn from your experience.

"Thanks for bringing it home Glen. I admire you and am proud to say I know Glen Ross."

"I told you I'd get it done, Croft. You owe me a drink."

"It will be my privilege."

When they unloaded the canister with Colonel Pennington's body, Croft stood at attention and saluted whispering, "You paid the price of a true hero. Thank You."

The eight specially designed ambulances snaked their way out of the complex and onto the highway to the hospital behind a cadre of police cars; and trailing behind the ambulances were TV crew vehicles.

Hundreds of people lined the roadside saluting and cheering the returning heroes.

Through their canister speakers the crew could hear the cheers and applause. Only Adam had trouble understanding what was happening. For him all the noises were strange, ever since he had been loaded onto the gurney. The whir of the wheels, the clack, clack, clack as the gurney was pushed over the separations in the cement, the banging of the axles against the bottom of the gurney as it was shoved into the ambulance, the strange faces peering at him through the window, the voice of the man welcoming him. Too many things, too many new things. We should have stayed in space, he thought.

Chapter 102

As the ambulances reached the hospital loading dock, Davis began telling the newspersons how proud he was to have been part of this great space mission.

"It's on days like this that the country can be proud and sure that the space programs are worthwhile. When I get to Washington, in January, I will devote much of my energy and time to enacting legislation that supports the work being done here at the Kennedy Space Center. As you watch them roll in the heroes of Venus X, salute them with your hands but do more than that. Salute them with the words you write or speak over the airwaves. They are the embodiment of all the pioneers that have made this country so great since Columbus made his first exploration."

At that moment the EMT's rolled Adam Ross's LSC onto the dock. He heard the last sentence and wondered who was speaking. Then he heard a mixture of many voices and thought how stupid it was for so many to try to be heard at once. One voice broke through the din.

"Congressman Davis, would you comment on the rumors of mutiny on board Venus X; allegedly led by Commander Ross? As well as possible physical harm to the three astronauts who died during the mission?"

"I assure you that I will be at the forefront of the investigation into this matter if any signs of wrong doing come up in the debriefing sessions that will go on for the next six months. I will personally see to it that whichever mutiny or crimes committed on board will be prosecuted to the fullest limit of the law. We must assure our future astronauts they will be safe on any mission they fly." Adam was stunned. There had been no mutiny or physical harm done to anyone. What's wrong with these people?

When Wade heard Davis pontificate about justice it was the last straw. He had not wanted to disrupt the arrival of the astronauts but this phoniness was too much.

"Let's take him now." The two detectives wormed their way through the news people. The EMT's began rolling Adam's gurney to the door. Donovan and Wade grasped Davis one on each arm. Wade spoke loudly, "Owen Davis, you are under arrest for the murder of June Landon. Anything you say may be used in a court of law. If you cannot afford an attorney, one will be appointed for you. Do you understand what I've just said?"

The doors swung closed behind the EMT. Adam never heard the answer. Thus began the earthenization of Adam Ross, first extraterrestrial earthman.

Front cover image photo courtesy of: http://science.nationalgeographic.com/science/ space/space-exploration/international-space-station-article.html